# IN OTHER NEWS

## A NOVEL

DALE ROBBINS

SEVENTEEN
PRESS

**SEVENTEEN**

**PRESS**

Cover design by Dale Robbins

Edited by Stephanie Cohen

Second Edition

ISBN: 978-1-7337157-0-6

Published by Seventeen Press
www.seventeenpress.com

# IN

# OTHER

# NEWS

DALE ROBBINS

*For the survivors. Keep fighting.*
*They can never take away our truth.*

CRIME HAPPENS WHEN THE VICTIMIZER CHOOSES.
JUDGMENT IS PASSED WHEN A COURT SEES FIT.
JUSTICE IS HARDLY EVER SERVED ON TIME.

## - SEAN MORALES

# CHAPTER 1

FOG BLANKETED THE BUSTLING, JAM-PACKED CAMPUS OF Pine State University. Whispers of students returning for the fall semester filled the crisp August air.

Marlon Woods approached the school with all eyes focused on him. Each group of students stopped what they were doing and stared at him as he trudged past. His dark jeans and ill-fitting T-shirt lay wrinkled on his hunched, lanky body.

In front of him, Laura Carpenter swatted her friend's arm, almost knocking the books out of her hands. "Oh my god. It's Marlon." Her quivering finger pointed at the shuffling figure. "I can't believe he's back."

Marlon glared as he passed the women and shoved through the entrance, inadvertently slamming into a female student.

Her glossy textbook and off-white coffee cup crashed to the ground. "Hey, asshole, watch where the hell you're walking!" she shouted.

Chills ran down Marlon's spine. It was Anna Moody.

"Marlon?" Anna's fingers touched her parted lips, and she gasped.

Marlon didn't respond. Instead, he stared at the ground, expecting she would take the hint and disappear. When she didn't, he glanced back up at her.

"I missed you so much." She hugged him, causing him to stagger backward.

She was almost unrecognizable, with her jet-black hair dyed a blazing shade of red and one of her pale arms covered in a colorful galaxy tattoo. He studied her, taking in her drastically changed appearance.

"Hey," Marlon said with a forced halfhearted smile.

Her grin melted into a frown. "I tried to reach you all summer. Where have you been?"

Marlon's cognac-colored eyes locked on the floor, and his ears reddened. "Ohio."

"Why didn't you tell me?"

"I-I needed to get away."

Her shoulders sank. "I'm so sorry about—"

"I'm late," Marlon said, his skin itching with anticipation. He couldn't handle talking to her about it. Not there, not then. He pulled her in for a quick hug. "I better get to class. See you around."

Anna smiled at Marlon, and her hazel eyes flickered. "Okay, let's hang out soon and catch up. Like the old days."

Marlon nodded, peered down at his smartwatch, and raced to Room 127 for his speech class.

His trembling hand twisted the classroom door handle. A wave of bright light flooded out into the hallway, halting Marlon in his tracks.

He stepped into the room and locked eyes with the professor. Since he was late, the only empty seat was at the front of the class. He walked through the aisles and sat in the chair without making eye contact with the other students. If he didn't look at them, maybe he wouldn't feel so awkward.

"Enough about the curriculum. We'll talk more about that another day. I'm so glad to be your professor this semester. My name is Dr. Shelly Watson, and I've been teaching at Pine State University now for, let's see, twenty-three years. My goodness, the time flies by, doesn't it? Now, I want to start with a fun experiment I try every year."

Marlon hunched in his chair. An experiment? This couldn't be good.

"Let's go around the room and have everyone stand and introduce themselves."

Marlon groaned, catching the attention of a few strangers sitting next to him. One of them cleared her throat to shut him up. His cheeks flushed, and he bit his lower lip.

"Doesn't that sound like fun? Now, I'd like you to state your first and last name, as well as something interesting about yourself. It should be a fact most people don't know. No secrets in Dr. Watson's class, you hear me?" Her eyes widened as she looked around and giggled. "Who wants to be my first victim?"

A man sitting two seats away from Marlon raised his hand. "I'll go."

"Go ahead."

He rose out of his seat. "Uh, my name is Frankie Baxter. I guess a fact most people don't know about me is I was in a diaper commercial as a baby."

"Great job, Frankie. That *is* interesting. Who's next?" Dr. Watson squinted toward the back. "You? Go on."

"Thanks. Name's Michael Donahue, but my friends call me Don."

"Yes, Don," Dr. Watson said. "What would you like to share about yourself?"

"Back in high school, I ranked number one in my wrestling division. Still got the trophies and everything. Cool, huh?"

Dr. Watson smiled. "Definitely. Thanks for sharing. Who wants to go next?"

"I would *love* to," a piercing voice said.

Marlon gulped and sank further into his seat. How did he not notice her when he walked in?

"My name is Courtney DuPont, and I ... Excuse me, Dr. Watson? Can I do this up there?"

"Great idea, Courtney," Dr. Watson said.

Courtney strutted from the back of the classroom in a

4

short plaid-printed skirt and a white blouse baring her midriff. When she passed Marlon, she paused and glared at him. That was his first time seeing her since the night of the party, but Courtney wouldn't dare say anything to him in class.

"Okay, so, I'm pretty much an open book."

Marlon's stomach ached. He wanted to stand and shout, "Nobody cares," but he knew he couldn't.

She ran her fingers through her flowing, golden-blonde hair, twirling a section of it as she spoke. "So, anyone who knows me knows I *love* shoes. I own, like, seventy-seven pairs. Nine pairs of Louboutin, seven pairs of Miu Miu, five pairs of Valentino, two pairs of Balmain, and two pairs of McQueen. Oh, and my absolute favorite—a pair of red suede Giuseppe Zanotti heels."

"Thank you, Courtney. I'm sure I speak on behalf of everyone here when I say I enjoyed hearing about your shoe collection. I bet it's beautiful," Dr. Watson said.

"Thanks." Courtney pranced back to her seat.

Marlon's flesh burned at the reality of sharing a classroom with one of his biggest enemies. He ignored the subsequent students' introductions. This meant he would have to see her face every week. It was only a matter of time before she had something to say to him.

After wallowing in his negative thoughts, the professor's voice recaptured Marlon's attention. "Since we had several brave souls volunteer to go first, I'll pick the next few. When I call your name, please stand and introduce yourself to the class."

Dr. Watson lowered her glasses at the group and dragged a finger over a clipboard. "Charlotte Knapp."

A loud sigh rang out from behind Marlon, prompting him to spin around in his seat.

Charlotte rose from her seat two rows back. "Dang. Okay, I guess I can go. I'm Charlotte Knapp, and I've been to eighteen countries."

Several classmates gasped.

A smile beamed across Charlotte's sun-kissed face. "Cool, right? My parents go on mission trips all the time, and I got to tag along for a few of them."

Dr. Watson nodded. "Impressive, Charlotte. Thank you for sharing. The next student will be ..." At that moment, her eyes locked with his. "Marlon Woods."

Marlon's heart sank right out of his body. There was no way he could stand in front of everyone and talk about himself. Everyone already knew his story—or at least what they thought they knew. Why would he need to say anything?

Hoping for a "gotcha" moment, Marlon blinked at Dr. Watson multiple times. But she didn't budge. As he tried to rise, his knees shook. He couldn't collapse because he'd become even more of a laughingstock if he did.

"My ... my name ... I'm Marlon."

The professor leaned in, pressing her hand to her ear. "I'm sorry, speak up. We can't hear you."

What was he supposed to talk about? What was an interesting fact he could share? *Hi, I'm Marlon, and I'm sure you've seen my face all over the news. Nice to meet you, and yes, the rumors are true.* No, he couldn't talk about it, let alone acknowledge its existence. His mind raced, scrambling to find a useless fact to share about himself.

"I'm Marlon Woods, and I collect vinyl records," he said, the words flying out of his mouth at lightning speed. He didn't think it was fascinating in the slightest bit, but at least he gave something.

Dr. Watson's short, brown hair bobbed as she rocked her head back and forth like a character in a stoner movie. "Far out, man."

Nobody laughed.

After an awkward silence, she chuckled. "I'm kidding. I love records. They sound so much better than the digital stuff most people listen to these days. You can feel the music more with vinyl."

A nervous smile formed on Marlon's face. "Yeah, true." He shot back down in his seat.

Dr. Watson looked at her wristwatch. "Well, that's all the time we have for today. Good job, guys. We'll pick back up on the introductions next time. Thanks for listening to me ramble earlier."

Students filed out of the room. Some stared at their phones in a zombie-like state, while others fumbled with their class timetables to figure out where they needed to go.

Marlon played it safe by allowing everyone else to leave the classroom before him so he wouldn't risk an awkward encounter. Once it was only him and Dr. Watson, he peered around and strolled to the door.

"May I talk to you before you go, Marlon?" the professor asked, shooting him an inquisitive look.

Marlon's shoulders slumped. "S-sure. What's up?" he asked, his voice weak and hoarse.

She scanned his face, her eyes piercing through his soul. "How are you holding up? What you must be going through is unimaginable."

Marlon's thumping heart almost deafened him. Oh, she went *there*. "I'm okay. Yeah, I've been doing better."

Was that the right thing to say? Was it what she wanted to hear? Why wasn't her face changing?

Her brows snapped together, and her lips pressed flat. "I'm not supposed to be talking to you about this, but I want you to know people support you. A lot of us do. Don't forget that. I'm proud of you for coming back."

Marlon breathed a sigh of relief. He didn't expect any of the college faculty to side with him. After all, Pine State University was partially responsible for what happened.

"Thank you so much."

"You're welcome. You'd better run to your next class. I don't want to make you late. Keep your head up, kid."

8

---

Chilly morning rain dampened Marlon's clothing as he exited his car. He paused inside the entrance of Noir Coffee to brush the beads of water off his oversized hoodie, which swallowed his body. An overwhelming aroma of fresh coffee smacked him in the face, intensifying his migraine.

"Good morning," a beaming redhead said from behind the register. "What can I get started for you?"

His eyes met the barista's and then the ground. "Um, hi. Could I have a medium pumpkin latte with extra spice and a vanilla scone?"

Once he finished paying for his order, he stood to the side of the counter and waited. The familiarity and ambiance of the coffee shop helped ease his mind.

Several people entered the shop and were engaged in an intense conversation with one another.

A raven-haired woman slapped her friend's arm. "Ew, gross. I would *never*."

Marlon turned to face them and locked eyes with one of the young women. Why were they so damn loud?

"Is that Marlon Woods?" the woman asked, squinting.

He gulped and shifted away from her as the barista handed over his order. How did she recognize him? "Thanks. Have a good one."

By the time he twisted around, the strange woman had

appeared beside him. "You guys, it *is* him."

He glared at her, and her eyes were unmistakable. It was Madison Benét, one of Courtney's best friends. Marlon clenched the hot cup tighter and walked past her toward the door.

Madison cackled. "The asshole is afraid of us."

One of the other women stepped in front of the door when he reached for it. "Not so fast."

He sighed and lowered his head. "What do you want?"

Madison walked up behind him, her voice drawing nearer with each step. "You owe Courtney an apology."

"Why?"

Madison's mouth hung open. "Because you lied about her boyfriend. You need to drop the charges. This has gone on long enough."

"Hey, leave him alone," the barista shouted. "If you don't stop, I'll have to ask you to leave."

That was his chance to run. The distraction caught the women's attention, allowing him to push past them. He bumped the girl away from the door and jumped in his car. Steering wheel leather squeaked beneath his tightening grip, and his eyes fixated on the café door, expecting the girls to run out and confront him again. But they didn't.

# CHAPTER 2

THE BLARING BUZZ OF AN ALARM DRAGGED MARLON OUT of a deep, tranquil sleep. Bold red numbering on the clock displayed the time as 7:15 a.m. He hopped out of bed and searched the room for an outfit to wear to school, settling on a pair of wrinkled jeans and a black T-shirt. He made a mad dash toward the bathroom to inspect his hair in the mirror. Tangled brown tresses fought through his fingertips as he attempted to smooth them out.

Today, he needed to give a lecture on a social issue in his speech course. Since it was the first real assignment of the year and the second week of class, the professor allowed the students to pick their topic. Everyone would expect him to discuss *that* night, but he wouldn't give them what they wanted. Instead, he picked bullying and how it correlated with the ever-growing suicide rate—how fitting for him.

He snatched his keys and research paper off the dresser and scrambled out of his apartment.

———————

Dr. Buchanan, his former English professor, smiled at him as he passed her in the lobby. He slipped into Room 127. To avoid attracting any unwanted attention, Marlon paused and looked around the room, taking in his surroundings.

At the front of the class stood Asher Davis, a guy with medium-brown skin who played on the university's football team and captured the hearts of everybody he met.

Marlon sat in an empty seat at the head of the room.

Asher turned and stared at him for a moment before returning to his speech. "And according to the same study, one in about 5,700 African Americans will die by murder. The scariest part is that ninety-three percent of murders are committed by someone of the same race as the victim. This is an unacceptable statistic, and we need to work on bringing these numbers way down."

Asher bowed, and applause filled the classroom.

Dr. Watson eyed Marlon as she neared her desk. "Good job, Mr. Davis. Those figures are, indeed, alarming. Who wants to go next?"

Marlon sank in his seat, hoping to avoid the professor calling on him again.

The place fell silent for several seconds. "Meee! I want to go," a shrill voice shouted from the back. Courtney DuPont rose out of her chair and walked down the aisle.

A knot formed in Marlon's stomach. He could only imagine what she was about to say.

She opened a neatly folded piece of white paper and glared out into the sea of students before directing her attention to Marlon. "My topic is lies. Yes, lies, and how dangerous they are."

The professor turned in her black leather chair and lowered her glasses. "All right, Courtney. Go ahead."

Marlon's pulse quickened. Was she about to talk about him? He was supposed to be safe in class, but this might have changed everything.

"How often do you think we tell lies?" Courtney's ice-blue eyes searched the room. "Would it shock you to hear sixty percent of adults lie at least once within a ten-minute conversation? Many people lie three to four times a day on average. Crazy, right?"

Marlon's face went blank, and his jaw clenched.

"Many lies are harmless, and sometimes, people don't realize they've lied until after they say it. Like, someone is talking about a popular show and asks if you've seen it. We've all lied about that. And a lot of lies are told to make ourselves more likable. Like, 'Babe, is my makeup okay?' and you respond with, 'Yes, you look fine,' when you know damn well her makeup is fugly, but you don't want to hurt her feelings."

Many students laughed, but not Marlon. He stared at the floor to avoid making eye contact. He was sure the bombshell was coming any minute now, and he didn't want to give her the satisfaction of shocking or embarrassing him.

Courtney smirked. "But some lies aren't so harmless. What if I told you only ten percent of lies are exaggerations, and sixty percent are total deceptions—false claims and made-up stories you know aren't true, but you tell anyway?"

She stopped to take a sip of water. "The most common reasons for lying are to make ourselves look better, to get out of trouble, and to avoid hurting a person's feelings. But lying is bad and can ruin someone's life. Did you know once a liar gets caught, seventy percent of them admit they would do it again? And that is why I'm a firm believer in the truth. After all, the truth will set you free."

Marlon rolled his eyes, appalled at her thinly-veiled attempt at belittling him through her speech. Why didn't anybody stop her?

Dr. Watson gave an approving nod. "Nicely done, Courtney. I must say, with this being your second time taking this class, you did an excellent job on your research. Who would like to go next?"

Marlon jumped up without giving it a second thought. "Me?" As soon as the word left his mouth, his blood ran cold. Why did he say that?

Dr. Watson grinned at him. "Of course. Go ahead."

He sipped from his water bottle, and his legs wobbled as he approached the front of the room. His eyes hunted for a friendly—or at least familiar—face he could focus on. A poster near the door at the back caught his eye and would have to suffice for calming his nerves. His sweaty hands fumbled with the crumpled sheet of yellow paper in his pocket.

"My topic is bullying." A wave of nausea rushed over him. Why did he volunteer to give a speech so early on? And why *this* subject? His eyes flitted up at the doorway several times, and he wanted nothing more than to run out of the classroom.

A lump formed in his throat. "Um, so I want you to look around the room. How many of you have ever bullied someone?"

Nobody responded to his question.

"A-and by that, I mean: 'A person using strength or power to harm or intimidate those who are weaker.'"

Several people hesitated to raise their hands. He made eye contact with Courtney, who was too busy playing with her phone to pay him any attention. She would never admit she was the worst of them.

"Why do we bully people? Could it be because we're insecure?"

His pleading eyes peered up over the paper. "One in three students will experience bullying in their lifetime."

His voice cracked from talking, so he clutched the bottle in his quivering hand and gulped down another sip. "What's worse is what we don't know about bullying. Did you know that sixty-four percent of bullying victims never report it? Or that more than half of the bullying situations stop when someone intervenes? This means if you see something, you *should* say something, because you might save somebody's life." He reminded himself he could do this. A few more lines and it would be over.

"Bullying victims are also three times more likely to attempt suicide. Let me break this down for you. Suicide is the second biggest cause of death for people aged fifteen to twenty-four. There are approximately 112 suicides per day, or about one every twelve minutes. For the fifteen-to-twenty-four group, there is one suicide every hour and forty-eight minutes."

Taking a breath, he pushed the hair from his face. "We have to do something. The change starts with you. All it takes is one comment to send someone over the edge. Stop spreading rumors about each other and making fun of people behind their backs."

Although there was still more to read, he gave up. He hustled back to his seat without taking a moment to relish in the spotlight.

Several of his classmates clapped, much to his surprise.

"That was fantastic, Marlon." Dr. Watson walked up to the podium. "Who's next?"

After class ended, Marlon collected his belongings and hurried out into the hallway. Before heading to his web design class, his aching stomach told him he needed to grab a bite to eat.

He hurried toward the vending machines down the

hall. As he pondered over which bag of chips to buy, the familiar clack of stiletto heels approached him from behind.

"That was *fantastic*," Courtney said, sarcasm dripping from every word. "Aren't you fucking special?"

Marlon turned around and stared at her. "What's your problem?"

"My problem is you, asshole. I'm tired of you and your lies. Nobody believes you. I'm surprised you even had the balls to show your face here again."

He looked away from her and left the vending area. He wished he could tell her what he thought about her and her rapist boyfriend, but the words wouldn't come out.

"Yeah, that's right. LEAVE. Why don't you do us all a favor and go? You better hope they don't convict Parker."

Marlon ran down the hallway, his face red and flushed—disappointed in himself for not fighting back and pissed at Courtney for confronting him.

"He's not even gay, and I don't know why you would think he's into *you*," she shouted, her voice fading in the distance.

He rushed into the first open door he found: the computer lab. The door slammed shut, and he took a moment to collect his thoughts. "Fuck her," he mumbled under his breath.

"Whoa, no thanks," a man said.

Marlon's eyes darted open as he twisted to see who said it. It was a man he had never seen on campus: an attractive guy with warm-toned skin, russet-brown eyes, acid-washed jeans, and a band T-shirt featuring The Cure. His curly hair was a rich brown, medium-length on top with the sides of his head cut short, similar to Marlon's own coiffed hair.

"I … I'm sorry," Marlon said, stunned by how handsome he found the man.

The mystery man beamed at him and pulled the second earbud out of his ear. "No, it's fine. I didn't mean to scare you." He straightened his posture and extended his hand. "Name's Quinn Beckham."

Marlon waved, missing the cue to shake hands. "Um, hi. I'm Marlon Woods."

"Marlon?" Quinn asked. "Like Marlon Brando? Awesome name. How long have you been at Pine?"

"Two years. How about you?"

"This is my first. Just moved here from Colorado. I needed to get away from my family."

The corners of Marlon's eyes creased from his grin. Someone who wasn't there last semester, meaning Quinn couldn't know who he was. "I get that. I moved from Ohio last year."

"Nice. So, what's got you feeling down?"

Marlon's hands ran through his faded brown hair. "People suck sometimes. It's okay. I feel a little better now. So, what's your major?"

"Political science with a minor in journalism. Exciting, right?"

Marlon chuckled. "That sounds ... Well, it's different."

"Yeah, sure it is." Quinn let out a self-deprecating laugh. "What's yours?"

"Graphic design, but I might switch to psychology next semester. Graphic design isn't really my thing anymore."

Quinn's forehead creased. "Makes sense. Well, best of luck to ya. Hey, maybe we can hang out sometime. You seem pretty cool, and, to be honest, you're the only person who has talked to me here."

Marlon pondered the idea. He had no friends there besides Anna, if she even still counted as one. But he wasn't too sure what Quinn's intentions were. "Oh, I ..."

"Sorry, is that a weird thing to ask someone you just met?"

Marlon's jaw tightened. "Uh, no, not at all. What's your number?"

"Here, type in your number, and I'll text you," Quinn said, handing his phone over to Marlon.

Marlon finished typing and smiled back at Quinn. "There. I'll message you soon, and we can work something out. Thanks for cheering me up."

"No problem. It was nice meeting you."

Marlon did it. He finally talked to someone, and it was a person who didn't know what happened to him.

―――――

Back in his apartment for the evening, Marlon browsed through his phone and came across Anna's number. How could he have been so cold and distant with her when he ran into her at school on his first day back? She was his best and only friend, and she deserved better than that. They needed to meet face-to-face to catch up.

His index finger quivered as he hit the dial button and waited for her to answer.

The ringing stopped, and a familiar voice broke through the silence. "Hello?"

"Hey, it's Marlon. What are you up to?"

A yelp on the other end of the call almost deafened him. "Oh my god. I can't believe you called. I didn't recognize your new number. I'm hanging out in my room, watching a movie."

"Yeah, sorry. I changed it … a few times." He nibbled on his bottom lip. "Can we meet for coffee or something?"

"Hell yeah! Let's do Noir Coffee tomorrow at seven. Does that work?"

"Yep. Cool. See you then."

How the hell was he going to talk to her in person when he could barely speak over the phone?

# CHAPTER 3

DURING THE SEVEN-MINUTE DRIVE TO NOIR COFFEE, HE speculated how his conversation with Anna would go. Did he owe her an explanation for why he disappeared and didn't respond to her messages over the summer? Should he explain what took place on that night in June? The thought of having to confront it was more than he could handle, but he couldn't continue running.

As Marlon pulled into the lot, he spotted Anna sitting at a bench outside the building. He found a nearby parking space, tucked his shirt into his pants, and shuffled toward the meeting spot. It was time to face his friend.

Anna caught him approaching, and she jumped up and embraced him with a hug. "I'm so glad you came." Her black jeans, off-the-shoulder maroon top, and smokey eye makeup complemented her new hair and curvy physique.

After embracing for several moments, they separated. His face flushed with an uncomfortable smirk. "Me too."

They entered the coffee shop, and the scent took his mind back to his run-in with Madison the week prior, freezing him in his tracks.

"Welcome to ... Marlon? Is that you?" Brandon shouted from behind the counter with a grin. His palm brushed against his short, clean-cut, brown hair.

Marlon gulped. It was so awkward to see him in public considering what had happened between them. "How's it going?"

"Good. Happy to be back in Washington. My family spent part of the summer in London, and I got bored fast. There is only so much you can do there." Brandon let out an amused chuckle.

Marlon nodded. He couldn't relate. He had never been to London, or even out of the country. "Yeah, I'm glad to see you're back."

A warm smile lit up Brandon's face. "I didn't think you'd come back after—"

Marlon flinched.

Without finishing his thought, Brandon shook his head and regained his composure. "What can I get for you guys?"

Anna stepped forward. "Hey, 'guy who pissed Dr. Stevenson off by not knowing who Charlie Chaplin is.' I'll take a large iced mocha, please."

"It's not my fault I don't watch old movies," Brandon said, laughing through his words.

Marlon's eyes tightened. "You share a class?"

Brandon cringed. "Unfortunately."

"Oh, um, I'll have the same," Marlon said.

The cash machine made a click as Brandon entered the order. "All right, your total is six dollars and seventy-nine cents."

After receiving their drinks, Marlon and Anna found a secluded corner of the café where they could talk in private.

"Sharing a class with Brandon—is that awkward?" Marlon asked.

"Why? Because we don't hang out with him anymore? No, but I miss the way things used to be."

His eyes locked on the table in front of him as he sipped his drink. Was he supposed to start the talk? Should he tell her? He needed to stop overthinking it. She was his friend.

At last, Anna broke the silence. "So, how's it been for you since you've been back? Have you had any … problems?" Leaning in, her hazel eyes searched his face.

His chin propped on his hand. "Things have been … different. Like, I haven't had too many issues, but people are acting weird around me. Courtney won't leave me the hell alone, and I had a run-in with Madison here the other day."

"What happened with Courtney?"

Courtney's contemptuous voice replayed in his brain, and his eyes rolled skyward. "She gave this speech in Dr. Watson's class about lying with some bullshit statistics, and then she confronted me in the hallway after class. I couldn't believe it."

"Really? What did she say? Ugh, I always hated that bitch."

His shoulders tensed. "She called me a liar, said nobody believes me, and told me to leave PSU. I'm starting to think she's right."

Anna rocked her head side to side. "Don't listen to her. She's mad because her dad's banging his secretary, and now the entire world knows about it."

He covered his mouth to stifle a gasp. "Where did you hear that?"

"I read an article about it a few days ago. It's not the first time he's cheated on her mom."

"Okay, I guess that makes me feel a *little* better."

"Good. So, what's new with you?"

He contemplated the question. Other than the obvious, what did he have going on in his life? Was that the part where he talked to her about *it*? His soul ached at the mere thought. "Not a lot. I don't go anywhere these days other than school, and I haven't hung out with anyone. But I met this guy yesterday in the computer lab. He seems cool."

Anna's brows raised. "Ooh, what's his name? Is he boyfriend material?"

He chuckled. "Shut up, Anna. His name is Quinn, but I'm not even thinking about dating right now. You already know why." He gulped. He hadn't intended on taking it there, but the damage was already done.

She lowered her head and grimaced. "Yeah, I understand. What's been going on with … you know?"

"The investigation? They don't really keep me in the loop, and it sucks. Last I heard, they were aiming for a trial date in the spring or summer."

Her eyes met with his and then darted to the floor. "I still don't know. I heard some different things, and I'm not sure—"

"You're not sure what happened?" The implication was like a punch to the gut. His stomach burned fiery hot, and he squinted at her as if it were an interrogation. "What did you hear?"

"I heard two versions. Version one is you and Parker Sullivan had sex behind the shed at Laura's party. The other story is … he forced you to have sex with him." She teared up, and her lip trembled as she stared at him.

Marlon cleared his throat and folded his arms, unable to suppress his anger. The implied accusation of him making the whole thing up cut deep. Why would he lie about something like that? What did he stand to gain from it?

"Which one do you think is true?" he asked.

"Why did you ignore me all summer? You know I'm here for you, no matter what. I wanted to help you, but you shut me out like you're doing now."

"It's been hard. Nobody knew that anything happened when I got home. I had to lie about how I got the bruises on my face. But a reporter called my house one day and asked my mom if her son was the Pine State University rape victim. And then someone posted the pictures on my social media accounts." Teardrops cascaded down his cheeks.

Anna frowned and rested her hand on Marlon's arm. "I'm so sorry. I can't imagine what you're going through."

He dabbed the stream of salty tears from his warm cheek. "Yeah, it sucks."

Anna's eyes locked on the thick pink scar on his left wrist as he wiped his eyes. She reached out for his arm, and her chin quivered. "Oh, Marlon. I didn't know …"

He pulled away and slid his sleeve back down, tucking his hand under his leg. "I don't wanna talk about it."

"I … I'm always here for you if you want to talk."

He shrugged. "It's like, I want people to know what happened, but why bother at this point if everybody's got their mind made up? I have so much to say, but nobody wants to hear it."

"The truth is the truth. Nobody can ever take that away from you. Who cares if they don't believe you?"

She had a point. He couldn't change people's opinions, so why should he try?

He sipped his iced mocha through a black straw. "You're right. It just sucks. God, I miss our little talks."

"Me too." After taking a deep breath and wiping the tears from her cheeks, she continued, "Think of it this way: regardless of what happens, they expelled Parker, and he can never show his face on campus again, so you don't have to worry about seeing him. As for everyone else, they'll get over it. It just takes time. People are assholes and only think about themselves."

"You're right, but I don't know what to do at this point. It's like I'm at a crossroads. Justice hasn't been served, and I'm still dealing with the backlash from something I had no control over. It's beyond unfair."

"It is unfair, but don't let it bring you down. We've gotta get through this together. Who cares what people think? Hell, if they didn't talk about this, they'd be talking about something else. Humans are gossipy little shits."

Marlon knew she was right, but not letting it bother him was easier said than done. He smiled. "That's why you're my best friend, Anna. You get it."

Anna chuckled. "Now, as your best friend, I'm obligated to ask what's going on with your hair? You're handsome, but that look isn't doing anything for you. Can I please do something with it?"

His cheeks reddened, and he laughed. Anna always knew what to say to ease his pain and make him laugh. "For real? We have a heart-to-heart, and you want to talk about my hair?"

She wagged her index finger at him in jest. "Someone had to. But you know I love you, and I'll always be here for you. We can make it through this."

The words were what Marlon had needed to hear for a long time. Coming from his best friend, they meant so much more than if anybody else had said them.

Anna swallowed another sip of her drink and continued studying Marlon's face.

"What? Why are you staring at me like that?"

"Sorry, I'm just glad we're talking again. These last three months felt like an eternity."

"I agree." Marlon sighed, trying to think of a way to take the conversation in a more lighthearted direction. "Are you seeing any new guys?"

"Nope, not yet. I didn't go on any dates this summer because of the whole Scott thing. It's whatever, but I'm over it now. There's still plenty of time and men this semester."

"I'm glad you're doing better now. You deserve to be happy."

"Thanks. Scott's still seeing that bitch. I did some creeping on social media a few weeks ago and saw pictures of them kissing. I hope his dick falls off." Anna scrunched her face.

"Wow, that's a little harsh, don't ya think?" Marlon laughed. "But you're right. You can *and* will do better."

"Anything's better than little Tic-Tac Scotty." Anna held her pinky up and wiggled it.

Marlon shook his head and continued laughing. "Ew, gross. That explains so much."

Anna's face relaxed. "How's your mom? Is she good?"

"She's Mom." Marlon bounced his shoulder. "Things have been weird between us lately. She didn't want me to come back. I had to tell her it's my life and my decision."

"Maybe the distance will be good for you guys. I'm proud of you for coming back. Call me selfish, but I sure as hell would have missed you."

They finished the last few sips of their drinks and walked to the parking lot. Relief washed over Marlon for the first time in months. The conversation went smoother than he had expected, and she seemed to understand his struggles.

Upon reaching her car, they hugged.

Marlon smiled. "I'm so happy we had this talk."

"Me too. We need to do this more often. Don't be a stranger."

---

Back in the comfort of his own bed, Marlon reached for the lamp on his nightstand. His encounter with Quinn replayed in his head. He grabbed the phone and tapped the screen before hitting the send button.

*Hey, it's Marlon.*

Marlon pressed his lips together. Would he be awake at that hour? Was it a bad idea to text Quinn in the first place?

A minute later, a new message displayed:

*Yooo. Wats up?*

Marlon sent his response:

*Heading to bed. Thought I would text you.*

Before he exited the thread, another new text appeared:

*Nice. Doing anything Friday?*

Marlon didn't know what Quinn's intentions were or if he was even gay, but he couldn't lead him on if he was interested. The thought alone made him nauseous.

*Not sure. I'll check and text you tomorrow.*

Once more, the phone beeped with a notification:

*K goodnight.*

# CHAPTER 4

MARLON SPENT MUCH OF THE MORNING CATCHING UP ON episodes of shows he had quit watching a few months prior. After moping around the apartment for several hours, his growling stomach told him he needed to eat. Since he hadn't gone grocery shopping, there was no food in the refrigerator.

Marlon sped off to Burger Hut. Their burgers always came out way too greasy and the fries a slight shade of gray, but he couldn't afford to be picky.

He pulled up toward the drive-thru, and the royal-blue sign outside caught his eye. Chipped paint exposed a rusty undercoat. Beneath the giant burger logo, the text read "New 3-for-$4 Combo." They were trying to compete with the major fast food chains, even though their food was gross.

He moved his car around to the extensive, faded menu.

The speaker box crackled with static until a woman's voice interrupted the noise. "Thank you for choosing Burger Hut. Would you like to try our new combo meal?"

Because of the dilapidated state of the board, he had to squint to decipher what it said. "Um, hi. One moment, please."

After placing his order, he waited in line. With two vehicles ahead of him, he reached the window within a few minutes. The sliding door screeched open when he drove next to it.

A young woman with chest-length black hair leaned out. "You ordered the large double cheeseburger combo with an orange soda? Seven fifty-eight, please."

He nodded as he passed his red debit card to her.

She ran it through the chip reader. As the receipt printed out, she glanced down at the card. After squinting at its small, worn text, her eyes sparked with recognition. "Here you go. Could you hold on for a minute?"

Marlon's forehead creased. Why did she make that face when she saw his card? He had never met her. Thoughts raced through his mind, causing his heart rate to accelerate. Was this a strange coincidence he was blowing out of proportion? He couldn't help how paranoid he had become.

Two other uniformed employees popped their heads around the corner, staring out the window at Marlon. One man whispered something to the other.

Marlon chewed on his bottom lip as he struggled to redirect his thoughts and justify the situation. There was no way they could have known him. None of the employees attended Pine State University, as far as he could tell.

The original female cashier reappeared and opened the window. "Sorry, Marlon. We're waiting on your fries."

Thank god, they were only waiting for the fries. *Wait, how did she know my name?* The hair on the back of his neck raised. She saw the name on his debit card. Pieces of the puzzle fell together. Did she recognize him from the news?

A menacing-looking man filled the window. He motioned for the woman to move. "Marlon? Is that you?"

"Yes." Marlon didn't dare turn and look at him.

Adam Poole leaned in, peered behind Marlon's car, and pointed at him. "Listen, you got some fuckin' nerve coming back to Pine. Nobody wants you here. We don't need scum liars like you ruining anybody else's life."

"I-I just wanted some food."

Adam's nostrils flared, and his face flushed. "Oh yeah? Go buy food somewhere else, faggot. You destroyed my friend's life."

Each word slashed through Marlon like a sharp, hot knife cutting through butter.

"How could you lie and tell everyone Parker raped you? If anything, *you* took advantage of *him*. It's just like you people to prey on straight guys."

Marlon turned to face him, tears burning their way to his eyes. "Please, give me my food."

Clenched teeth showed through Adam's parted, crusty lips. "Explain what the hell your endgame is here. Are you trying to have him locked up for the rest of his life? You're disgusting. I see the way you stare at all the guys."

What did he mean? He barely spoke to Adam, let alone his other friends. They only saw each other in passing at school and parties.

Adam clapped his hands together three times. "Are you going to say something or continue to sit there looking stupid? Hello? Do you hear me, faggot?" When he didn't receive the response he had expected, he slammed his fist on the counter. "Just get out of here."

Tears burst from Marlon's eyes. He crumbled into his seat. "You don't understand."

"What is there to understand? Parker didn't like you back, and you tried to get him into trouble."

Marlon shook his head, and his palm pressed to his lips to stifle a whimper. "Please stop."

Why couldn't he say what was on his mind? He hated Adam, and he hated Parker. He never found the rapist bastard attractive.

"Get the hell out of Pine," Adam said in a contemptuous tone.

The cashier from earlier reappeared behind Adam, holding the food and drink. She pouted as she nudged his arm. "I think you've said enough. Give him his meal and let him go."

Adam growled as he snatched the soda and bag from the girl's hands. He hurled the bag of food into the car, sending French fries and condiments all over the floor. With his other hand, he chucked the drink at Marlon, splashing orange soda all over his clothes. "Have a *great* day."

Marlon looked down at the mess on his floor with an incredulous stare and back up at the window as it slammed shut. An onslaught of tears streamed down his face, and his lip quivered as he coasted out of the parking lot. He drove home without stopping to clean the debris out of his car.

———

Marlon stood in his living room in shock for several minutes. Nothing he said or did provoked Adam to do that. Had he made a mistake going back to Pine? It had only been a week since he returned to the university, and he still had to face an extensive trial.

He collapsed on the floor and curled up in a ball. The pain hit like a truck, and the feelings he suppressed over the last few months festered inside of him. The next year would be exhausting, and he didn't know how he could push through and persevere. All he wanted to do was sleep for-ever. That way, he wouldn't need to deal with the embarrassment the trial would cause him. But he had al-ready tried in vain to kill himself over the summer. This added to his ever-growing list of failures.

When he mustered up the strength to crawl into bed, he sobbed himself to sleep.

———

Marlon walked through the entrance of the school, and his body became heavy and lethargic. It was a bizarre sensation he had never experienced. Everyone passing in the hall whispered and stared at him, but he couldn't make out what they were saying. His eyes darted in both directions as he tried to find an empty room to hide in. All he wanted was to escape. The encounter with Adam had left him unable to breathe.

The further he moved into the building, the more people he encountered. They snickered and taunted him as he trudged through the crowded hallways. At the end of the hall stood his second worst nightmare: Courtney DuPont.

Marlon's knees weakened.

"Oh, look, it's the *victim*." Her bony face wrinkled as she grinned at him. With each step she took, her heels clicked on the hard floor.

She stared at his face and let out a loud cackle. Her neon pink nails shimmered when she snapped her fingers. "We don't want you here. Why don't you disappear?"

"Why are you doing this to me?" he asked, his tired voice reduced to a whisper.

A figure emerged from the shadows behind him. "The real question is, why did you do this to yourself?"

Chills struck Marlon's body. No way, it couldn't be him. He spun around toward the mystery person.

Parker Sullivan flashed a toothy smile. "Miss me?" He was wearing the same outfit as the night of the assault—a bright-red polo shirt and light-wash jeans. His blue eyes glowed at the sight of Marlon's terror.

Marlon's head exploded with racing thoughts. This couldn't be real. No. Parker wasn't supposed to set foot inside the school. He had to run away. His pounding heart thumped in his ears.

Courtney plucked a knife out of the waistband of her skirt and wagged it in his tear-streaked face. "Where do you think you're going, faggot? You wanted attention, and now you can have it." With the scene growing tenser by the moment, an audience gathered, and many students applauded.

Parker lit up with a devilish smirk. "Yeah, we had a good time, remember? I know everyone else here does."

"Oh, god, someone help me." Marlon dropped to the ground and guarded his face with his arms. His voice trembled as he attempted to ward off the assailants. "Leave me alone. Stop it."

With her arms crossed and eyes rolling, Courtney stared down at him and groaned. "You're such a pussy."

Marlon squeezed his eyes shut. Maybe if he didn't acknowledge their presence any longer, they'd leave.

When his eyes opened after a few seconds, Anna stood above him.

He almost choked gasping for air. "Oh, thank god you're here. They're trying to kill me."

Her hand flew up in his face to silence him. "Get over yourself, Marlon," she said, her voice similar to the barking of an aggressive dog. "It's always about you. That's all you ever think about."

Marlon's ears rang. "I thought you were my friend."

She flung her head back and uttered a mischievous laugh. "I don't associate with liars, dumbass. You got what you deserved."

Marlon rubbed his eyes, and Anna disappeared.

Courtney stepped closer to him and reached out. Her hands grasped his messy brown hair, and she yanked him up to his feet. She held his head as she forced the knife against his neck.

"I've wanted to do this for a long time. Give me one reason not to," she said, words filtering through her gritted teeth.

They were about to kill him. He had thought about taking his own life, but he didn't want to give them the satisfaction of being the ones to decide.

"Please. Don't do this," he said, hyperventilating through every other word.

Courtney hissed and hurled him backward. "You're pathetic."

When Marlon regained the courage to stand, Parker emerged in front of him. Marlon scurried back against the wall to move away, but Parker kept staggering closer.

Parker unbuttoned his pants and yanked the zipper

halfway down. "What's wrong? Scared?"

Many of the nearby students raised their cell phones to film what was about to transpire.

Marlon closed his eyes, preparing himself for the imminent attack. "Please, Parker. You don't have to do this."

———————

A loud buzz woke Marlon from his nightmare. He lurched forward in bed, panting. "It was only a dream," he whispered, repeating the words to himself a few times before he believed them.

# CHAPTER 5

**OVER THE NEXT FEW DAYS, MARLON SKIPPED OUT ON ALL** of his classes. He spent his time escaping via trashy reality television shows, which helped him momentarily forget about the tragic state of his life. Any thought of leaving the house brought to light the memories of what happened at Burger Hut and reduced him to tears.

After several days like this, he ended his pity party and returned to school on Friday. By remaining home and skipping class, he was letting the bullies win. Wouldn't they love to have the satisfaction of running him off for good?

---

Marlon's phone lit up with a text message from Quinn after his last class. His face flushed at the realization he hadn't texted the guy throughout the week. He drafted a reply:

*OMG. So sorry I forgot to text you.*

About a minute later, another new message appeared:

*No prob. Doing anything fun tonight? It's Friday, after all.*

This made Marlon laugh, since he hadn't gone out on a Friday night in almost four months.

*Nope, I'm staying home and studying. You?*

The phone vibrated again.

*Not studying lol. Wanna grab dinner tonight?*

For the next ten minutes, Marlon clutched the phone in his unsteady hand and contemplated going out to dinner with Quinn. Considering what happened to him the week prior at the drive-thru, he couldn't risk running into another one of Parker's friends. He could have made up an excuse and asked for a rain check, but the guy did nothing wrong. Marlon decided he needed to give him a chance.

*Sure. What are you thinking?*

Marlon hesitantly pressed the Send button.

*How about Mad Taps or Café Confidante?*

Marlon sighed and tapped his response:

*Let's do Café Confidante.*

Within seconds, a new notification came through:

*Cool. Meet u there at 8?*

Before he agreed, he peered at the clock and discovered he had plenty of time.

*Sounds like a plan. See you soon.*

That left enough time for him to take a shower, style

his hair, and settle on an outfit. After careful consideration, he picked out an olive-colored sweater, indigo jeans, and black combat boots.

Once he finished getting ready, he checked the time. It was twenty to eight. He ran out of the doorway and sped down I-90 toward Seattle.

———

Marlon arrived at Café Confidante in time to catch Quinn exiting his vehicle. Relieved to see Quinn was also running a little late, Marlon parked next to his car as best as he could in the crowded parking area. He struggled to catch up to him and almost tripped on the curb.

"Quinn," Marlon said, greeting him from behind.

Quinn jumped and spun around. "Oh, Marlon. Glad you made it."

Although it was a casual dinner between two strangers, Quinn had dressed to impress. The outfit he wore consisted of a form-fitting navy-colored suit, a maroon tie, and brown Oxfords.

Marlon had underdressed. After looking him over, he nodded with approval. "Wow, I love your outfit."

Quinn put his hand to his chest. "Oh, this old thing? Thank you."

They walked inside, and the hostess seated them toward the rear of the restaurant. The venue featured a beautiful black-and-white herringbone pattern imprinted on the walls and a blue curtain dividing the main room from the private dining space. A familiar jazz song hummed over the radio.

"So, what have you been up to?" Quinn asked, breaking the silence.

Since Marlon needed to keep the previous week's events a secret, he threw out the first thing that came to mind. "Not a lot. Class and readjusting to school. Pretty boring. What about you?"

Quinn's suit shifted as he shrugged. "Hey, nothing wrong with that. I'm trying not to suffocate with the number of assignments I have. But I will say my American politics class is cool, at least. Well, it is to me."

A twenty-something brunette dressed in a black pencil skirt and a white button-up shirt approached the table. "Welcome to Café Confidante. My name is Amira, and I'll be taking care of you gentlemen this evening. What would you like to drink?"

"I'd like water, please," Quinn said without hesitation.

If Quinn ordered water, Marlon couldn't follow it up with a soda. Awkward social cues like this contributed to why he dreaded going out with people. "I'll take a water."

Amira jotted down their drink order. "Are you ready to order your meals, or do you need a few minutes?"

Quinn slid the menu forward without opening it. "Yes, I'd like the Confidante house burger and sweet potato fries."

Amira smiled back at him before she turned her attention to Marlon. "And for you, sir?"

His eyes stayed focused on the menu, and he picked the first thing he saw. "I'll have the plum pork with broccoli."

Amira collected their menus. "Thanks. Be right back."

"So, what do they teach you in American politics?" Marlon asked.

By the look on Quinn's face, the question came as a pleasant surprise. "Lots of things. We're currently learning about all of the different political parties and how they shaped America's history. I'm writing a report on how the Republican and Democratic parties traded platforms throughout the 1900s and what I think led to the change. Sounds fun, right?"

"It sounds interesting. What made you major in political science, if you don't mind me asking?"

Politics had never interested Marlon, and he turned off the TV whenever campaign ads came on. But he couldn't let Quinn know that.

"I wanna change the country. I'd like to not be one of those people who sits on their ass and complains about how things should be. I want to be the person making the changes happen. It's sad that so many people are still fighting for equal rights."

"Wow, that's amazing. What do you want to do after graduating?"

Before Quinn answered, the waitress returned to the table with their drinks. "The food should be out soon."

Quinn nodded at Amira and continued, "I think I'll start out as a campaign manager and work my way up through the ranks. Hopefully, I can run for office someday. Who knows, maybe I could be president."

Marlon laughed. "Whoa, don't get ahead of yourself there, buddy."

Quinn shot a bashful smile at Marlon. "Hey, a boy can dream. Maybe I'll be the first gay president."

*Gay.* Marlon was right, and hearing that word was a relief. "Don't you think we've already had a few of those?" Marlon said, raising a brow at him. "I'm kidding."

"You're not wrong, though. Anyway, enough about me. Tell me about you."

The moment Marlon had been dreading. How should he respond to this loaded question? *My face is plastered all over the news because of a horrific summer night that continues to haunt me to this day. I lost most of my friends and the respect of everyone I know because of it.* No, he wouldn't dare say such a thing, let alone think about explaining the story. He needed to play it cool.

They locked eyes for several seconds until Marlon looked away. "Oh, there isn't a lot to know about me. I grew up in a small town in Ohio. I'm an only child. Boring, I know. I've lived in Washington for almost two years, but I haven't spent too much time in Seattle, which is a bummer because I'd love to explore the city. I like indie-pop and nineties rock music."

Quinn leaned in. "Nice. Who are your favorite artists?"

"Um, in terms of nineties bands, I would say Hole, The Cure, Smashing Pumpkins. There are tons of recent artists, too, like Sharon Van Etten, Twin Shadow, Diana Gordon, Sky Ferreira, Mary Lambert. I could go on for days."

An impressed smirk spread across Quinn's face. "Great taste. I like a lot of those artists. My all-time favorite is The Cure, which I'm sure you could tell from my shirt when we met at school."

Marlon's shoulders relaxed as the discussion steered into a less invasive direction. "Oh, yes, I remember. What's your favorite song of theirs?"

"Easy. It's gotta be 'Lullaby.'"

"Yeah, right. The correct answer is 'Close To Me.'"

"I mean, it's a good song, but not as good as some of their others."

Marlon chuckled and shook his head.

"If that's how you feel, then this friendship is over. I can't take that kind of negativity in my life," Quinn said.

"Not so fast, mister. We haven't talked about movies yet." Oh god, was he flirting with Quinn? He thought so.

"You sure you want to? I might judge you more." Quinn made a cringing face. "Kidding. My favorite is *The Breakfast Club*. Didn't expect that, did you?"

"I could see that. I get a *Breakfast Club* vibe from you."

Marlon looked him up and down twice. "Mine is *The Shining*. I think it's the weirdest, most interesting movie ever."

"You know, I haven't been able to sit through the whole thing. Maybe I don't understand the story or something, but I guess I need to give it another chance. We should watch it together someday."

Marlon's chest tightened. Something must have been going right if Quinn was talking about a second hang out already. "I'm always down to see it again. I've seen it at least ten times, so what's one more?"

"Yeah, true." Quinn paused and stared at him as his brows drew together. "It's like I recognize you from somewhere. You've never been to Colorado, have you?"

Marlon's expression dulled. Maybe Quinn recognized him from TV. He couldn't handle that, not after what happened last time. "Nope, never. Maybe you met someone who looks like me or something?" Why was he overexplaining and overthinking this? He reminded himself to calm down before his cover was blown.

"Probably, but it's cool since we've met now. I can tell you're a sweet guy."

Marlon beamed at him. "Aw, thanks. So are you."

Amira appeared at the table, holding two plates similar in pattern to the walls. "Enjoy your dinner, gentlemen."

Aside from the occasional small talk about school and hobbies between bites, the two men ate their meals in silence. After they finished eating, they split the bill, paid the waitress, and walked toward the parking lot.

Quinn smiled. "Glad we came here. The food and vibe are perfect."

Marlon breathed a sigh of relief. "Thanks for inviting me. I've wanted to check this place out for a while."

"We need to do this again soon."

Both men stood silent for a minute before Marlon found the right words to say. "I agree." Ending a conversation without seeming weird was always difficult for him.

Quinn shrugged. "Well, have a good night. I enjoyed hanging out with you." As he leaned in for a hug, he caught Marlon off guard, resulting in an awkward half-hug.

The two parted ways as they headed to their cars, and Marlon waved goodbye. "Thanks again for the invite."

As soon as the coast was clear, Marlon grinned. He wasn't nervous during dinner. Why did he feel so comfortable around Quinn when he hardly knew him?

# CHAPTER 6

**ON MONDAY MORNING, MARLON GLANCED AT HIS ALARM.**
The time displayed as 10:45 a.m. He had slept through his
first two classes, and the next class of the day didn't begin
for several hours. Sleep would be impossible given the number of hours he had slept over the weekend, so he wandered
into the living room and plopped down on the couch. His
stark white apartment walls sat bare; any shred of decoration
packed away in the closet—a painful reminder of the person
he once was. Light peeked through the dusty vertical blinds
to the side of the couch.

He grabbed the remote off the coffee table and turned
on his television. He flipped through a few channels before
settling on a local news station for the weather report.

A bubbly reporter smiled into the camera, her blazing
red lips glistening. "And this is the third murder to rock the
small town this year. I'm Monica Robertson with Channel
3 News. Back to you, Donna."

Marlon's brow arched at the screen. Those news people were so insensitive, talking about murder and rape with the same happy faces they used to talk about funny cat videos.

The show panned to a different anchorwoman, who shifted in her seat as she adjusted her dress. "Thank you, Monica. In other news, we have an update on the Pine State University rape case. Parker Sullivan, former student and quarterback of the PSU Bears, was indicted in a King County courtroom this morning."

Marlon's stomach twisted in knots. He leaned in and increased the volume.

"The charges included one count each of rape in the second degree, sexual battery, and voyeurism. For the viewers who aren't aware, Parker Sullivan is the son of former Washington State Governor Walter Sullivan. He is accused of sexually assaulting a male student at an off-campus party in June. The trial date is set for May 23. If convicted, he faces the possibility of several decades in prison. This news comes a week after learning the victim returned to the university to resume his studies. No word yet on if the student plans on speaking to the media about the indictment."

The TV powered off as he tossed the remote aside. His shoulders slouched, and he sat frozen on the couch, unable to process the fact it was finally happening. Kenneth Hughes had told him the indictment was coming, but hearing it on the news made it so much more official. He might actually receive justice. But with this came the thought he would also need to relive the assault during the trial and experience intense scrutiny and shame along the way. They had video and photos the entire courtroom would see. He wanted to be excited about the recent developments as there had been no news in months, but it was bittersweet.

He wandered into the bathroom, still in a daze. Now that the courts had set a date for the trial to start, Marlon faced potential questioning by drama-seeking reporters and classmates. Everyone expected him to act either thrilled or frightened by the news, and he couldn't give them the reactions they wanted. No, he needed to change something to show the world he was more than an ongoing news story.

He plugged in his electric clippers and checked himself out in the mirror. He rubbed the skin below his eyes, examining the dark circles that had formed in recent months. He didn't look like the handsome, vibrant man he had been months ago. His fingers fumbled through his tangled tresses. What was once a well-kept style with shaved sides and some length on top was now a jumbled mess, making him appear deranged. The remnants of his May dye job still showed, as his roots were several shades darker than the rest of his hair.

Desperate in his hunt for a pair of scissors, he dug through the medicine cabinet above the sink. The memory of the last time he cut his own hair replayed in his head— he was seven years old, and it was the day before picture day. The photos turned out terrible, and his mother was pissed at him for days. He chuckled as he slid his fingers into the handle of the scissors.

Marlon tried to recall how his barber used to cut his hair. He pulled a chunk in front of his eyes and trimmed the ends. As he made the final cut, he glanced down at the small pile of hair in the sink. He let go of the hair and smiled at how perfect it turned out. He worked with diligence to cut the remaining hair several inches shorter. To finish, he used the clippers to trim the hair on the sides to its usual length. When he finished, he brushed off the trimmings and gazed at his reflection.

The look wasn't complete without a new color. He found the box of bronze-brown hair dye Anna had left under the sink in May. How hard could it be to dye your own hair? It appeared identical to his natural shade, so if it turned out disastrous, he could at least cut his hair off and start over.

He pulled out the bottle of toner, colorant, a pair of gloves, and the instructions, which he read over several times to ensure he didn't miss a single step. After mixing the ingredients together and giving the bottle a gentle shake, he moved his hair back and squirted the mixture on his roots.

With the color applied all over his head, he set a timer on his cell phone for twenty-five minutes. To pass the time, he sat on the couch and played a game on his phone.

Once he grew tired of it, he flipped through the television channels for several minutes. Nothing was worth watching at that hour, as it was news programs, soap operas, and infomercials. *The Judy Faith Show* would have to suffice.

"Yes, Judy, I feel a conviction is likely in this case. All the evidence points to Mr. Sullivan's guilt. I mean, pictures, video, and a rape kit. What more would you need as a juror?" a bald man in his late fifties said.

Marlon nodded at the television.

The loud-mouthed, larger-than-life host gawked. "Listen, Mark, I get what you're saying. There is so much evidence against him, and I hope they convict him. What kind of person does something like this to a defenseless young man? But we need to consider something else here: Parker has a lot of family connections. When the kid got arrested, his daddy bailed him out. We can't expect Walter Sullivan to let his baby boy get humiliated on the stand. I don't think he'll testify. Also, what happens when that poor boy testifies? They're going to destroy him. Mr. Sullivan has David Samberg, one of the nation's best defense attorneys."

Marlon gulped as he leaned closer to the television, and his pulse quickened. Destroy him? He was already stressing over the trial, and that was the last thing he needed to hear.

"You're right, Judy, but even if there isn't a conviction, Parker is expelled from the university. And there's no—" Mark said.

Judy rolled her eyes. "Are you kidding? As if expulsion is punishment enough. The man should be executed! Joining us now is Defense Attorney Connor Phelps. Connor, what are your thoughts? How would you handle this if you were Mr. Sullivan's attorney?"

Marlon bit his lip in anticipation. Parker deserved so much more than expulsion, and the thought of that being his only punishment left him sick to his stomach.

The first expert's image vanished off the screen as a mid-thirties attorney replaced him. "Thank you, Judy. The issue here is perception. Yes, there are photographs and videos, but what do they show? A young man who went too far and had some regrets, or someone unable to consent?"

Connor paused and continued, "I would say Parker has a favorable chance. The Sullivans are a powerful family. Susan is a philanthropist, and Walter is the former governor of Washington. Parker's defense just needs to pick the right witnesses and experts, and he could beat this. It'll be interesting to see how the prosecution presents its case."

Marlon shook his head. There was no way they would acquit Parker. He told the truth, and they had evidence.

Judy tilted her head side to side, weighing the statement. "Great points, Connor. But do you honestly think the jury can see through Mr. Sullivan's guilt by overlooking the photographs and videos, regardless of what they're purported to show? And this young man, the victim, started back at the school this semester. Do you think this recent development will impact the case?"

"Anything is possible. For the first week after the story broke, we didn't have many of the details until someone close to the Sullivan family leaked the video and photo evidence. So, expect the unexpected. I'd say the victim returning to the campus says a lot. It either shows his incredible strength and bravery, or it's proof we may not know the full story."

Marlon scowled at the TV. 'Says a lot'? He was trying to move on with his life, not stir up controversy.

"You're right. I can only imagine what he's going through. Thank you, Connor. Let's go back to the story of the missing three-year-old taken from his home last week. Police have been questioning his mother, Claire Ackerman, who claims the child was with a babysitter for several days while she was partying out of state. We received word earlier that police interviewed the so-called babysitter, and she claimed she had never even met the child's mother." Her hands flew up as she rolled her eyes.

Marlon turned off the television and sat in silence. No matter where he went, he couldn't escape it. He couldn't turn the TV on without hearing about it. And why did they say those things about him when he was telling the truth? Why would he lie about something like that? What did he stand to gain from it?

An alarm buzzed on his phone, letting him know he needed to rinse the dye out of his hair. He rushed to the bathroom, turned the shower on, and yanked his pajamas off as fast as he could before stepping into the cold water.

He shifted the water off, and the last few soap bubbles

swirled down the drain. Thoughts of the reactions of his classmates played in his head. Connor Phelps thought it said a lot that he was back at school. A hairstyle change couldn't be a big deal, right? Maybe he'd blend in with the rest of the students if he looked nothing like the boy everyone grew accustomed to watching each day.

He tiptoed across the chilly tiled floor toward the mirror. A thick layer of fog hid his image. He rubbed the steam away with his hand and smiled at his transformed reflection. He looked human again. And more importantly, he *felt* human again.

———

Marlon's car engine powered off in the campus parking lot. He opened the car door and stepped out in his favorite black boots, which had been collecting dust in the closet for months. He swung his brown leather backpack over his shoulder and walked toward the building.

Crisp green grass glistened under the warm September sun. The stench of a lit cigarette crossed his path as he strolled along the sidewalk. Several students stared at him. Knowing it would shut them up, he grinned and waved.

A girl he recognized across the lawn caught his eye. "Hey, Charlotte," he shouted.

She turned to face him, and her pearly white teeth almost blinded him when she flashed a halfhearted smile.

"Oh, hey, Marlon."

Marlon was already cringing inside since he never particularly liked her. He thought she was two-faced and fake. During the second semester of his freshman year, he caught her texting Anna's ex-boyfriend. And rumors swirled on campus about the possibility of Charlotte's father pulling her from the school after she maxed out a bunch of his credit cards on a weekend shopping binge. He laughed at the memory.

"It's been so long," he said, softening his voice. "How have you been?"

Charlotte winced. "Great. I spent most of my summer in Dubai with my family. How about you?"

His forehead creased, and he gave an impressed nod. "That's awesome. I went home for the summer, but that's about it. Glad to be back in school."

Her eyes narrowed as she stared at his hair. "Did you change your hair, or something? Something's different."

"Yep. Thanks for noticing. What do you think?"

Charlotte placed her hand on her hip. "It's ... cute. I like it."

"Thanks," he said, the pause in her compliment making him chuckle. "I gotta go to class, but it was nice talking to you."

"See you around."

Marlon turned and walked away, muttering to himself in a mocking tone, "I spent the summer in Dubai."

He pushed through the doors of the university, down the hallways, and into the Web Design classroom. As he moved to his usual seat in the room, all eyes shifted toward him. He flipped through his papers as the professor jotted notes on the board. Someone made a faint *psst* noise from behind.

Blake Porter leaned in and whispered to him, "Looking good, Woods."

"Thanks, Blake," Marlon said with a smile, not wanting to appear rude.

"Who studied their HTML codes?" the professor asked, interrupting their whispering.

Marlon raised his hand as he pulled out his notes.

A grin lit up Professor Gasteu's face. "Excellent. What do you remember?"

# CHAPTER 7

DURING THE HOUR-LONG BREAK BETWEEN CLASSES, Marlon retreated to the student lounge. He leaned back in the overstuffed armchair at the far side of the room with his headphones in and listened to Sharon Van Etten. He closed his eyes as the music roared in his ears.

A few minutes into his relaxation, a hand grasped his shoulder and made him jump, almost knocking his phone to the floor. His eyes darted open.

Behind him stood Anna, with her fist over her heart. "Sorry. I didn't mean to scare you."

"Damn. It's all right," Marlon said, almost breathless.

Anna looked him over, concentrating on his hair. "I love the new hair. It's fab."

"When did you start saying that?" Marlon chuckled.

She sat in the chair next to him, propped her chin on her hands, and leaned toward him. "What made you decide to do it?"

Marlon gave an 'are-you-kidding-me' stare and ran his fingers through his dark brown tresses. "I looked like shit."

"I'm glad to see you're coming back to life. You've been through so much."

"Did you hear the news?"

"Yes. How do you feel about it?" Her top teeth bit into her bottom lip.

"Good, but a little nervous. Did you watch *Judy Faith* this morning?" His eyes met hers, and he frowned.

"No. What did she say?" Anna asked, lowering her tone to match his.

"She had some experts on there, and they talked about the potential verdict. They said, on the one hand, the evidence should help me, but the defense could always twist the story around."

He huffed and continued, "I'm worried about testifying. I don't think I can do it. The thought of facing Parker and his lawyers is scary."

Anna rested her palm on his shoulder. "Don't worry about that. You have months before the trial starts, and I'm sure they'll prepare you for it. There's no way anyone can hear all the facts and find him innocent."

"How is Courtney going to react? I can't face her again. It's crazy I even have to worry about this."

Anna glanced around. "She missed all her classes today. I overheard Charlotte talking to someone earlier, and she said Courtney's freaking out. She doesn't think she can stay with Parker if he's convicted. I'm happy that bitch is suffering. She deserves it."

"That makes me feel a little better. I shouldn't let her get to me like last time." He shrugged. "But anyway, what are you doing this weekend? We need to hang out, and you have to meet Quinn. I'm sure you'll love him."

"Hell yes. My apartment on Friday? Please?"

To see his friend so ecstatic brought a smile to his face. "It's a date. I have to head to class now, but I can't wait for Friday."

"Me too. Love ya," Anna said.

Marlon grabbed his textbooks and wandered out of the lounge and into the corridor.

———

On the drive to Quinn's dorm the next day, Marlon cranked the music up and played several scenarios in his head. Should he tell Quinn about what happened to him? What if he already knew? Marlon was trying to move on with his life and make friends, not burden people with his problems. He couldn't bring anything up.

Marlon pulled his car into a parking spot outside the dorm, slammed his door shut, and strolled up to the second floor. After a deep breath gave him the courage he needed, he tapped his fist on the metal three times.

"Yeah, one sec," a voice called out from inside.

*Stay cool, and don't act weird*, he repeated in his head.

The knob rattled, and the door eased open.

"Hey, you. Welcome to my humble abode," Quinn said, grinning.

Marlon smirked back at him. "Thanks for the invite."

"So, do you want to come in or just wait outside?" Quinn looked around behind Marlon and chuckled.

"Oh, I figured we would talk in the doorway for a few hours. My bad." There he went with his flirting again.

Quinn stepped backward and welcomed him inside.

The apartment resembled a typical dorm—beat-up furniture that had seen better days, poor lighting, plain-colored walls, and what barely qualified as a kitchen. The sweet scent of patchouli filled the air, and the wooden octagonal coffee table featured five lit candles of assorted shapes and sizes.

They neared the tan sofa, and Quinn tapped on the rear cushion. "Have a seat. Are you thirsty? I have water, sparkling water, and—"

"Let me guess, more water?"

Quinn gasped, pretending to act surprised. "How did you know? Did you break into my house and raid the fridge or something?"

"I'll have plain old water." Marlon's smile faded, and his tone mellowed out. More flirting. He had to stop reciprocating before he crossed a line.

The boxy, white refrigerator cracked open, and Quinn

dipped his head inside, muffling his voice. "So, what do you wanna do?"

The question made Marlon's stomach burn. Not what Quinn had in mind, he was sure. "How about that movie you wanted to watch with me?"

Quinn passed a bottle of water to him. "Ooh, *The Shining*? I would love to."

"Is it cool if I run to the bathroom first?"

"What kind of fancy mansion do you think I live in?"

Marlon laughed. "I'm sorry I overestimated your wealth. Now, could you tell me which door it is?"

"Sure, second door on the left," Quinn said, motioning toward it with his head.

"Be right back." Marlon didn't need to go, but he wanted a moment alone to collect his thoughts. Being there was more stressful than it should have been.

He strutted inside the bathroom, closed the door behind him, and exhaled. He stared into the mirror, his fake-happy expression vanishing in an instant as thoughts dashed through his brain.

He was there, hanging out with someone—a boy. But he couldn't lead him on. He was a friend, and that's all he needed. He reminded himself of what happened to him last time. And with the whole impending trial thing, what would people say? Just a friend, nothing more.

To keep up the illusion he needed to go to the restroom, he flushed the toilet and washed his hands before returning to the living room.

Quinn clicked on the remote. "Oh, hey. You're back in time for the movie."

Marlon flashed a smile, eyeing the cushion-sized gap he'd keep between Quinn and himself. "Awesome."

———

An hour into the film, Quinn twisted around toward him. "Sorry to interrupt, but I've got a question for ya."

Marlon's shoulders tensed with anticipation. "Sure, what's up?"

"When did you come out to your family and friends? Sorry, is that too personal?"

He shook his head. The question wasn't as personal as the ones he had grown accustomed to in recent months. "No, not at all. Um, I was like fifteen. What about you?"

Quinn's brow furrowed. "Wow, you're brave. I waited until I was seventeen, so it's still kind of a new thing for my family. How did yours take the news?"

"Most of them were cool with it. The only person who acted weird was my grandma. She's what my mom calls *old-fashioned*—as if that's an excuse—but she eventually came around."

"Ugh, I hate that word—old-fashioned. But I'm glad they took it well. Mine was super accepting. My mom is bi, which I didn't find out until after I came out to everyone, and my sister is trans. So yeah, they're pretty awesome. Things have been good."

Marlon smiled. He was lucky to know someone like Quinn and not have to fear feeling judged. He wished he could have known him before everything happened, back when he was a normal, social person with friends.

"Aw, that's amazing. Good for you. There aren't many of *us* at Pine State, unfortunately," Marlon said.

"There are more than you'd expect. Some people stay locked in the closet forever or wait until way later in life to come out. It's sad."

Marlon closed his eyes for a second. "Yeah, that's so true. How do you like Pine so far?"

"So far, so good. I haven't met many people as cool as you yet, but there are a few classmates who I wouldn't mind hanging out with. Everyone seems a little on edge here, though, and I'm still trying to put my finger on it."

"Hmm, I wonder why. Maybe you feel that way because you're new and are still getting used to everyone," Marlon said, catching himself overexplaining again.

"Yeah, true. It's a new experience for me. Anyway, sorry for interrupting the movie. What do we have, like, seven hours left?"

Marlon nudged Quinn's arm with his elbow. "Oh, come on. It's more like ten."

Once the film wrapped up, the two strangers-turned-acquaintances sat in silence.

Goodbyes were always so awkward for Marlon. Why couldn't he tell Quinn he wanted to leave like any normal person would?

"So, uh … what now?" Quinn asked, breaking the uncomfortable quiet between them.

Marlon's heart lurched into his throat. "Um, I should probably go home."

"Sounds good. Thanks for coming over. Hope to hang again soon."

"Me too."

As they walked to the door, a question struck Marlon. "Hey, why don't you have a roommate? Are you an undercover cop or a rich person in disguise or something?"

"Oh, I wish. No, they didn't assign anyone to me this semester. I guess I'm lucky. I've heard horror stories. Nothing as bad as hotel ghosts, though."

Marlon laughed. "Yes, you *are* lucky."

Quinn's warmth enveloped Marlon as they hugged goodbye, the most he had felt from a hug in a long time.

*Just friends*, he replayed in his head.

———

The highly anticipated night of his planned hang out with Anna and Quinn had arrived once class let out on Friday. A flood of students filled the cramped hallways. Marlon was one of the last to leave, hanging back to avoid the swarm of people.

"Hey, you got the time?" a woman asked, clutching her books to her chest.

Marlon looked around, thinking there was no way she was talking to him. When she continued staring at him, he realized she was. "Oh, sorry. Hold on." He tapped on his smartwatch and read the time. "Yeah, two-thirty."

"Thanks," the woman said with a smile. "Nice shoes, by the way."

Marlon grinned back at her and glanced down at his watch again. When he looked up, a tan man with short, black hair stood in front of him.

"Hey, why are you talking to my girl?" Nathan Cartwright asked.

Marlon swallowed hard. "Excuse me?"

"Why were you talking to her? She doesn't need to talk to pieces of shit like you."

The scenario was too similar to Marlon's reoccurring nightmare for it to be real. He blinked several times, willing himself to wake.

"We all know you're lying. You can have your *Judy Faith* and fake news, bro, but you better stay the hell away from Andrea or so help me God," Nathan said, his face glowing red.

Marlon couldn't process what he had done to piss him off like that. "I-I'm sorry? I don't understand—"

Nathan stepped closer. "You're lucky they even let you

back in. I swore I wouldn't say anything if I ran into you, but man, you are testing my patience. If there weren't all these people around, I'd knock you out," he said, his voice low and breathy.

Marlon's stomach burned as the urge to turn and run became stronger by the second. But he hadn't defended himself in the previous confrontations, and he couldn't risk his ego taking another beating like that. He had nothing left to lose. "Do it, then."

Nathan clenched a fist and curled his lips. "You don't want those problems."

"I don't know what's wrong with you. Your—that girl asked me what time it was. If you have a problem with me, that's on you," Marlon said, a lump forming in his throat as he instantly regretted saying those words. He didn't need another drive-thru incident.

"Nobody trusts or likes you, okay? You should—"

Austin Hooper approached Nathan from behind, clutched his shoulder, and squeezed. "Hey, leave him the hell alone. Okay?"

Marlon had never spoken to Austin before, but recognized him from a class the previous year.

Nathan turned to face him. "Yo, Austin, he tried—"

"I don't care what he tried to do. Leave it alone. Do you really think this is a good idea?"

Nathan glared at Marlon and stormed away, saying nothing.

"Thanks for helping me, I—"

Austin's head shook, silencing Marlon. "Don't thank me. It's the right thing to do."

Marlon clasped the straps of his backpack tighter with his thumbs.

The two men nodded at each other and took off in different directions. Another day, another run-in with one of Parker's friends. When would the madness end?

# CHAPTER 8

A CHIRPY RINGTONE BLARED ON MARLON'S PHONE, AND his mother's picture flashed on the screen. He tapped the Answer button several times. "Hello?"

"Hi, sweetheart. How's it going? Are you, how do you say it, slaying those classes?" his mother asked, her mellow voice echoing through the speaker.

He chuckled at her attempt to use slang. "I've been trying to keep busy. I'm about to go hang out with Anna and Quinn."

"Aw, that sounds like fun, sweetie. That's the guy you were telling me about, right? I'm so proud of you."

He grinned at the phone. "Yep. Thanks, Mom. Things have been okay for the most part."

"I know when we talked the other day about the trial announcement, you were hanging in there. Keep your head up, kiddo," his mother said, her voice like honey.

The clock was ticking, and he needed to finish preparing for the night. "Thanks, Mom. Hey, I have to go now. I need to get ready. Maybe I can call you tomorrow."

His mother made kissing noises into the phone. "All right. Take care, sweetie. I love ya bunches."

The call ended, and he sifted through his wardrobe to find the perfect outfit. Not that he wanted to impress anybody, but he didn't want Quinn to upstage him with his exquisite taste in fashion once again. Marlon selected a simple midnight-blue polka-dotted dress shirt, blue pleated pants, and brown shoes. That ought to do the trick.

———

While he waited in the parking lot at Anna's place, he took a minute to fix his hair in the rear-view mirror. A car pulled up beside his, and he recognized Quinn sitting in the driver's seat. The two men exited their cars.

When Quinn saw Marlon's outfit, he stepped backward and put his fist on his chin to gaze at him like a painter studying their finished piece of art. "Wow, nice choice."

Marlon checked out Quinn's simple blue jeans and white T-shirt, and his face flushed at the realization he had overdressed. "Thanks. You aren't so bad yourself."

They strolled up to Anna's apartment, and Marlon knocked twice. Footsteps stomped their way to the door, and it burst open. "Hey, guys. I'm so happy you came. Good to meet you, Quinn. I've heard lots about you."

He glanced at Marlon. "All good things, I hope."

Anna gave them both hugs and motioned for them to sit on the long, gray couch against the wall.

"Nice place you got here. Do you have a roomie?" Quinn asked, his eyes filled with wonder.

"Nope, just me. I didn't want to do the dorms this year. No offense if you live in one, but I hate how crowded they are. Ugh. I made that mistake freshman year," Anna said.

Marlon laughed. "Jeez, am I the only one who didn't ever do dorms? As soon as I told my mom I wanted to go to college, she said we needed to find an apartment nearby be-cause—in her words—'Dorms are scary and gross and those parties are insane, honey.'"

"Your mom wasn't wrong," Anna said. "I *hated* my roommate. It was this girl named Sloane Larson—she was a mess. She never picked up after herself, and she got all weird a few months into the semester. It was a nightmare."

Quinn's eyes tightened. "Wow. Thanks for making me feel better about this, guys."

"You don't have a roommate, so I don't wanna hear it."

"Is that true?" Anna asked, laughing. "Tell me about yourself, Quinn. I wanna know *everything*."

"Yeah, no problem. What do you wanna know? I'm eighteen. I'm a Sagittarius. I'm majoring in political science. I grew up all over Jefferson County, Colorado. Um, other than that, I'm a huge movie and music fan. I guess I've seen about fifty concerts so far."

Anna's brows raised, and she gave an impressed nod. "Damn, that's amazing. I've been to, like, three. How can you afford it?"

"My dad knew a guy who gave away tickets when concerts wouldn't sell out. That's how I got into a lot of shows for free." Quinn's left shoulder raised and fell. "What are you majoring in?"

"Graphic design, with a minor in business. It's my third year, and I can't wait to finish."

"I bet. I'm only in my freshman year, and I'm ready for it to end already. Sometimes I wish I could change my grades like I … Never mind." Quinn smirked.

Marlon and Anna gasped. "What?"

"It's not a huge deal, but when I was a junior in high school, I found a way to change some of my grades. They made one of the administrative passwords something super basic: admin. How stupid is that? At first, I wanted to see if it did anything, so I fixed a few of my friends' grades. When the teachers didn't notice anything, I did mine. It wasn't anything crazy like all A's, but I changed a C to a B and a B to an A."

"That's pretty badass," Marlon said, his expression softening. "Did they ever catch you?"

Quinn chuckled. "Did they catch me? No. But they changed the password, and I pretended it never happened. I didn't think it was a big deal to change a few grades. Nobody can ever find out about this, though. Promise?"

Marlon and Anna glanced at each other and bowed their heads in compliance.

"Do you guys wanna play Cards Against Humanity? It could be fun," Anna said.

Quinn nodded. "Oh, hell yeah. Prepare to lose."

"Because *I'm* going to win," Marlon said.

Anna shook her head. She grabbed the box of cards from under the coffee table and distributed them amongst the three.

After a few rounds of the game with Quinn winning more than the other two, they relaxed and put on a movie. Anna sat Marlon and Quinn together on the couch and rested on the loveseat nearby. Every so often, she peered over toward Marlon and winked.

Marlon's mind kept drifting from the film back to the predicament Anna had put him in. Was he overthinking the whole sitting together thing? There was no way this would end how she was hoping since Marlon wasn't interested. At least, that's what he continued telling himself.

"So, Quinn, are you seeing anybody?" Anna asked, breaking the quiet in the room during a boring part of the movie.

"Nope. Truth be told, I've never been in a relationship," Quinn said.

She huffed. "You've never been in a relationship? Why not?"

"That's rude, Anna. You can't just ask someone why they're single," Marlon said.

"I mean, I've been with a few people, but no strings attached. None of the people in my town were relationship material, but maybe things will be different here in Washington. Who knows?" Quinn shrugged.

Anna smiled at Marlon. Her motives became clear to him at that moment.

He flashed a glare at her. "Yeah, I'm sure you'll find someone, Quinn. You're a nice guy."

"Thanks. The right man is out there somewhere. What about you? Are either of you dating anyone?"

Butterflies danced around in Marlon's stomach. This question had the potential to go into the danger zone. It was the one thing he couldn't discuss in front of Quinn.

"No, I got dick on the regular last semester but haven't put myself out there lately. Classes are extra shitty this year, and I just don't have the time anymore," Anna said.

Both men chuckled, and Quinn covered his ears. "That was more than I needed to hear. But I appreciate the honesty."

Anna bounced her shoulder. "Hey, I'm not one of those girls who is ashamed of her body. I know what I've got, and I'm proud of who I am."

"And that's one of the reasons why you're my best friend," Marlon said.

Quinn turned toward Marlon. "What about you? Are

you talking to anyone?"

The tension grew on so many levels with his question, a knife couldn't cut through it.

Anna's eyes met Marlon's, and her tone dropped to a mumble. "Does he know—"

"About Marcus Bradshaw? No, Anna, you're so silly. I haven't mentioned it," Marlon said quickly, the words slipping right out of his mouth. It was a closer call than he ever hoped to encounter.

Quinn scrunched his face. "Who is Marcus?"

Since Anna left Marlon speechless by her near exposure of his deepest, darkest secret, she took the cue to answer on his behalf. "His ex. They broke up in March."

Quinn frowned at Marlon. "Oh, damn, sorry you guys split up. How did things end?"

"He cheated on me with someone from another college, and then he transferred there not long after."

Quinn winced. "Aw, man, sorry if I brought up a touchy subject for you. Can't say I know how a break-up feels, but it's gotta suck."

"Don't worry, it's not that big of a deal. It was a long time ago, and I got over it pretty fast." *Because something worse happened.*

———

Quinn let out a yawn as the film credits played. "Sorry, guys.

I gotta go. I'm exhausted."

"Aw, okay. It was really nice meeting you, Quinn. We'll have to hang out again soon, and I *will* beat you at the next round of Cards Against Humanity," Anna said.

Quinn laughed. "We'll see about that. Nice meeting you as well."

Marlon and Anna walked with Quinn toward the front door and hugged him goodbye.

Quinn disappeared down the steps, and Marlon stuck around to talk to Anna.

"What did you think of him?" Marlon asked as the door clicked shut.

"I liked him a lot. He seems like a great guy."

Marlon flashed a shy smile. "Yeah, he is."

"Do I hear wedding bells?"

"I saw what you were doing earlier. I'm still not interested in dating. There are too many things I need to work through."

"I didn't hear a no."

"Shut up, Anna."

The two friends laughed at each other.

Her mouth snapped shut, and she stared at him. "Uh, so you didn't tell him about—"

He shook his head and pressed his hand against the side of his neck. "No."

"When are you going to tell him? He's bound to find out sooner or later, and I would hate for someone else on campus to break the news to him."

"I don't know him well enough, and we're both new to this whole friendship thing. I'm not even sure if I can consider him a friend yet. I'm still learning to trust him. Besides, he's the only person in my life not hounding me about the trial—no offense—and once he finds out the most personal thing about me, it's over. I guess I'm holding on to this for as long as I can."

She nodded. "Yeah, I get that. Sorry. You know I love you and support you. Whenever you're ready to tell him, I'm sure he'll understand."

# CHAPTER 9

MARLON'S PHONE VIBRATED, AND HE TAPPED THE GREEN button and answered. "Hello?"

"Yo, Marl, it's Quinn," the voice said, surrounded by background noise.

Marlon chuckled. "Don't call me that. What's up?"

"Are we still on for coffee later?"

"Sure. Is three all right with you?"

Quinn hummed into the phone. "Hmm, I'm not sure. I'm suuuuuuper busy with my exciting life. I'll have to get back to you."

"Oh, shut up. You wish."

"Maybe I can move some things around and find the time. But on one condition."

Marlon's palms became sweaty, and his mind raced. Was Quinn about to cross the line? "And what is that?"

"Anna has to come with us."

Marlon's body untensed. "She'd love that. I'll text her

and let her know."

"Cool. See you then?" Quinn asked, his tone revealing a hint of excitement.

"Yes. Talk to you later."

———

Marlon parked near the entrance of Noir Coffee, turned off the engine, and sat in silence. He reminded himself he shouldn't stress because they were his friends. He was doing normal things with people, and he should be proud of himself because he came so far. And so what if he hadn't told Quinn about what happened? He wanted to hold on to that carefree feeling for as long as he could before reality crept back in and snatched it away again.

Marlon flipped the visor and stared at himself. He knew he needed to fake a smile and go in there. That wasn't the time or place to think about Parker or the trial. He adjusted his hair with his fingers and closed the mirror.

Once inside, he spotted Anna and Quinn sitting in the corner, chatting with each other.

Anna pointed at him. "Late as usual, huh?"

"You know me too well. Time for new friends."

Quinn thrust his palm over his chest as if hit with a bullet. "*Ouch!* That quick, huh?"

Marlon stood in line behind a middle-aged blonde lady

and looked back at his friends. "Did you guys order already?"

"Yep, like ten minutes ago," Anna said.

Marlon's cheeks turned rosy. If they were there for that long alone, had she already told him about *it*? No, Anna would never do something like that. "Oh, sorry—didn't realize you would show up so early. I'll go order."

When the woman ahead of him finished ordering for her entire office, it was his turn. He stepped up in front of the red-haired cashier he saw on many trips to the coffee shop. His eyes fixated on her name tag, which read "Katie."

"Hi, what can I get started for you?" she asked, grinning.

He shook the blank expression from his face and smiled back. "Hey, could I please have a medium iced vanilla latte? Thanks, Katie."

She plucked a clear plastic cup from the holder next to her as her other hand tapped on the screen. "Sure. Anything else?"

"No, that's it."

He paid for his drink, waited for another barista to finish making it, and walked back over to his friends.

Quinn flailed his hands around. "And that's why I'll never try it again."

Marlon's forehead creased. "Uh, what did I miss?"

"His story about going vegan for three days," Anna said.

Marlon slid the chair out at the four-seat table and

plopped down. "So sad I missed that exciting story."

Quinn reclined in his seat and sipped from his cup. "Sorry, we're not all interesting and mysterious like you."

Marlon shot him a look that said, '*Oh, please. A simple Google search will tell you all there is to know about me.*'

Anna cleared her throat. "So, I have a secret to share with you guys, but you have to swear you won't tell anyone."

"What? No, I'm planning on telling all thirty of my friends in class. Sorry to spoil the surprise."

"Shut up, Quinn. I'm serious. This is juicy," Anna said.

What could this news be? She wouldn't keep something a secret from him. Marlon leaned forward and reduced his voice to a whisper. "What's the tea?"

"So, you guys know Pierce?" she asked, her voice so quiet it was almost unintelligible.

"Of course I do. No, never heard of the guy. Should I know him?" Quinn asked, shrugging. Quinn's constant playfulness gave Marlon the realization there was no way he could handle his truth.

"Wait, you mean Pierce Barnett?" Marlon asked.

"Yep. We hooked up last night."

Marlon flashed a suspicious glare. "Whaaaat? I thought you hated him."

"Who said anything about liking him? I gave him the best night of his life, though."

Quinn burst into laughter. "I'm not sure who he is, but that's hilarious. You go, girl."

She held her hand to her chest and smirked. "Thanks. I gave him a piece of the ol' Moody booty. Wham, bam, thank you ma'am."

Marlon chuckled. "God, I love you, Anna."

"A girl wants what she wants. Thanks for not slut-shaming me, guys. This is why you're my friends."

Quinn's facial expression shifted, and his voice changed into a strange combination of a Southern accent and a drunk person slurring their words. "Hot dog, we got a Jezebel and two hummersexuals over here thinking they can do whatever they want with their lives. I'll be damned. Someone lock 'em up. Burn 'em at the stake."

Marlon loved how Quinn could make him laugh without even trying. "What the hell was that? Is that how you think Southerners sound?"

Quinn shrugged. "Are you not entertained?"

Anna pointed at him with finger guns. "Ah, I get the reference. Marlon, can we keep him?"

Marlon clasped his chin with his fingertips. "I'll have to talk to your mother about it, but I don't see why not."

The three friends laughed.

Anna glanced at Quinn. "So, do you have any scandalous stories you'd like to share with the group?"

"Um, no, I don't. Sorry. Does destroying a pint of ice cream by myself in one sitting count? If so, I did that last night. Hope you can forgive me," Quinn said in a serious tone, followed by laughter.

Marlon shook his head. "What a skank."

Quinn sipped his drink. "So, Marlon told me before that he's an only child. Do you have any siblings, Anna?"

Marlon's eyes darted toward Anna's. Quinn shouldn't have asked that question.

She sighed and glanced at the ceiling, tapping her fingertips against the coffee cup. "I had a sister who passed away in March. Her name was Whitney."

Joy melted from Quinn's face as his head lowered. "I'm so sorry. I didn't mean to bring up something so painful. How are you dealing with everything?"

"This is weird to say, but her death didn't come as a surprise. She became addicted to drugs two years ago, and her life spiraled out of control pretty fast. It's still a little hard for me to talk about sometimes, but I'm at peace with the whole thing now because I know she's in a better place."

Marlon patted her arm with his hand. "Anna's been through so much, and she always bounces back."

Quinn's lips pressed together. "Yeah, I can see that. Have you considered becoming a counselor or therapist or something, Anna?"

"No, I'm the worst at giving advice and listening to people talk about their problems. I'll stick with burying my own feelings, thanks." Anna laughed in an attempt to lighten the mood.

The chair screeched as Marlon slid backward and stood. "Sorry to ditch you guys for a minute, but I have to run to the bathroom. Be right back."

Anna's chin rested on her fists. "My dear, your idea of 'a minute' is so different from mine. But take your time."

After another sip of his drink, Marlon grinned sarcastically at her. "Whatever."

The restroom door creaked open and slammed shut. He waited for a second to see if anyone else was in there, but he was alone. He entered the stall furthest from the entrance, twisted the lock, and stood there for a moment to collect his thoughts. *Wow, this is normal. Look at you, hanging out with your friends. Yes, that's right: you have* friends.

He flushed the toilet and approached the sink. After lathering his hands up several times, he rinsed the soap off and fumbled with the paper towel dispenser. The door slammed open, and he needed to hurry because hanging out in the restroom while someone completed their business was weird to him.

He tossed the dampened paper towel in the trash can and almost ran into the person who entered. "Oh, sorry."

"No problem, man. Whoa, Marlon, is that you?"

Where did Marlon recognize his voice from? "Uh, yes. Hi." His eyes raised to meet the man's face.

Asher glanced at the two empty stalls behind Marlon. "You got a minute?"

What would he want to talk about? They hardly knew each other, and he was friends with … Oh no. Marlon gulped. "No, my friends are waiting. I should go back."

"I wanted to talk about the whole trial thing. It's crazy, man. Are you really going forward with this? If so, I—"

Marlon's eyes squeezed shut. "I don't wanna talk about it. Please, let me leave."

"All I wanna know is the truth. I've heard so many things, and people are talking. The least you can do is tell me what happened."

What if he didn't? Did he owe anyone an explanation? The thought of being grilled about his sexual assault was unbelievable to him.

His palms faced Asher to silence him. "No, the truth is already out there. What you believe is up to you, but I'm asking you to move so I can leave."

A frown covered Asher's face as he stuck his arm up in the doorframe, blocking the only other path out of the room. "I'm trying to help you, but you won't say—"

"Leave me alone. What are you doing to *help* me? Harassing me in a bathroom after I asked you several times to move so that I can go back to my friends? Believe what you want, but I'm done with this conversation."

Before Asher could react, the door opened.

"Hey, Marlon, are you in here?" Quinn called out.

Marlon glared at Asher and then at the doorway. "Yes, I was just leaving."

Asher's expression dulled as he lowered his arms and unblocked the exit.

Quinn almost collided with Asher's back as he turned

the corner. His eyes widened. "Sorry. Did I interrupt something?"

"No, I was telling Asher about how you guys were waiting for me. Sorry I took so long."

"Who is he?" Quinn whispered as Marlon grabbed his arm and pulled him out of the restroom.

"Someone I share a class with. Don't worry about it."

They returned to the table with Anna.

"Took you long enough, diva."

Should he tell her? No. If he did, he'd owe Quinn an explanation on the reason for the confrontation.

"Takes one to know one," Marlon said in a mocking tone.

# CHAPTER 10

**ON OCTOBER 24, MARLON AWOKE TO A FAMILIAR DINGING** on his phone. Sleepiness fought back as he struggled to open his eyes. After taking a few moments to wake up, he snatched the phone off the nightstand and brought the screen to life.

A white notification box alerted him of a new email from Pine State University. He found it odd the school would email so early in the morning. Unable to fight the exhaustion off, he fell fast asleep once again.

A short while later, his phone vibrated several more times. He reached for it again, groaning to himself. It was an incoming call from Anna.

"Hello?" he said, his voice tired and faint.

Anna panted into the receiver. "Marlon? Are you okay?"

Uncertain if it was a dream, he peered down to double-check the time. "Uh, yeah. Why?"

The line fell silent for a moment.

"You haven't heard, have you? Oh, god."

What was she talking about? His heart plummeted into his stomach. "What's wrong? Did something happen? Am I missing something?"

She sighed. "I'm not sure how to tell you this. It's going to hurt."

"Say it, Anna. Don't do this to me."

"Someone hacked the university website and posted some pictures. The, um, the ones with Parker. I don't understand how this happened, but—" she said, her voice cracking as she sniffled.

"Wait a second. What did you say? If this is a joke—"

"I'm so sorry. I wish I were kidding. I can't figure out who would do this. What kind of an asshole blasts photos of a rape all over a university email?"

His face turned pale, and the hair on his arms raised. "They sent out an email?"

After the words left his mouth, he recalled the notification he received about an hour earlier. He yanked the phone away from his head and scrambled into his email. Sure enough, an unread message appeared in bold lettering at the top of the list from the Pine State University administrative account, which faculty used for notifications.

Anna let out a loud gasp, causing Marlon to almost drop his phone. "Did you get the email? Please, whatever you do, don't open it. It's bad. You don't need to see that. I wish I could make this all go away."

He stared wide-eyed at the unread email, losing focus on his friend's words. The only way to satisfy his curiosity and figure out what it said required opening the email. No, he couldn't do it. But how would he know if he didn't?

Anna cleared her throat and shouted, "Hello? Are you still there? Please, don't hang up on me. Say something."

His eyes fixated on the title of the email:

*PINE STATE SUPPORTS RAPISTS*

A lump formed in his throat as his trembling hand squeezed the phone. He whimpered as the tears poured down his face. "I-I'm trying not to open the email."

"Don't do it. I'll come over to your apartment to be with you. We can figure this out together."

Frozen with fear and unable to respond, he nodded. But she couldn't hear a nod. "Okay."

Car keys clattered in the background. "I'm on my way now. Be there in ten. Don't go anywhere."

He gazed at the phone for a minute until the screen timed out and darkened. What was he going to do? Suffering through the sexual assault and having the pictures and video leak was bad enough, but now they were shoved in front of the hungry eyes of the entire school. He didn't want to be in Washington anymore. Why did he come back here in the first place? This was so *wrong*.

Unlocking the phone once again proved to be a struggle as his hand shook while he entered his lock code. Once more, the email lit up in front of him. Why would somebody do that? Did they think they were helping him, or were they trying to exploit him and his assault further?

Curiosity got the best of him as his index finger dangled over the email. After a few deep breaths, he clicked on it. It was too late to turn back. The screen lit up with a white background and the familiar red Pine State University logo and header. Based on the first glimpse, he could only see the title and school emblem.

Several more gasps of air later, he scrolled down.

*Pine State University protects their beloved sexual predator, former quarterback Parker Sullivan, after allowing him to rape multiple students. Director of Admissions Dr. Allison Hubbard was caught on tape defending her favorite rapist with two other faculty members after his indictment. On the tape, she can be heard calling the victim a liar and a conman. Tell me, does this look like an innocent person?*

*- #QBJUSTICE*

Marlon didn't intend to move the screen down further, but he couldn't stop himself. Four full-color photos displayed his rape. When someone posted them on his social media accounts, he had avoided seeing the pictures before deleting his accounts. Not this time, though.

For several minutes, he sat there numb, his eyes glued

to the screen. The first two images showed him lying face down on the ground with his pants pulled around his ankles as Parker forced his way inside of him. The third image was a close-up of his battered face at the end of the assault, and the last one showed the monster's face mid-orgasm. The pictures appeared to be screenshots from a video.

The sight made Marlon touch the deep scar on his wrist and brought dark feelings to the front of his mind as he re-traumatized himself. He wished he'd never been born. His stomach quivered with the urge to vomit.

The screen closed out because of inactivity, and the front door flapped open.

"Hey, it's Anna. I used my key. Are you in here?" Upon opening the bedroom door, she found him lying in bed, fixated on his phone. "Tell me you didn't look."

Not even a single eyelash batted in her direction to acknowledge her arrival. The blank screen still held his attention. His eyes became bloodshot from the dried tears and not blinking for so long.

Anna burst into tears. "You saw them, didn't you? I told you not to look. I'm so sorry you had to see that." Within moments, she turned into a blubbering mess.

"Q.B. It's Quinn. He sent the email."

Anna exhaled, her eyes wide and shimmering with tears. "What? Why would you think he did this?"

He glanced up at her with a pleading gaze. "It's him. The hacker signed off with QBJUSTICE. His initials are

Q.B. Quinn Beckham. Remember, he told us about hacking the computer system in high school to change his grades?"

"You're right, I forgot. But why would he do this to you? You're friends, and he moved here in August, so he wouldn't have any reason to do something like this," she said, a hint of doubt in her voice.

"Think about it. He's a political science major, and he told me he wanted to get into politics to help people. I ran into him in the computer lab a few days after the fall semester started, and he tried to start a friendship. He texted me all the time. What if he knew about what happened all along, and he used me for a news story or something?"

"I think you're overwhelmed and aren't thinking this through. Quinn wouldn't do this to you. And why would he sign off the email with his own initials? That's stupid."

Marlon glared at Anna. "Shut up and listen to me. I know he used me, and I should have known better than to trust someone like him."

Anna frowned. "But I can't think of what would have prompted this. He doesn't seem like the type of guy who would intentionally hurt anyone."

He shrugged as the tears welled in his eyes once more. "Maybe he thought he was helping me by doing this. I remember he mentioned something about hating crooked rich people when we hung out for the first time."

"If this is someone's idea of helping you, they're an idiot. How do you want to handle this?"

"I don't know anymore, but I'm done. If this is how it's going to be, I don't wanna play this game. The trial hasn't happened yet, and I'm already dealing with all of this shit."

Anna reached toward his shoulder, but he swatted her away. "Don't give up, Marlon. This is just another bump in the road, and I'm so sorry you have to deal with this. Things will get better. I know that sounds cliché, but it's the truth. I'm not going anywhere. I'll miss class today if I have to."

Both of their phones vibrated, and they locked eyes before reaching for them.

She shook her head. "It couldn't be. It must be a stupid sales promotion from a store or something."

Marlon gazed at his phone for several seconds before he rushed into his email in a frenzy. He needed to know what it was.

Her hand flew up over his screen. "What if it's something bad again? What if they—"

He shifted the phone away. "It's from the school. The subject is 'Please disregard the last email.'"

The two sat in silence until Anna grabbed her phone and searched through it. "Oh, thank god. There's nothing bad in this one. I'll read it to you. 'Please accept our sincerest apologies for the previous email. An investigation is pending to locate the source of the hack. All university servers, websites, and email accounts were verified to be secure and safe by our IT group.' Bring on the damage control."

"I'm gonna tell them who did it. This needs to stop."

Her jaw clenched. "Are you sure? We still don't know if Quinn did this, and we need to think things through before we—"

Without giving her a chance to finish, he scrunched his face. "Yes, I'm positive, Anna. He used our friendship to seek revenge against someone he's never met. Either you're with me on this one, or you're against me."

With a hesitant nod, she agreed with him.

———

Two hours later, after calming down, they drove to the campus to meet with the administration. Although they still hadn't called Marlon to discuss the hack, he needed to talk to them.

Marlon struggled to leave the car. The pressure of being on campus hit him with brute force.

A fair number of students lingered outside the administrative building and, as Marlon and Anna approached, stared with mouths agape. Whispers echoed through his ears and reminded him of his first day back at Pine State University after the assault.

Without so much as a second thought, Marlon forced through the doors and into the administrative offices. "I need to speak with Dean Hamilton immediately."

Recognition dawned on the executive secretary's face, and her eyes widened. "Oh, uh ... yes. Yes, sir. One moment while I notify her."

She peered down at her phone and back up at Marlon several times, covering the side of her mouth as she whispered into the receiver.

A minute later, a middle-aged woman with brown skin and a shoulder-length black bob strolled out from behind the door. "Pardon me, Mr. Woods? Yes, please come in and have a seat."

As he and Anna entered, the dean locked eyes with Anna. "Is this necessary?"

The words inflamed Marlon, making his skin hot. "I won't talk to you without her."

"Very well." Dean Hamilton motioned for them to sit in the room. "Mr. Woods, I am sorry we have not reached out to you yet. As I'm sure you can imagine, these things are delicate, and we wanted to conduct an investigation first. Now, I want to let you know we have suspended Dr. Hubbard and those implicated on the tape without pay until the investigation finishes, and we hope to—"

"Cover it up?" Marlon's jaw clenched as he scowled at her. "Listen, I'm not here for an apology. I came to tell you who did it."

"Oh? How do you know?"

"I just know. Do you want their name or not?"

"Tell me, and we will look into it. If it is a student, we won't tell them you told us."

"Quinn Beckham. He did this."

The dean placed her fingers to her chin. "I am not familiar with that name. Where did you get this information from?"

As Marlon took a sharp breath, Anna stepped in for him. "The email ended with QBJUSTICE, and Q.B. are his initials, and his major is political science, hence the 'justice' part. That's Marlon's theory, at least."

Dean Hamilton leaned in and raised an eyebrow. "And how do you know him?"

Tears rushed to Marlon's eyes. "I thought he was my friend, but I guess not."

Dean Hamilton jotted notes on a piece of paper. "Well, don't you worry. We will look into this and get to the bottom of things."

He flashed an intense, fevered stare at her. It reminded him of how little the school had done for him so far. What made this any different?

"Right, because you've all been so supportive. Your students are bullying me, and nobody has done anything to stop it. I suggest you do your job for once and put an end to this shit."

Anna and Dean Hamilton stared at each other until the dean said, "Sorry you feel that way, or if we gave you the impression we don't care. Again, as I am sure you are aware, an institution such as ours cannot make statements or assumptions based on allegations of a sexual assault without a formal investigation. I wish you would have reported it to us first and given us a chance to investigate."

"Had I reported my rape to you, there wouldn't be a trial, and Parker would still play for the Bears. Goodbye."

With that, he grabbed Anna's hand and stormed out of the office.

———

Back at Marlon's apartment, they streamed a few shows to pass the time and distract themselves.

Marlon's phone vibrated with a call from Quinn. When he rejected the request, a text message popped up:

*Call me.*

# CHAPTER 11

THE TWO FRIENDS EXCHANGED GLANCES, AND MARLON contemplated what he should do. There were so many questions he needed answers to.

"Should I call him back? I'm too upset to talk to him right now."

Anna gave him a concerned once-over. "It's up to you, but whatever you say to him won't translate well over a text or phone call. You're better off doing it in person."

Marlon's shoulders slumped. "But what if I can't start the conversation? Or what if he gets pissed off and punches me or something?"

"He doesn't seem like the fighting type to me. You should be safe, and I'll be with you to make sure nothing happens."

"You're right. Can you set it up for me?"

She grabbed her phone and tapped on the screen. "Sure. Let me see if he can meet us at the park."

A few minutes later, a notification appeared, and she read it aloud. "Okay, he responded and said he could meet us there in fifteen. Does that work for you?"

Marlon hadn't expected the meeting to take place so soon. The notion of their inevitable confrontation happening within the next twenty minutes left him shaking.

"Sure, I guess. Let's go."

———

The gray, cloud-filled sky brought a haze over the park. Anna pulled into a parking spot, and Marlon spotted Quinn sitting at a picnic table under a tree. "There he is."

As they approached, Quinn rose out of his seat and waved. "Thanks for coming."

A fire raged inside of Marlon, and he wished nothing more than to scream at the top of his lungs. He hated him. How could Quinn do something like this? He was supposed to be Marlon's friend.

"What did you want to talk about?" Anna asked after a quick glance at Marlon.

Quinn stared at the people strolling by. "Did you guys get that email earlier? What the hell was that about?" he said, his tone hushed and filled with suspicion.

Anna raised an eyebrow at him and lowered her voice. "Yes, we did. What do you think about it?"

Quinn shrugged. "It's messed-up that someone did

that, and I feel bad for the guy. I hope this gets people talking about what happens at colleges."

Marlon's blood boiled. Was Quinn serious? Was he turning this into some stupid silver lining?

Anna's expression hardened, and she glared at Quinn. "By blasting photos of somebody's sexual assault? How is that helping?"

"Yeah, it's wrong," Quinn said, "but I think it gives you some perspective. Like, when there's a hurricane and the pictures are everywhere for weeks. It makes you realize how lucky you are not to have to go through something like that, and it makes you want to help."

Unable to hold back his irritation and resentment, Marlon's teeth gritted together. "You did this, didn't you? Admit it. Don't I deserve that much, at least?"

Quinn's face scrunched. "Huh?"

"The hacked website and emails," Marlon shouted, pointing at Quinn.

Quinn's eyes flitted between Anna and Marlon. "Why would I do that? I don't even know—"

Marlon's face turned scarlet. "You pretended to be my friend and used me for your little social justice fantasies."

Quinn plopped down on the picnic bench as his fingers settled over his heart. "I'm confused."

Both of Marlon's hands shot up in the air. "You knew all along what happened to me, and you didn't bring it up because you wanted me to be the one to share all the details."

"Parker raped Marlon, and he's the person in the photos," Anna said after sitting in silence and bouncing her eyes between the arguing men.

Quinn's eyes and mouth widened as he heaved. "Wait, what? That's *you* in those pictures? I had no idea, and I'm so sorry for—"

Marlon raised a finger to hush him. "For sending them out to thousands of people? Your apology means nothing to me. The dean already knows what you did."

"I didn't know it was you, I swear. The first time I found out about the case was right before I started here after my mom saw the story on the news. I didn't know it was you. And I promise you, I didn't hack or leak anything."

Anna rolled her eyes. "Well, to be fair, you told us about how you hacked your grades in high school."

Quinn's face flushed. "You didn't tell anybody, did you? I could get in huge trouble if you did. Look, I don't know how you want me to prove this to you, but I wouldn't do something like this."

"We'll see about that." Marlon snatched Quinn's notebook off the table and held the book with locked arms against his chest. "If you have nothing to hide, you won't mind me looking."

Quinn's eyes skimmed over Marlon holding the private notebook, and he reached several times to seize the item back. "Trust me, I didn't do it."

In a fit of fury, Marlon flipped through the pages,

searching for the smoking gun. His eyes stopped on a printed article taped to a page. The face on the page caught his eye, as it was his own. Behind the paper was a scanned copy of the local newspaper, *Pine Daily News*, with a headline reporting the charges against Parker Sullivan. The discovery sent a flood of tears rushing down his cheeks. "What the hell is this? Why is this in here?"

Anna grabbed the paper from his hands and read it over. "I can't believe you."

"Okay, listen to me." The revelation left Quinn speechless for several seconds. "After we went out for dinner the first time, I told my mom about you, and she recognized your name. That was when I found out you were the one Parker assaulted. I never brought it up because why the hell would I do that? You didn't mention anything, so I figured you didn't want to talk about it."

Marlon couldn't handle any more of Quinn's lies. With a sickened expression on his face, he tossed the book, sending pages flying to the ground. "Were you trying to get a story out of me so you could run to Judy Faith or Karen Kennedy or something?"

Quinn's head shook wildly, and his brow furrowed. "No, no, of course not. I started reading about the case a few weeks ago. That's why those papers are in there. It sounds crazy, but this, um, your story needs to be shared so our system can be fixed."

Marlon glared and backed away. "Well, you can kindly

go fuck yourself. My story is my own to share."

The argument caught the attention of some bystanders, who stared at them.

Quinn rose from his seat and stepped toward him. "Please, I swear, I didn't do it. Our friendship means so much to me."

Anna shook her head. "Honestly, you aren't proving your innocence, buddy. The hacker signed off the email with QBJUSTICE, and those *are* your initials. I didn't want to believe Marlon at first, but there's too much evidence."

"Yeah, those are my initials, but why would I use my own initials if I hacked the school? That doesn't make any sense. Why would I leave evidence of my guilt? To help them find me if I did it?"

Marlon rubbed the glimmering stream of tears from his dark pink cheeks. "Either way, you used me as a pawn in your little game. How could you do this to me? Haven't I suffered enough?"

With his eyes bouncing between Marlon and Anna, Quinn's expression dulled. "Trust me when I say I didn't use you. Why would I get close to you just to hurt your feelings? Give me a chance to make things right with you again."

Anna walked between the two men and put her hands up in front of their faces. "Stop. You've both said enough. We need to leave. If you did this, Quinn, I hope you get what you deserve and realize how fucked-up this is."

Quinn stepped back and frowned. "I swear I didn't do this. I'll do whatever it takes to prove it. Someday you guys will realize I'm telling the truth. I just hope the bridge isn't too far burnt by then."

———

Hours later, Marlon's phone vibrated on the coffee table. His eyes bounced up to meet Anna's, and she nodded at him.

"Hello?" she said into the receiver. "One second."

She pulled the phone from her ear and covered the microphone. "Dean Hamilton. She wants to talk to you."

Marlon snatched the phone from Anna's hand. "Hi."

"Hello, is this Marlon?"

"Yep."

"This is Dean Hamilton. I'm calling to let you know our team is still looking into the matter, and I wanted to suggest you miss class for the next few days until this resolves itself. That is, if you're okay with that."

Marlon sighed. "Fine."

The university finally listened to him and was looking into who was behind the hack. The pain of Quinn's betrayal weighed heavy on Marlon's heart. How could he be so stupid to overlook the signs that Quinn had been using him? He kept telling himself he should have known better, considering what happened the last time he trusted someone.

# CHAPTER 12

**EACH DAY BLENDED INTO THE NEXT AS MARLON EVADED** phone calls and text messages. Bored one morning, he waited for *The Judy Faith Show* to start and flipped to it.

Judy's light brown hair shimmered as the screen lit up with her smug face. "… sent out sexually explicit—and disturbing, might I add—photographs of the sexual assault involving Parker Sullivan. The hackers also shared a secret recording of a conversation between Director of Admissions Dr. Allison Hubbard and two other faculty members. The university is still investigating the hack, and while we don't have an update, they released a statement on how they're dealing with the scandal. I'll play the clip for you first."

A stock image of a cassette player materialized on the screen, and the text read, "Pine State Univ. Faculty Caught On Tape Bashing Alleged Rape Victim." Subtitles narrated the verbal exchange.

*ALLISON HUBBARD: Listen, I don't*

know [redacted] well, but I can tell he comes from a [expletive] home. His father isn't in the picture, and maybe that's why he ended up this way.

KIMBERLY RAMIREZ: What do you mean?

ALLISON HUBBARD: You know what I'm talking about. He's gay. A lot of people from bad homes end up that way.

MARSHA BLACK: [laughs] You're not wrong.

ALLISON HUBBARD: Okay, I'm not a judge or anything, but if this case were in front of me, I'd throw the thing in the trash where it belongs. It's obvious what we're dealing with here. He just wants attention. I mean, he wishes someone like Parker would have sex with him. Right? Sorry, but somebody has to say what everyone else is thinking.

KIMBERLY RAMIREZ: Well, they obviously had sex if there are pictures of it. Did you guys see them? Not gonna lie, I got curious, and I know Dean Hamilton released that staff memo about it, but I had to. And I couldn't believe my eyes. Parker is a freak, and not in a good way.

MARSHA BLACK: Ew, no, I'd never search

*for gay pornography. I'm sorry, but that's what it is.*

*ALLISON HUBBARD: Sure, they had a sexual encounter of some sort, but it wouldn't surprise me if [redacted] was the aggressor. I've heard so many stories about the gays preying on drunk straight men and trying to take advantage of them. His whole 'help me, I didn't want this' [expletive] story is ridiculous, though. Own your [expletive]. If you sleep with someone, you don't need to put them on blast when they don't want a relationship with you. Get over yourself, kid.*

*KIMBERLY RAMIREZ: What's his endgame? Is he gonna sue the school? God, I hope not.*

*ALLISON HUBBARD: Who cares? It wouldn't shock me if he tried to, but a jury wouldn't side with a conman. I'm still pissed we had to expel Parker in the first place because of some outlandish accusation. He was a damn good quarterback, and he wasn't bad to look at either.*

Marlon's skin turned hot. There was no way he could ever show his face at Pine again. He needed to go back home to Ohio.

Judy's image returned to the screen, and she shook her

head and wrinkled her nose. "Cut the tape. We've heard enough. They get the gist. As you've just heard, Pine State University Director of Admissions Dr. Allison Hubbard was caught describing the victim in a less-than-favorable light. I mean, the things she said were disgusting. The school suspended her and the other two staff members without pay while they investigated. Today, they issued a statement. Here's what they said."

The screen cut to another dark backdrop and a message from the university appeared in white text:

*The vulgar comments made by Dr. Allison Hubbard, Kimberly Ramirez, and Marsha Black are not in line with the Pine State University Code of Conduct. They are also not an accurate representation of our ethics. Because of their disturbing remarks, we terminated all three faculty members today and replacements will be hired in the coming weeks. We would like to extend our sincerest apologies to the student mentioned on the tape and are working with law enforcement to expose the source of the recent cybersecurity breach.*

When Judy appeared on the screen once again, her fire-red lips separated, and she let out a sudden huff. "Is that a legitimate apology? Come on, you have all this money, and this is the best you can come up with? If I were them, I'd be rolling out the red carpet for the survivor."

Marlon's shoulders tensed. What a terrible apology. And they didn't do a damn thing to help him.

"Joining me is legal analyst Mark DeLaurie. Mark, what are your thoughts on this?"

The camera panned to the familiar bald gentleman regularly featured on the show. "Thanks for having me, Judy. Over the last few months, controversy after controversy has rocked this institution. First, sexual assault allegations came forward against one of their most admired students, Mr. Sullivan. Now, they get hit with an explosive exposé, someone hacked their servers, and photos of the assault were sent out to their entire student body. What surprises me most of all is how long it took them to fire the employees. There is no doubt these were the people heard on the recording, so why did they only suspend them?"

Marlon shook his head, barely able to contain his emotions.

Judy's eyes widened. "I know, it's ludicrous! If you're so intent on covering your ass—pardon my French—why wouldn't you pull the plug sooner? A viewer who attends several classes with the victim called in a tip earlier, and she stated the young man hasn't been in class since the leak. Do you think he will leave the school once and for all?"

"It's possible. If I were him, I wouldn't want to stick around that campus any longer than I needed to. I can't imagine he feels too safe, especially if things like this keep happening."

————

A few hours later, Marlon's phone vibrated. He recognized the number as the university administrative line and took a deep breath before answering.

"Hello, is this Marlon?" a familiar voice asked on the other end of the call.

"Yes," Marlon said. Why would she be calling again? He did what she suggested by staying home and missing class. Did she finally have an update on the hack?

"This is Dean Hamilton. Could you please meet with me this afternoon? There are details I would like to discuss with you in person."

"Okay, when?"

"Hmm, could you meet me at my office at noon?"

"Sure."

————

The same secretary from his previous visit greeted him with an uncomfortable smile. "Welcome, sir. You may enter the office to your left."

Marlon stepped into the room, and Dean Hamilton peered up from her desk and grinned at him. "Thank you for taking the time to meet with me today, Mr. Woods."

"Yeah, no problem. What did you want to talk about?" He rested in the chair and crossed his arms.

The dean cleared her throat before acknowledging his question. "Well, as I'm sure you are aware, we launched an investigation into the recent hack. We have worked painstakingly with the authorities to expose the person who did this. Now, the man you brought to our attention—your friend, Quinn? Detectives inspected his computer."

"And?" He waited with bated breath for Dean Hamilton to confirm his suspicions. Her potential responses dashed through his head: her saying they had Quinn in police custody, or that his expulsion papers were being filed as they spoke.

She tightened her posture. "We appreciate you reporting your suspicions to us, and it helped to narrow down our investigation. But I wanted to inform you—off the record, if you will—that he isn't our guy."

His heart thumped hard and fast in his chest. It couldn't be true. Quinn had to have done it. "Wh-what do you mean?"

Dean Hamilton looked over Marlon's shoulder at the door. "I shouldn't be sharing this information with you, and I hope you can keep this confidential, but they found no evidence on his hard drive. It looks like he researched for an assignment around the time of the breach and took several Skype calls."

Although a reasonable explanation, it made little sense

to Marlon. It had to be Quinn behind the attack. Too many signs pointed to his guilt. "But what if he used a different computer? It's gotta be him, Dean Hamilton."

She raised the glasses from her face and rubbed her eyes. "It doesn't sound plausible for him to be working off two different computers at the same time. Plus, his dorm only pinged one device on our Wi-Fi."

He could no longer contain his irritation. "But the hacker tagged their email with Q.B., his initials. How do you explain that?"

The dean winced. "Yes, they tagged the letter with that. However, our team believes the Q.B. stands for quarterback, as in Parker Sullivan's old position on the team. They're basing this theory on the other evidence they discovered. Again, I shouldn't be sharing this information with you."

Tears welled in his eyes. Why didn't he think of that? "Do you have any other suspects?" he asked, his voice trembling.

Dean Hamilton bounced her head from side to side in contemplation. "There are some leads we're working through, and we will keep you updated."

"One more thing. I listened to the tape on *Judy Faith*. Why did you take so long to fire them?"

Dean Hamilton's calm expression faded, and she squirmed in her chair. "I cannot comment on that, but we apologize for all you've gone through."

"That's all you have to say?" He rubbed at the tears

flowing down his cheeks and stared up at her. "Is that what the other staff members think about me?"

"Of course not. The things they said were egregious, but again, I cannot comment any further."

His mouth quivered. "All I wanted was to come back to college and hope for some part of my life to return to normal. It's not fair."

"Person to person, I would see a professional and talk to someone about all the things going on in your life," Dean Hamilton said, softening her voice to a whisper. "They might also be able to put you on a prescription. It might help you cope."

His mouth dropped open at the implication. "I don't need therapy, Dean Hamilton. I need to feel *safe* coming to school and to know the university has my back."

"Let me know if you have any other problems on campus, and I'll take care of them."

He glared into her eyes as he brushed away the salty tears. "So, what am I supposed to do now? I've missed a week of classes."

She glanced down at her desk and shuffled her papers to break eye contact. "You are free to return to class as early as tomorrow, if you'd like. The media attention appears to have died down, and I don't foresee any threats to your safety."

He rose and trudged toward the door. "Thanks."

———————

Marlon sat in silence in the parking lot of his apartment complex for several minutes. He contemplated how his life ever reached this point. Things were somewhat normal for him again a few weeks ago, and now he had to deal with this. The media was breathing down his neck, administrators were talking about him, and the pictures ... Oh god, the pictures. The first time they leaked over the summer was bad enough, but now, the entire university was forced to see them. How was he going to face anyone again?

The upcoming year would be a disaster. He needed to decide if he wanted to go back to Ohio and leave this mess behind or continue pushing through and dealing with it. But he didn't want to think about that. The situation left him physically tired and mentally exhausted.

# CHAPTER 13

**THE STEADY HUM OF VOICES IN THE CRAMPED UNIVERSITY** hallway disoriented Marlon. Two days had passed since his conversation with Dean Hamilton, and although his emotional state displayed only a slight improvement, he couldn't afford the risk of affecting his grades any more than he already had. For his first day back, he donned a beanie and sunglasses to avoid the bulk of the university students identifying him.

As he moved through the building, a commotion from behind distracted him, causing him to crash into somebody.

"What the hell?" the man groaned.

"I-I'm so sorry." The force of the impact knocked the shades off Marlon's face, and he leaned over to pick them up from the floor.

The man dusted off his slacks. "Marlon Woods?"

Marlon's heart almost stopped. It was somebody he knew: Blake Porter, a guy from his web design class. The last thing he wanted was to run into someone who recognized him. "Oh, hey, Blake. How's it going? Sorry for running into you."

Blake shrugged off the hostility and smiled at Marlon. "No, it's cool, buddy. Don't worry about it. So, how have you been?"

Uncertain of whether to give an authentic answer or the short one everybody wanted to hear, Marlon settled on the latter. "Okay, I guess."

"Sorry about what happened with the email and stuff." Blake patted Marlon's shoulder.

The contact made Marlon's body shudder. "What?"

Blake pulled his hand away and bounced his shoulders. "Nothing. I meant I'm sorry you went through that."

"Oh, thanks." Marlon's stomach twisted in knots. These were the encounters he dreaded. He couldn't survive five minutes back at the campus without someone bringing *it* up.

"Doesn't it piss you off?" Blake asked in a monotone voice, leaning in toward him.

Chills coursed through Marlon's veins. He didn't understand why Blake acted so weird toward him all the time. "What are you talking about?"

Blake sighed. "All the things that happen in this school. Can you believe they said that stuff about Parker? They love covering shit up. They're gonna piss off the wrong person someday."

"Yeah, it's sad," Marlon said, growing more suspicious by the moment. It was a strange thing to discuss with someone he'd hardly ever spoken to.

As if waiting for a better response, Blake glared at him before shaking the expression off his face. "If you ever wanna talk, I'm here for you, buddy."

Marlon peered down at his smartwatch and back up at him. "Thanks, Blake. I gotta go, but I'll see you around."

———

Later in the afternoon, Marlon swung his backpack over his shoulder and scurried into the student lounge. His eyes darted around, making sure none of his hunters were nearby. When it became apparent the coast was clear, he retreated to the corner of the room and sank into the oversized brown chair.

A group of students engaged in a loud conversation nearby. Marlon pulled his earbuds out, plugged them into his phone, and put on a playlist of his favorite artists. His eyes clenched shut, and he let the music fill his ears, making all his worries disappear in an instant.

He sat with the music playing for several songs. His mind kept drifting back to the leak and how he still had no clue who was behind it. Was he wrong for turning Quinn in without evidence? It made too much sense that Quinn did it, given how fast their friendship developed and all the weird tidbits of information he gave Marlon. How was he going to make things right after being so wrong?

"Pictures of You" by The Cure played, and goosebumps raised on Marlon's arms. Quinn's favorite band coming on was almost a sign of sorts, the lyrics describing their situation so well.

His eyes welled up with tears, and he clicked on the Gallery icon on his phone. He scrolled through all the selfies he had taken with Quinn, some including Anna during their hangouts. After the assault, Marlon gave up on taking pictures, but his friendship with Quinn had changed his mind about that.

Marlon wondered how terrible of a friend he was for turning against Quinn like that. The guy was one of only two people to treat him like a normal, decent person since he returned to Pine.

A photo of Marlon and Quinn in the same student lounge he was sitting in loaded; Quinn leaning against the back of the chair in the photo—his tongue poking out of the side of his mouth—and Marlon's face featuring a half-smile. One of the most sincere, natural ones he had shown in ages.

His finger traced over the screen, pushing the picture around. He longed for a chance to redo everything. Maybe if he had been upfront with Quinn about the assault, things could have been different. They'd have more honesty between them, and Marlon would have known he wasn't behind the leak. It was too late to fix it now, though.

Marlon pushed the Skip button, and the music changed to an upbeat indie-pop song by Twin Shadow. His eyes closed again, and when they opened, the people sitting at the table across from him were all staring at him—two guys and two girls.

Their stares made him shift in his chair, turning away from them enough to where he could refocus. When he glanced up once more, they were still looking. This time, one guy had his phone out and was holding it up to the three other people.

Marlon's pulse quickened, and he gave into temptation by pulling out the headphones to listen to them.

"… you it was him," the guy with the phone whispered.

"*Shh*, he can hear us," one girl said in a loud whisper.

Marlon's jaw clenched. They *were* talking about him. She must have recognized him from the emailed photos. It was almost worse than his sexual assault case making headlines. At least back then, most college kids had no interest in the news and therefore didn't know he was the Pine State University victim. This time, everybody on campus knew, and any shred of anonymity vanished.

"Are you sure? I think he's getting ready to leave. Hurry and get a picture," the other girl said, with little effort to lower her voice.

Marlon's cheeks reddened, and he shoved his phone in his pocket, snatched his backpack off the ground, and charged out of the lounge. These paparazzi-like run-ins were becoming old fast. He never asked for this and wanted nothing more than for everything to go away.

———

A few days later, after finishing speech class, he waited for everyone to leave before walking into the hallway.

"Hey, asshole, I hope you're happy," a shrill voice shouted from behind him.

Marlon stopped dead in his tracks, and the hair raised on his arms. "What do you want?"

Courtney's heels clicked at the ground as she strutted toward him. "I know you had someone hack the server. Do you feel better about yourself now?"

He twisted around and scowled at her. "How do I know *you* didn't do that?"

Courtney let out a hearty chuckle. "Oh, please. If I wanted to do something, it would have happened by now."

"What's your problem, Courtney? Why are you always such a dick to me?" Marlon asked, stunned by the fact he worked up the courage to say what had been on his mind.

She stalked closer, pausing within a foot of Marlon. "You're a whiny bitch who thrives off the attention he receives from his bullshit little 'I'm a victim' story."

"You and I both know it's not bullshit."

"Parker would never rape somebody. Besides, he

doesn't even like guys."

Marlon's mouth fell open. Why was she such an idiot? "Then how do you explain what happened? If he didn't rape me and doesn't like men, why are there pictures and videos that prove otherwise? And why would I lie about what he did to me?"

She shrugged. "I don't know what you did to him, but you better hope he's not convicted."

He couldn't hold back any longer. The hate-loaded words gushed out of his mouth like hot lava. "Fuck you, Courtney. You and your dumbass friends need to leave me the hell alone."

Courtney arched a brow. "Really? What are—"

"I'm sorry you peaked in high school and can't accept the fact that your boyfriend is a rapist. I did nothing but try to give you the benefit of the doubt and avoid a confrontation. It's obvious you don't have any gay friends because you can't coordinate an outfit for shit. And don't get me started on those eyebrows."

"Wow. Real mature."

"Says the girl with the knockoff Louis Vuitton bag." He hadn't meant to say that, but the damage was already done.

Her cheeks glowed as she peeked down at her purse and clasped it to her side. "This is the real thing. My daddy bought it for me in Paris."

He squinted at the bag and pointed at the lettering. "Tell Daddy he got scammed because the *L* and *V* are way too far apart. If you knew anything about designer clothing, you would know that."

Courtney swung the fake handbag over her shoulder, grunted, and tramped away from him.

# CHAPTER 14

PUMPKIN-SCENTED CANDLES FLICKERED ON THE COFFEE table in the dimly-lit apartment. Marlon shoveled another scoop of vanilla bean ice cream into his mouth as his other hand jammed the channel button on the remote control. Dozens of programs flashed across the screen since he gave each one a fraction of a second to load before skipping it.

Marlon leaned back on his stiff couch. This almost ritualistic method of attempting to clear his mind and pretending everything was okay was becoming more exhausting as the days dragged on. School and home, that was it. Even grocery shopping at Safeway turned into a quick dash through the store and a final stop at self-checkout.

He blinked, bringing his attention back to the television. The channel he stopped on was *The Karen Kennedy Show*—Judy Faith's blonde, more annoying counterpart. The two were like the Wicked Witch of the East and West. Last Marlon had heard, Karen said unfavorable things about him on her show, and he swore he'd never watch it again.

"And we're gonna take it to legal analyst Paul D'Amati now. Hi, Paul. What are your thoughts?" Karen asked, her voice as fake as press-on nails.

A man in his mid-thirties, dressed in a dark shirt with a bright red tie, nodded at the camera, his sculpted, gelled sandy hair not moving an inch. "Thanks, Karen. It's an interesting point you bring up. And I want to start by saying I have nothing but love for Pine State University. It's a wonderful college, and my little cousin even went to school there."

Marlon's face tightened, and he stared at the headline bar below on the screen: *LATEST UPDATE IN PINE STATE ALLEGATION.*

"I agree. They have one of the lowest numbers of sexual assaults per student of any college in the United States. They're also champions of diversity and have a lot of programs and policies in place for the students," Karen said with a shrug.

Marlon's nostrils flared, and his stomach churned.

"They do, and that's why this is so confusing. Why would somebody breach their security systems to send out something like *that*? It doesn't make sense, and as you've said on here time and time again, the hacker's letter is clearly pro-victim, anti-truth." Paul shook his head.

Marlon stared at the television. He couldn't wrap his brain around what Paul meant by 'anti-truth.' Marlon had been honest about what happened to him and didn't understand why people couldn't accept that.

Karen's eyebrows pinched together. "I know! Whatever happened to 'innocent until proven guilty'? Nobody lives by that statement anymore, it seems. And it's sad they are dragging this prestigious university's name through the mud for the sake of shock value."

"That's why I don't understand why critics are blaming the school for this social media group. We cannot hold the university responsible for what students do in their free time," Paul said.

Marlon leaned closer and increased the volume. Group? What group?

Karen shook her head, swaying her long, blonde hair side to side. "Yes, let's talk about that a little more in-depth. From a legal standpoint, what are the consequences of this? Are there any at all?"

"No, but it's a gray area. One could argue it's protected under the First Amendment, and others might say it borders on harassment. But either way, I think this is a case of 'kids will be kids,' and everyone is blowing it out of proportion."

Being a Sunday, Marlon didn't have class and hadn't spoken to anyone in almost two days, so he wasn't aware of what happened. He muted the audio, grabbed his phone from the cushion next to him, and searched "pine state university group" on the search engine. An assortment of news articles appeared, all posted within the past few hours. He had ignored several of Anna's calls and text messages earlier in the day and now wondered if that was what she was calling about.

He tapped on the first article he saw, and he read over the text.

> *A private social media group created by a Pine State University student brings to light questions regarding a student's expectation of privacy on campus and whether people have gone too far. A group titled 'I saw the PSU victim today' was brought to the public's attention this morning by someone who joined the page and screenshotted several posts, resharing them on their own account. The group focuses on taking candid and unauthorized pictures of the man believed to be the sexual assault victim of former Pine State University quarterback Parker Sullivan.*

Marlon held the phone tighter, his hand shaking, and his teeth clenched. He wanted to stop reading, but he couldn't.

> *Several students even took to bashing the man on the group's page, calling him a liar and using homophobic slurs, amongst other things. The reason for their belief is, in their own words, 'he doesn't act like a victim because if he was one, he wouldn't have come*

*back.' After the group went viral earlier, the administrator of the page deleted it, and it is no longer accessible. Since the victim hasn't stated his desire to share his name, we won't be mentioning his name in any articles on the case.*

The screen faded to black, and he tossed the phone aside. What more did they want him to do? Even when he quit talking to everyone and allowed his true, dark feelings to show, it still wasn't enough to satisfy everyone's ideal victim criteria. Things were only getting worse for him at Pine, and he wasn't sure how much longer he could live like this.

———

The low gas symbol flickered on Marlon's dashboard. "Great. Just great," he whispered. Breaking from his usual plans, he swerved into the gas station near Pine State University and stopped at pump six. He avoided this place at all costs because of the inevitability of running into classmates or worse, Courtney and Parker's friends. Still, he couldn't afford to run out of gas and find himself stranded along the side of the road.

No other car parked within several pumps of him, so he figured he should have enough time to fill up the tank and bolt out of there before anyone recognized him. He lifted the gas door handle inside the car, glanced around, and hurried out toward the pump screen. He inserted his card, typed in his pin, and hit the Unleaded button. The twist cap fought back against his hand at first before breaking free, dangling against the vehicle. He shoved the gas pump in and clicked the autofill latch. Gas flooded into the car, and the dollar counter ticked up the price.

His mind drifted as the familiar and comforting pumping noise permeated the air. Two men walked into the store holding hands, something Marlon wasn't used to seeing around PSU. Washington was supposed to be one of the more liberal and LGBTQ+ friendly states in America, but he had only ever experienced hatred and bullying in recent months because of his sexuality. The thought of loving somebody in such an open way without fear of repercussions brought a smile to his face.

The latch on the handle snapped back into place, startling Marlon. He swallowed hard and spun back around. He locked eyes with a full-figured brunette woman at the pump next to him. She didn't move or say anything, just gaped at him. That was what he feared happening had he ever stopped at that gas station. She recognized him from somewhere, and he had to leave before something bad happened.

He broke eye contact with the strange woman and fumbled the handle back into the holding slot. A prompt appeared on the faded digital screen, asking if he wanted a receipt, and he pressed on the 'no' button several times until it reset to the main screen. Finished, he twisted the cap back on his car and slammed the compartment shut.

"Excuse me, are you Marlon Woods?" a woman asked.

Marlon gripped his chest and gasped. He turned and faced the person asking the question—the woman who stared at him moments prior. "Y-yes. Why?"

"Oh my god. It's really you."

Marlon's blood turned to ice. Who was she? Was she a reporter who hung around the campus hoping to catch him off-guard? Or somebody acquainted with one of his enemies?

Her eyes widened. "Sorry, I didn't introduce myself. I'm Eva. Eva Gonzalez. I also go to PSU."

His worst fears manifested. There was no telling who she was and why she was trying to talk to him. He jiggled his keys and reached for the door handle.

"Wait. I wanted to tell you something." She grasped his wrist, stopping him in his tracks.

"What?" he asked, his tone harsh.

Eva moved her hand away and peered at the ground. "I'm sorry. I, uh, I believe you ... about the whole Parker thing. The guy's a scumbag."

Marlon's expression hardened. "What did you say?"

"Parker—he's a rapist. I know you're telling the truth."

If this was a prank or a game, it was the cruelest one yet. Marlon had only heard those words a few times since he came forward and spoke his truth.

"I didn't realize how awkward this was, confronting you like this. Sorry. I'll leave you alone now," Eva said.

"No. Th-thank you. That means a lot to me. Nobody believes me."

Eva offered a comforting smile. "I do. He'll pay for what he did."

Marlon's skin itched and burned with revulsion. "Do you know him?"

"Yeah, we shared a few classes freshman year. I know all about him," she said, inhaling deep. This made the situation even weirder. There was something she wanted to say but wouldn't. Not yet.

He squinted at her. "Did he do this to someone else?"

"I'd better get going, but I'll see you around." Without allowing him to stop her or say goodbye, she abruptly raced back to her car and sped off.

Someone knew something, and the full story would come out at some point.

# CHAPTER 15

OUTSIDE THE STUDENT LOUNGE ONE DAY, MARLON SAW
Quinn standing at the end of the hallway. He hesitated to
approach him, unsure if Quinn still resented him for reporting him to the administration. Several weeks had passed
since their falling out, and Marlon didn't know if that was
enough time for him to apologize and try to fix their relationship.

After giving himself a pep talk, Marlon strolled over.
"Hey, how's it going?"

Quinn jumped and almost dropped his phone. "Hi."
His sad expression said more than words could.

"How have you been?" Marlon forced a small smile.

Quinn stared into the distance. "Fine." His tone was
cold and sharp.

"I wanted to say I'm—"

"Don't bother. I thought our friendship meant something, but I guess the feeling wasn't mutual."

"It was. I—"

Quinn shook his head. "No. You thought I'd try to hurt you by sharing pictures of your assault with the entire school."

"Pl-please, it was because of the initials and what you said—"

"The cops took my laptop and searched through all my files. They basically destroyed my dorm room, trying to find evidence." Quinn's eyes met his, and he squinted.

All Marlon wanted was a chance to make things right. He frowned. "I'm sorry. They told me you were innocent."

"Yeah, funny how that works, huh? You had to hear it from them to believe it rather than from me, your friend. What did they ever do to help you?"

Marlon swallowed hard, and his hands moved as he spoke. "All I want is to be—"

"Yes, what *you* want. It's always about what you want, isn't it? I'm so happy you showed me your true colors."

"I was confused and—"

Quinn waved his hand. "Stay confused, my friend."

Marlon's jaw dropped as Quinn disappeared into the crowd. Had he ruined things to where Quinn couldn't accept an apology? Did he miss out on any chance of mending their relationship?

Another student stopped in front of Marlon, breaking him from his daze. His eyes darted to meet theirs, and he stumbled away before they said or did anything. He didn't want another awkward run-in like what had happened at the gas station.

——————

The next morning, as Marlon finished scarfing down a Pop-Tart, his phone lit up with an incoming call from Anna.

He tapped the green button. "What's up?"

"Are you watching *Judy Faith*?"

His eyes rolled, thinking about her calling to talk about the news. "No. Why?"

"There's another victim, Marlon. This girl who went to high school with Parker called in and talked about it."

Marlon sat up in his chair and concentrated on the conversation. "Huh?"

"He raped her in high school when they were on their way to see a movie. It happened in a parking lot."

His heart dropped into his stomach. "Is she pressing charges against him?"

"I don't know. She talked about it with Judy, but it was confusing."

Marlon huffed. "It couldn't have been that long ago."

"She said it was four years ago, but Judy was saying the laws recently changed in Washington, so there isn't a statute of limitations since she was under eighteen."

"What else did she say?"

"He did the same thing to her as he did to you. There

were pictures, and I guess his friends spread them around the school," Anna said.

"How come no one said anything about this sooner?"

Anna exhaled. "Parker's family paid her off. I missed some of that part because I was brushing my teeth, but something about a non-disclosure agreement."

Marlon's forehead creased. How was that possible? It made no sense. "If she signed a contract, how is she talking about it on *The Judy Faith Show*?"

"She gave the money back to them and is trying to end the agreement. She's staying anonymous for now, but Judy said she wants to interview her when she's ready."

"I'll check Judy's website and see if it's on there."

"It should be. So, are you going home for the winter break or staying in your apartment?" Anna asked, her voice perking up at the change of subject.

The realization of the impending holidays hit him. The thought of returning home was both exhausting and exciting. "Ohio. What about you?"

"Staying here. It's the first Christmas without Whitney, so Mom and Dad didn't plan anything. I'm pretending I have things to take care of here. Besides, Mom made it clear she does *not* want to celebrate."

"Well, don't get yourself into any trouble while I'm gone."

Anna laughed. "No promises. How have your classes been?"

"Not too bad, but I ran into Quinn yesterday. It was so awkward."

"What happened?"

"He's pissed at me. I can't say I blame him. I tried apologizing, but he didn't want to hear it."

"Give it time. It's only been a few weeks."

Maybe he was unrealistic for expecting Quinn to forgive him so fast. Still, he longed for that normalcy again. "You're right, I need to give him space for now. It's—"

"Holy shit. Turn your TV on right now. *The Judy Faith Show*. Trust me," Anna said. Several voices spoke over hers in the background.

Marlon's pulse quickened. It must have been urgent if she was rushing him like that. He fumbled with the remote and clicked through to the proper channel. Judy's face loaded on the screen mid-eye roll.

"What is—" Marlon said.

"Parker. He's on the phone with her," Anna said, her voice shaking.

Chills danced up Marlon's arms. This was bad. Could he handle hearing Parker's voice for the first time since the night of the attack? He didn't give himself enough time to think about it before he jammed on the volume button.

"… you call in?" Judy asked, squinting.

"Because this is so unfair. You fake news people keep lying about me. I can't take it anymore. I didn't 'rape' anybody," Parker shouted, his voice hard to distinguish due to the diminished quality of the call.

Marlon's eyes widened. His phone slipped through his hands, crashing into his thigh. He didn't flinch.

Judy let out a sarcastic chuckle. "Well, then how do you explain what happened? Huh?"

"We had sex. So what if I hooked up with a few people? It's not that big of a deal."

A devilish grin covered Judy's face. "So, you aren't denying the young woman's story about you taking her to a movie, stopping along the way, and forcing her to have sex with you?"

"I didn't force anyone to do anything. I don't have to. It's not my fault it was consensual, and she changed her mind afterward 'cause she wants money. She's lying, and you're stupid if you can't see—"

"Hold on. What lies would you like to clarify?"

Marlon gasped. Was this real, or was it one of those weird nightmares he kept having about Parker? The lines between reality and imagination blurred more as the days dragged on.

"Oh my god, there's so many of them! Let's see, you lied about me raping Marlon—that never happened. Me being gay, because I sure as hell am not. This made-up story about me hooking up with that girl and her calling it rape. The list goes on and on."

Judy's lips pressed together. "So, you mean to tell me everyone is lying? Everyone?"

"Yes. If you really look at the facts, you'll see none of it adds up. They're trying to make me look like a monster, but I'm not. I'm a good Christian. A good student."

"Why would two different people have these similar stories about you when they don't know each other? It makes no sense, Parker."

"They're trying to get famous by making me look bad. Everyone always believes the so-called victims and never considers what the actual victim goes through—all the men who are lied about. It's not fair. Look at everything that happened in Hollywood. Anyone can lie and say someone did something to them, but nobody ever stops and thinks about what innocent guys like me have to go through."

Marlon's trembling fingertips pressed against his lips. He wanted to look away and turn the show off, but he couldn't. He needed to hear what else Parker had to say. That was his first taste of what the trial would be like.

"And what *are* you going through?"

"This lie ruined my life. I can't finish college now, I'm stuck in the house all day, and my family is always worried that somebody's gonna do something bad to us. It's so wrong, and fake news people like you make it so much worse. You're a piece of—"

"So, all you've got to say for yourself is people lied about you? That's it?" Judy asked.

Marlon gripped the couch pillow closer to his chest, squeezing hard. Judy's apparent baiting technique worked, as Parker couldn't keep his mouth shut and continued snapping at her, making himself look worse by the minute.

"I've said that a hundred times now. They're trying to destroy me, but you'll all realize the truth when I'm found innocent."

Judy raised a carefully-drawn brow. "It sounds like you think you're the victim here. Correct me if I'm wrong."

"I am! I don't deserve this, and … Mom, stop. I'm talking to Judy Faith. No, I'm not gonna calm down. Leave me alone." Background noise ensued as Parker shifted the phone. "Judy, it's fucked-up how you won't report the truth because you only care about your ratings. You're ruining my life, and I won't—"

Parker's voice vanished, and silence lingered both on television and in Marlon's living room for several seconds.

"Parker? Are you still there? Hello?" Judy said, her voice calm and assured. "Looks like he hung up. Well, as you just heard, Parker Sullivan, accused Pine State University rapist, called in for an unplanned and, might I add, unhinged impromptu interview. Let's take it over to Defense Attorney Connor Phelps. What are your thoughts on that call?"

Connor's brow furrowed. "Wow, Judy. In all my appearances on your show, I have never witnessed anything as messy as this. I can't believe he did something so stupid and ill-advised. This will hurt his defense and publicity, no doubt about that. Why didn't somebody stop him sooner?"

The television clicked off, and Marlon sat frozen on the

couch. Although Connor referred to the phone call in his last comment, the question resonated with him: Why didn't someone stop Parker sooner?

# CHAPTER 16

A FEW DAYS BEFORE CHRISTMAS, MARLON FLEW HOME TO Ohio to visit his family. The trip would be the first time he saw any of them since he had returned to the university.

Upon landing at Hopkins International Airport in Cleveland, his mother greeted him with a radiant pink "WELCOME HOME MARLON" sign near the baggage claim area. Her wavy, champagne-blonde hair gleamed under the bright lights.

Marlon flashed an embarrassed grin as he neared her. "You didn't have to do this."

She winked at him. "Sure, I did. I couldn't risk my baby boy not being able to find me."

They collected Marlon's luggage, strolled toward the parking garage, and headed home.

"So, honey, how have things been going for you?" she asked, breaking the silence between them.

Unsure how to answer her question, he glared at the

road. "Okay, I guess."

She glanced at his face and settled her hand on his. "Don't lie, sweetie. I know it's been tough, what with the hack and all. Once they figure out who did it, though, I'm sure you'll feel a lot better."

"No, it doesn't matter who did it. They ruined my life." He yanked his hand away from hers. His mother was one of the last people he wanted to talk about this with.

"It's tough to see things this way, but hear me out. Maybe this happened because God, or whoever is out there, knew you could deal with it. You could be the face of change in this country. You're so brave, and I'm really proud of you."

"But …" He couldn't say what was on his mind. "But what happens if all this is for nothing? What if this goes to trial, and he isn't convicted?"

His mother's hazel eyes bounced over to his, and she shrugged. "Well, honey, at least you tried. Would you want to live with the fact that you spoke your truth and left it in the hands of the law? Or would you rather give up and live with the 'what ifs' for the rest of your life?"

He rolled his eyes and let out a quiet laugh. She had a point. Why was she always right about this stuff? "Quit being so rational, Mom. It's nauseating."

"Hey, it's what moms are for. What I'm trying to say is it's all in how you deal with it. The fact of the matter is you have no control over what happens with your case now. Are you going to let it eat away at you, or are you going to accept that this horrible thing happened and grow from it?"

"What about the people who won't leave me the hell alone?" These words reminded him of a time in middle school when he told his mother about a student bullying him. Her lecture then had gone much of the same way.

She flicked the wipers as small snowflakes billowed from the sky, leaving wet spots on the windshield. "Sweetie, if they weren't talking shit about you, they'd do it to someone else. If people are talking, let 'em talk. It's human nature, and you can't change it. Instead of focusing on the bad things they're saying about you, give them something positive to talk about. Do something nice for someone or go out of your way to be kind to strangers. Your granny used to tell me that growing up."

He mulled over her remarks. Maybe he focused too much on all the negative experiences he had with people on campus rather than the good ones. Still, he couldn't shake the negativity plaguing him. "Sometimes, I think it'd be easier to come back home and live in Salem again. Things were so much simpler here. I wouldn't need to worry about people knowing my name, and I could go to Kent State or something."

His mother honked at a herd of deer along the side of snow-covered State Route 14. "Aren't you the one who sat me down and yelled at me about why you needed to return to Pine State in the first place? I'll be honest with you, I thought it was a terrible idea. After everything that happened, I couldn't risk sending my baby back to that hellhole. But you told me it was the right thing to do. You needed to confront your demons and prove to the world you are more than a blip in the news. Didn't you say that?"

His cheeks burned crimson red. "Yes, but that was before I—"

She raised her palm to silence him. "When things got rough, you stuck it out and waited for the storm to pass. Hell, I didn't know about half the stuff that was going on until long after it happened. You kept those things a secret to protect me, and I trusted you because I knew you could handle it."

Marlon sank into the seat. It was true. He had so many chances to run away from Pine, but he stayed and figured it out on his own. While they used to talk every other night during his first year at Pine State University, they spoke only once or twice a week this semester. And he kept most of what happened from her, out of fear she would force him to return home. But if he despised it so much, why did he stay?

———

Pasted across the vibrant sapphire walls of his bedroom were the posters of several of his favorite musicians he had hung up a few summers before the attack happened. His sheets and blanket lay in a wrinkled mountain, just the way he left them. Assorted clothing covered the floor, making the place resemble an abstract art painting. It was clear his mother hadn't set foot in here. She kept their promise.

A neatly-folded white note sat on his bare, brown desk. His brow furrowed, and he walked over to read it. The paper trembled in his quivering hand, clinging to his sticky palm.

*If you're reading this, you either made it through the semester, or you couldn't handle the pressure of returning to Pine. Either way, you are alive, and I want you to know how proud I am of you. By saving yourself, you saved me. I'm not sure if life is any easier for you than it was for the person writing this, but I can only hope so. See how far you've come.*

*Sincerely,*

*You from August*

Hot tears burned their way to his eyes, but he blinked them away. Before Marlon flew back to Washington to begin the fall semester, he had written that note to himself as a reminder for when he returned to Ohio. It put into perspective how much he had gone through over the past four months.

Only months prior, he couldn't leave the house without triggering a panic attack. But somehow, some way, he managed to return to school, reconnect with Anna, and throw himself back into the lion's den. And still, he came out stronger than before. He wasn't sure how he did it or where the strength and courage came from, but he did it.

———

After settling back into life in Ohio, his Aunt Gretchen and grandmother came to the home to see him. His other family members would be over for the holidays, but he and his aunt were always close. She became very protective of him after the assault.

The two sat at the kitchen table to chat while his mother and grandmother spoke in the living room.

Gretchen's long eyelashes fluttered as she beamed at him. "I'm so happy you're here. I've missed you."

"I missed you too. It's nice being back. I don't feel like I have to pretend or hide like I do back in Washington."

"I'm sorry, sweetie. If it makes you feel better, I love you for who you are. Don't ever think you have to be someone else around me."

Marlon smiled. "Thanks. You're the best aunt ever."

"*Shh*, don't let Aunt Tina find out." Aunt Gretchen winked. "So, how's the love life? Have any of those Washington boys caught your eye?"

"No, I'm not interested in dating anybody."

"There aren't any boys you're talking to, even as a friend?" Aunt Gretchen asked, her eyes focused on him.

Marlon rattled his head. "There was one guy I considered a friend, but I ruined it. Remember Quinn?"

Her hand settled on his shoulder and gave it a few reassuring pats. "Yes, I remember you telling me about him. Are you two still not talking?"

"He hasn't talked to me since I turned him in for the hacking thing. I took Mom's advice and tried to apologize, but he wouldn't let me," Marlon said, sighing.

"It's never too late to right your wrongs. If he were ever a real friend, he'd forgive you. But you gotta be the one making the first step and admitting your mistake. You understand?" Aunt Gretchen's floral perfume overwhelmed Marlon, causing him to cough as she leaned in closer.

The voices of his mother and grandmother drew nearer as they reached the kitchen.

"Call me old-fashioned, but I'm still getting used to this whole *gay* thing. Back in my day, it didn't exist," his grandmother said, her Southern drawl dragging out every other word.

Marlon tensed. Now wasn't the time for her homophobic remarks.

"Yes, it did, Mom. People just didn't talk about it. Rock Hudson was gay," his mother said.

"And we didn't know about it until years later, now did we, Rachel?"

The exchange made Marlon and his aunt giggle.

Recognition dawned on his grandmother's wrinkled

147

face as her eyes widened at Marlon. "Hi, sweetheart. I didn't realize you were sitting there."

"I was talking to Aunt Gretchen," Marlon said.

His grandmother winced. "I don't know how much of our conversation you heard, but I'm still learning how this whole thing works. I love you and will support you no matter what, darling."

"Thanks, Grandma. It means a lot coming from you." To make light, he grinned at her. His grandmother had always been a little homophobic and bigoted, but he knew her heart was in the right place. When Marlon was younger, his mother used to explain that her strong opinions on things were due to generational differences. That was never a valid excuse, though.

She smirked back at him and squinted, her expression dulling. "And I'm sorry, pardon my language, but that Judy Faith bitch needs to mind her own business. She thinks the sun comes up just to hear her crow."

Aunt Gretchen gasped. "Mom!"

Grandma rolled her eyes and flopped her hand forward. "Don't act like you don't feel the same way. I can't stand to listen to her voice. It's like nails on a chalkboard. I wish she never would've solved that Nashville serial killer case. Maybe then the woman would've been a nobody, and some other poor broad would be in her spot. Couldn't be any worse than her, that's for sure."

His mother chuckled. "Oh, stop it. You watch her show

all the time."

"And that's why I can't stand her. Do you know who else makes my skin crawl? That rich son of a bitch's parents. I always thought Walter Sullivan was a terrible governor. You ought to sue the dickens out of them 'til they don't have a pot to piss in."

"I would never win against them. They're millionaires, and I'm a nobody," Marlon said.

His grandmother's thin, coral-colored lips parted. "Never gonna get anywhere with that attitude, now are you? People like them have done stuff like this for centuries, and it's time we put a stop to it. Now, I'm not saying take 'em for all they've got, but they need to pay for the pain and suffering they've caused you."

His eyes darted up at hers. Was she suggesting money would make this whole thing go away? How ignorant. "No amount of money will take away the pain, and I don't want people thinking I did all this for money."

"You're right, honey. But it sure would feel nice to stick it to those assholes, now wouldn't it?" Grandma asked.

"But it won't erase what happened or make people respect me again," Marlon said, his voice cracking.

Grandma flashed a halfhearted smile at him. "Don't take this the wrong way, Marlon, but it's all in the attitude. My mother, your great-granny, used to say, 'You can catch more flies with honey than vinegar.' What it means is people will like you more if you have a positive attitude than if you are a negative person who dwells on the bad stuff. Do you get what I'm saying?"

"I get what you're saying, but it's easier said than done." Did she have an old Southern saying for every little thing?

His grandmother's wrinkled hand clasped his shoulder. "You may be right, but the change starts inside of you. When you start feeling down or think things are bad, look back at the happy times and think of the better days ahead of you. It's not going to be a walk in the park, but it gets easier over time."

"She's got a point, sweetie. Remember when you first came home after it happened, and you couldn't talk about it at all without shutting down? Well, look at you now," Aunt Gretchen said.

He hated to admit it, but they were right.

———

The next day, while he waited for his family to come over for Christmas dinner, Marlon searched through the drawers in his desk. He had stowed his journal away in it somewhere before returning to Pine. His hand slid across the embossed letters on the leather cover as he reached up into the secret compartment.

After some fumbling around, he yanked the diary out. He didn't remember everything he wrote in there, but he yearned for the familiarity of the past. What was Marlon from the summer thinking about? That whole period in his life was a blur.

He flipped through the first few pages, labeled with the months leading to his trip to Pine for freshman year. Gross. He didn't want to relive those days. He was so awkward back then.

At last, the red ink on the cream-colored page caught his attention. It was the bad one. He took a deep breath and braced himself for what he was about to read.

> *It happened to me. If you're reading this, whoever you are, I'm sure you know what I'm talking about. I'll try to be honest and detailed, but it's hard when you're crying your eyes out and trying not to get the pages wet. Here is my side of the story, not that I owe it to anyone.*

His stomach quivered, and his jaw clenched. Those words. They were about to come.

> *I was raped. Parker Sullivan raped me. If two weeks ago someone told me I would say those words, I never would've believed them.*
>
> *All I wanted was to go to the party with Anna and have a good time. No, I wasn't "asking for it," and I didn't lead him on.*

Guilt flooded his veins, and his pulse pounded in his ear, deafening him. How did he put himself into a situation like that? It was supposed to just be a party. After collecting his thoughts, he continued.

*I'll spare you the graphic details since I'm sure the talk shows will gladly provide those. He tried to kiss me, and I said no. He beat me until I gave up on trying to resist. In those next few minutes, he ruined me. Who knew going for a walk with someone and listening to their hopes and dreams would lead to this? Apparently, being a decent person and making small talk is considered consent. The reports will say I flirted with him or wore something that gave some indication I was an easy target. That's what they say about women all the time, right?*

His hands rested above his knees, his chilly fingertips stinging his warm, bare flesh. It was true. Not only did people say that about women, but they also started saying it about him—that he flirted and hooked up with Parker.

*Anyway, that's my story. Pine State University's beloved quarterback raped me and shared it with the world. Since I'm a nobody, people won't care about what happens next. Everyone is defending my rapist, and I don't want to live through the smear campaign of Marlon Augustine Woods. So, this is the last you'll hear from me. I hope I've done a good enough job of telling you the truth.*

A tear dripped from his eye. He had been in such a dark place. What the hell happened?

*Please, make sure this doesn't happen to anyone else at Pine State University or any other college. Nobody should suffer the way I have. Let my death serve as a grim reminder of the reality victims face in a country that favors the perceived innocence of the attacker over the safety and sanity of the victim. I'm giving up before the real shitstorm begins. To my family and the few friends I have left, I'm sorry this crappy note is all you're left with. Don't cry for me. Goodbye.*

Reading the words brought back the memory of chugging down a bottle of pills in this very room after writing the note, only to wake fourteen hours later with a splitting migraine. That was June, and this was now. Things weren't great in his life, but he was nowhere near as low as he was back then. Maybe he had been thinking of things the wrong way. He said it himself in the note: nobody should suffer the way he did, and things needed to change. So, what was he doing to make that happen?

His fingers traced over the raised scar on his wrist, another reminder of the worst summer of his life. He clutched the book to his chest and inhaled through his congested nose. He needed to do this for the Marlon who wasn't strong enough to live to see another day.

A knock on the door dragged him out of his thoughts. "Sweetie? They're here."

His fingertips brushed the tears away as he shoved the book back inside the desk. "Be down in a minute."

He could do this. Happiness wasn't a distant dream.

———

After the start of the new year, Marlon had to fly back to Washington before his next semester started. The car halted at a red light several blocks from the airport, and his mother shifted to face him. "I'm flying into Seattle a few days before the trial, and I'll try my hardest to be there for the full thing, sweetie."

The more he thought about it, the more he decided he didn't need her there. He could handle the trial on his own. With the recent developments, the thought of having his mother in the audience witnessing everything churned his stomach. "It's okay, Mom. Coming home, I've realized while things seem bad sometimes, they could be a lot worse. And during the trial, they're gonna describe a lot of stuff that you don't need to hear. Maybe it would be best if you don't come. If it's all right with you, of course."

It was clear he confused his mother as she cocked her head toward him. "You don't want me there? Are you sure? It's gonna be stressful for you to handle it alone."

"I'm sure. I have Anna, and once I get past the initial awkwardness of my testimony, the rest of it won't be so bad. Plus, I don't want to inconvenience you, with work and all."

"Honey, I want to be there for you."

Marlon twisted in his seat to look at her. "I know, but I think I can get through this one on my own."

# CHAPTER 17

**SNOW CRUNCHED UNDERNEATH MARLON'S DARK BROWN** boots as he sauntered up to the school entrance. Most students didn't pay him any attention or glance in his direction. Their hushed conversations about the anticipation of returning to class brought a wave of relief to him and contrasted with his first day of the fall semester. His vivid blue jeans and mustard sweater fit tight on his thin frame as he strutted along. He pushed through the front door, and someone caught his eye.

"Hi, Marlon," Anna said as they locked eyes.

Marlon smiled. "I've missed you. Thanks for meeting me here."

It turned out he wasn't the only one who experienced a winter break transformation. She had brightened her hair to a rich shade of golden brown with a subtle blonde balayage and made up her face with a muted-plum lipstick.

"You look *gorgeous*," Marlon said.

"Aw, thanks. How was Ohio?"

"Beyond amazing. It gave me a different outlook on things."

She peeked up at him. "Are you serious?"

His cognac-tinted eyes twinkled as he nodded at her. "I am. Being back there made me think about everything, and I realized I need to try harder if I want things to go back to normal again. The only way to heal is to try."

"Oh, wow. I'm glad to hear that. But please don't deny yourself the space to experience negative emotions. Can you promise me you won't? You have every right to get upset and be pissed off at the world sometimes."

Without acknowledging her question, he tugged her toward him and wrapped her in a hug. "I'm happy I got to see you. We'll hang out soon. Promise."

Marlon roamed through the doorway of Room 113 for his Introduction to Sociology course. He walked to the back of the room and found a seat near the window.

A red-haired man stopped writing a welcome message on the board and turned to face the class. "Good afternoon, everyone. I'm Chadwick Brown, and I will teach you all about sociology. To start, let's go around the room and say our names. Let's start with you in the front corner."

"Leighton Fletcher," a woman said.

A dozen other people gave their names, and Marlon tuned out most introductions until a recognizable voice disturbed his thoughts.

"Quinn Beckham."

Chills raced down the back of Marlon's neck. His eyes shifted over in Quinn's direction, and the two gazed at each other for a moment as other classmates continued their introductions.

Marlon's eyes widened, and he looked down at his hands. No way. They shared a class. How did he miss seeing Quinn when he walked into the room?

"And you, sir?" The professor pointed at him.

"Um, I—my name is Marlon Woods."

Marlon wasn't sure if it was fate or something else, but there was a reason they shared this class. He needed to apologize to Quinn, or else he would have to suffer through seeing his former friend's face every week and thinking about what could have been. But their last conversation didn't go so well. Maybe he shouldn't bother him. Still, all he wanted was a chance to apologize again.

When class concluded for the day, students flooded out into the hallway. After watching Quinn stay seated for a few minutes, Marlon gave up and stepped out of the room.

A moment afterward, Quinn crashed into him as he left the classroom. "Sorry."

The two stared at each other until Marlon spoke. "Hey. How's it going?"

"It's fine," Quinn said in a caustic tone.

Marlon flashed a warm smile. "I'm glad. Listen, I wanted to apologize. I know I tried talking to you about everything around Thanksgiving, but I'm really sorry."

Quinn's eyes locked on to the floor as he backed away. "Yeah, it's cool. Don't worry about it. I gotta go."

"Please stop. I messed up. Big time. There's no excuse for what I did. I was confused and pissed, but I had no reason to throw you under the bus. You were nothing but sweet and considerate, and you went out of your way to not bring up the assault. You're a damn good friend, and I would hate to lose you over this. I'll do whatever it takes to make things right between us."

Quinn shrugged. "I appreciate that, but it's not that easy. It hurt. Bad."

"I know it did. I had no right to snap like that. I was an idiot."

"No. You were just going through a lot."

Marlon pressed his lips together. "Going back to Ohio made me think about how much I want to be here and beat this thing. But I want—I need—you in my corner. Life isn't as fun without you."

Quinn's face relaxed. "Thanks."

"So, what do you say? Can you give me another chance?"

"Yeah, of course. I forgive you and appreciate the apology," Quinn said.

Marlon beamed. "Thanks. Does this mean we can hang out again and argue over music?"

"Only if we both agree I'm always right."

"Oh, I don't know about that." Marlon raised his brows.

"I'm glad you stopped me today. Winter break was ... something," Quinn said.

"Why? What happened?"

Quinn rolled his eyes. "My sister broke up with her boyfriend, and our mom got into this huge argument with his mom in their front yard. It was like an episode of *Jerry Springer*. The moral of the story is, don't tell a woman how to parent her sixteen-year-old daughter."

Marlon chuckled. "Jeez, and I thought my family was messy. Sorry. At least you had entertainment, right?"

"Yeah, I've had enough to last a lifetime." Quinn sighed. "I ... I missed you. I mean, I missed our friendship. I felt bad about not listening to your apology sooner. Let's be honest with each other from now on, so something like that doesn't happen again. Okay?"

"Deal," Marlon said.

# CHAPTER 18

MARLON RELAXED IN HIS CAR OUTSIDE THE UNIVERSITY. An indie-rock station played on the radio until his phone vibrated, echoing through the Bluetooth system. He jolted forward in his seat and stared at the caller ID. Quinn? Why would *he* be calling? "Hello?"

"Yoooo. What are you up to at this fine hour?"

"Getting ready to go to my drawing class. How about you, slacker?"

Quinn yawned. "Who, me? Oh, nothing. I don't have class today, so I'm gonna take an epic nap."

"Jerk. Wanna trade?" Marlon said.

"No, thanks. But what do you say we hang out later? Maybe we can go to Mad Taps?"

Marlon's face flushed. He needed to sneak Anna into the equation. "I'm always down to hang out. Want me to text Anna and invite her?"

Silence filled the line until Quinn hummed. "How

about just the two of us go out tonight? We can grab coffee or something with her tomorrow. Is that cool? I feel like I haven't had much alone time with you since classes started back last month."

Marlon sighed. How could he say no to him? "I'd love to."

"Yay, great. See you there at six?"

"Perfect. Talk to you later." Beeping signaled the end of the call.

Marlon clenched the phone in his hand and swallowed hard. Would it be awkward hanging out with Quinn alone again? And this time, with no movie or third friend to make it less uncomfortable.

———————

Along the way back to his car after classes finished later in the day, he spotted Courtney's friend Madison Benét reading a book on a bench. She had been so nasty to him last time he saw her, but he couldn't blame her; maybe she didn't know any better.

Marlon shifted his facial expression into a beaming smile and stopped within feet of where she sat. "How's it going?"

Her eyes darted up from the red hardback book in her hands. She glared at him for several moments. "Good."

What could he say? Oh, her hair was different. He

pointed at her hair and smiled again. "Your hair looks amazing. Brown is totally your color."

The comment left her furrowing her brow and glancing around. "Uh, me? Thanks."

"Yes. Nice book, by the way."

"I love it so far." She grinned back at him. "Most people don't know this about me, but I'm a sucker for a good book. Everyone thinks I'm some rich idiot who spends all her money on clothes and stuff, but really, I spend most of my free time reading."

Marlon wasn't expecting that from her. Maybe he was no better than her and the others for judging someone he didn't know. "I don't think that about you. And if you ever want to swap book recommendations, let me know."

She glanced down at the book and up at him again. "I'd love to. Thanks, Marlon."

He nodded at her as he stepped away. "No problem. Have a nice day."

Before he could take more than a few steps, she stopped him. "Thanks for the compliment. I'm, um, embarrassed to admit this, but I'm having a rough day. I needed that."

As he spun around to lock eyes with her, a smile lit up both of their faces.

"Glad I cheered you up. Return the favor to someone else today."

She nodded in acknowledgment.

———————

A few hours later, he peered at his watch. He needed to leave within fifteen minutes to meet Quinn.

He hurried to the bathroom, fixed his hair, and brushed his teeth. The next task was to find an outfit to wear. During their friendship, he and Quinn had developed an unspoken fashion competition. Today, he couldn't let Quinn win.

He dug through his closet and settled on an off-white button-up dress shirt, dark jeans, and black dress shoes. To tone down the look, he rolled the sleeves up mid-arm. That ought to blow Quinn away.

He left the apartment and hopped into his car.

While driving out of Pine and down I-90, his mind took him back to the events of the past few months. He couldn't believe he was on his way to hang out with Quinn—something they had started doing on a regular basis again with Anna. A matter of months ago, he ruined the friendship. He had two best friends again, was doing well in school, and was happy. Yes, happy. Did he ever think he'd use that word to describe himself post-rape? No, never.

A pothole on the highway swallowed his front tire, rattling the car, and redirecting his attention to the task at hand.

When the GPS alerted him of his arrival at the restaurant, his eyes danced around, trying to find a place to park.

"Where the hell is it? I don't see a ... Oh, there."

To Marlon's surprise, someone was leaving a spot as he turned into the back lot. He shut the car off and peered down at his phone, reading a new message from Quinn.

*Go through the doors and make a right.*

He took a deep breath, opened the car door, and strolled up to the entrance. The words "Mad Taps Beer & Burgers" greeted him in large mustard-colored lettering.

A man on a mission, he walked past the rows of patrons until the smiling face of his friend caught his eye in the back of the restaurant.

Quinn rose from his seat and opened his arms. "Look at you. Nice outfit, Mr. Handsome."

He gulped as they embraced. Here came the flirting. Marlon didn't want to act weird. "Thanks. Back atcha."

Quinn stepped back, allowing Marlon to take in his whole outfit: black dress pants, olive-colored button-up shirt, and suede shoes of a similar shade of green. "Do you like it?"

"Love it."

The two men sat in opposing seats at the booth.

Marlon picked up the menu and scanned over the options. "So, what should I order?"

Quinn bit into his lip. "Uh, yeah, about that. I ordered for you already. Hope you don't mind."

"Oh, am I not cool enough to order for myself?"

"No, you're the worst. I'm kidding. I wanted you to try

my favorite burger."

Marlon chuckled at him. "As long as it isn't gross. Don't disappoint me."

Quinn gasped, clutching his hand to his chest. "Me, disappoint you? Impossible."

"But you invited me to a restaurant with 'beer' in its name when neither of us can drink. Strike one against you. You might as well have taken me to Noir or Donna's Diner."

Quinn's brow furrowed. "Yeah, you're right. Sorry for teasing you with delicious, sinful alcohol. I hope you can forgive me."

Marlon flapped his hand at him.

"Weird question," Quinn said, "but why do you go to Noir Coffee so often? Not that I mind, but it's like your second home."

"Oh, I don't know if I told you this, but I used to work there. Yes, Marlon Woods held a job for a whole year."

Quinn sipped on his drink, and his brows raised. "Wait, what? I didn't know that. Why didn't you work there when school started up again?"

Marlon exhaled through his nose. That was the one thing they hadn't talked about in their friendship. Marlon needed to work on being more open about it. "The, um, sexual assault. I couldn't imagine having a job, going to school, and dealing with a trial all at once."

A frown formed on Quinn's pillow lips. "I'm so sorry,

I didn't mean to go there. But I understand. I think you're doing a great job of keeping your shit together. Takes a lot of bravery to push through the madness and work on finding happiness for yourself."

Marlon smiled. Why had he been so afraid to bring this up with him? Quinn was one of the least judgmental people he had ever met. Although he knew about the case before, he didn't let it impact their relationship. "Thanks so much. I'm trying as hard as I can."

"I'm glad. Sorry if this isn't okay to ask, but are you nervous about the trial? You're gonna nail your testimony. I can't wait to see them convict that asshole."

Why was everyone so naïve about the case? He was happy people thought he would do a good job testifying, but it wasn't a slam dunk. Marlon rattled his head to shake the thoughts away. "Nervous? Yes, I'm terrified. Do I think they're going to convict him? Not sure. These cases almost always play out in the rapists' favor."

Quinn lowered his head. "I wish you weren't right, but you are. There's a lot of evidence in your case, though, so that'll help."

"I've done a lot of research on it and am coming to terms with the justice system. I read a statistic somewhere that said they only convict seven out of a thousand rapists of a felony. Crazy, right? But I'm not giving up hope. Who knows? Maybe my case will be one of the lucky ones."

"Yeah, I read that too. But that's the spirit. Keep your

head up and stay focused on healing. Don't worry about numbers and figures."

"So, what are your plans for the summer? We're still a few months away, but I'm curious," Marlon said.

"Going back to Colorado, unfortunately. Don't have much of a choice. You?"

Marlon hadn't thought about this. Did he want to go back to Ohio or stay in Washington? The trial would determine which one he chose. Time would tell. He shrugged. "Don't know yet. My family will want me to go home to Ohio, but I still have plenty of time to think about it."

A bleach-blonde waitress interrupted the conversation as she approached the table with two white, rectangular plates in her palms. "Two Mad Cow burgers cooked medium-well."

Quinn put his finger up. "Thanks."

Marlon glanced around and leaned closer to Quinn, lowering his voice to a whisper. "Did you really order me something called a 'Mad Cow burger'?"

"I did, and you will love every delicious bite."

They ate a few bites in silence before Quinn gulped down his food and waved a fry in the air. "I think you're a pretty amazing guy."

Here it came. They were about to enter another danger zone. No, he wasn't ready for that. Marlon's cheeks flushed as he peered up at him. "So are you ... buddy."

# CHAPTER 19

ON A SUNNY MORNING IN LATE MARCH, MARLON RAN INTO Laura Carpenter at the university bookstore. They hadn't spoken since the night of her party when Parker assaulted him.

"Laura?" Marlon said, approaching her in an aisle of books.

She glanced up from a textbook, grinning at him. "Oh, hey, Marlon. It's been a while."

Once the sincerity in her smile became clear to him, he smiled back. "I'm so glad to see you. Sorry for not talking to you sooner. It's not like you did anything wrong, but—"

Laura shook her head. "It's fine. I understand why you wouldn't want to talk. How have you been doing?"

"Honestly? This semester has been great so far. I almost feel like a different person. Life is getting better for me, and I'm not so bothered by everyone else's bullshit."

"I'm so happy for you. I never got the chance to tell you

this, but I believe you. I cut off Parker and any of the friends who sided with him. I'm so sorry it happened at my house. I can't help feeling like I'm somewhat responsible."

"I don't blame you. There's no way you could have known," Marlon said.

"Thanks. Hey, I don't know if this is appropriate, and if not, please don't be afraid to say no," Laura said, hesitating for a second. "I'm throwing a spring break party this Saturday night if you wanna come. You can invite Anna and that guy you've been hanging out with."

Joy was the initial reaction to hit him, but nausea soon followed as he contemplated going back to her house and the site of the attack. "Um … I … Well … Can I get back to you on that?"

Her face slackened. "Sure. I'm sorry if I made you uncomfortable."

"Oh no, you didn't. It's … I need to make sure Anna and Quinn don't have any plans. Otherwise, I'm totally down." To comfort her, he smiled and shrugged.

"Makes sense. It is kind of short notice. If you wanna go, feel free to show up. No pressure, though, and I'll understand if you don't come."

He hugged her. "Thanks."

———

Throughout the drive to Noir Coffee for his scheduled

hangout with his two best friends, Marlon speculated how they would react to his interest in attending the party. How the hell was he going to bring it up? Anna would love the idea ... Not!

As Marlon entered the coffee shop, Quinn turned and pointed to him. "And speak of the Devil, there he is."

"I heard that," Marlon said, playfully flipping his middle finger up at them behind his back. "I'll be over in a sec. I need to order first."

Brandon Kennedy beamed at him from behind the counter. "Look who it is."

"Hey, stranger. How's the business major going?"

"Awesome. This time next year, I'll be planning for graduation. Can you believe it?" Brandon asked, chuckling at himself.

"Congrats. I know you've worked really hard. I guess we don't share any classes since you're a hotshot junior now, huh?" Marlon lowered his sunglasses at him and laughed.

Brandon's forehead creased. "While that may be true, I'll never be as fabulous as you. Anyway, what would you like to order?"

When Marlon finished ordering his drink, he strolled over to Anna and Quinn's table. "Thanks for waiting up for me."

Anna wagged her hand at him. "Hey, it's not our fault you're fashionably late all the time."

With his chin rested on his fist, Quinn leaned in.

"Where were you?"

It was time to tell them. Marlon glanced around to see if anybody could overhear him whispering to his friends. "You guys won't believe this, but I talked to Laura at the campus bookstore."

A gasp slipped from Anna's mouth. "What did she say?"

Marlon pressed an index finger to his lips to hush her. "*Shh!* She apologized for what happened at the party. She said she blamed herself, and she stopped talking to Parker and all his friends."

"Who is this?" Quinn asked.

Quinn was so out of the loop because Marlon kept forgetting he wasn't there last year. Marlon peered at him in acknowledgment. "And she invited us to her party this weekend."

Anna leaned closer. "Are you kidding? You aren't considering it, are you?"

And there was that classic Anna answer he knew she'd give. Marlon twitched his shoulders. "Why not? I mean, it's obvious why I wouldn't go, but I'm torn. A part of me wants to go, and if I do, you guys should come with me."

A smile radiated across Quinn's face. "Oh, a party. I'm down if you are. I think it could be good for you."

He had a point.

Anna stared at him. "Quinn, I'm sorry, but you weren't there that night. I don't think it's a good idea to put Marlon back in that place and situation. It hasn't even been a year yet, and he has made so much progress over the last few months. I'd hate to see it ruined."

She also had a point. Marlon shook his head. "I'll be fine, Anna. If both of you go, nothing bad can happen."

Anna let out a perturbed sigh and flashed a halfhearted smile. "If you think this won't set you back, I'll go."

———

On the afternoon before the party, Marlon and Quinn drove to Northgate Mall in Seattle to buy outfits for the evening. After two hours of browsing, they picked out their selections and rode to Anna's apartment.

Anna opened the door. "Hello, boys. Oh, you brought goodies."

With his arms bogged down with shopping bags, Quinn smiled back at her. "Of course."

Over the next hour, they scrambled to get ready.

Anna stepped out of the bedroom and donned a form-fitting burgundy sweater, dark blue jeans, and black heels. A few moments later, Quinn walked out of the bathroom in a sky-blue button-up shirt, blue slacks, and mocha dress boots. Marlon entered the living room in a denim button-down, skinny maroon pants, and Oxford shoes.

Anna looked at her two buddies. "Damn, we clean up nicely, don't we?"

The three friends loaded into Anna's jeep and headed

to Laura's home on Mercer Island, about twenty miles from the university.

As they neared their destination, Quinn patted the back of the passenger seat, shaking Marlon's body. "You guys didn't tell me this girl is a millionaire."

Anna laughed. "When we went to one of her parties last year, I got curious and searched for her house on Zillow. They bought it for over a million dollars a few years ago. Can you imagine having money like that?"

Quinn's mouth dropped open. "What does her family do for a living?"

Marlon chuckled. "Her dad is a film producer, and her mother runs an accounting firm in Seattle."

"Wow. I bet she's a spoiled brat, huh?" Quinn asked.

The assumption prompted an exasperated sigh from Marlon. "No, she's one of the nicest people you'll ever meet. And she doesn't use any of her family's money. She pays for everything herself."

Quinn's eyes widened. "That's something you don't hear every day. Good for her."

———

Slate-colored horizontal siding covered most of the exterior of the home, and the corners of the house featured a brick pattern with varying hues of gray. Vibrant yellow lights glowed outside the garage. Several cars sat parked on the long, freshly sealed pewter-toned driveway, a sign they weren't the first to arrive at the party. Pine trees peeked out from behind the silhouette of the home as the setting sun painted the sky various shades of peach.

Marlon's heart pounded fast and hard. Being where his assault happened less than a year prior terrified him. Parker wouldn't be there, but he still didn't feel safe. It was too late to turn back, though.

"Are you okay?" Anna asked, interrupting his thoughts.

He shook his head to rattle the worries away. He needed to snap out of his fog. "I'm fine. Let's go."

They strolled up to the entrance, and Anna rang the buzzer.

Laura peered through the window before the door opened. "Glad you guys made it. Come on in and make yourselves at home."

Upon entering the house, the buzz of music and guests engaged in conversation left Marlon stunned.

Quinn glanced around and beamed. "Wow. I can honestly say I've never been to a house this nice before."

Laura's cheeks flushed, and she shot a sheepish smile at the two men. "Aww, thanks."

Most people in attendance Marlon had only spotted in passing on campus and hadn't spoken to, which brought a wave of relief to him.

Once they settled in, the three friends parted ways with Anna and Quinn walking around to explore the home and find the booze. To play it safe, Marlon plopped down on the extravagant steel-colored couch in a quieter section of the downstairs and sipped on a glass of water. He couldn't risk getting intoxicated and someone taking advantage of him again.

"Whoa, Marlon? Didn't expect to see you here," a man said from behind him.

Marlon swiveled around on the couch. His heart sank when his eyes met those of the speaker. "Oh. Hi, Asher."

Asher Davis stuck his hand out and pulled Marlon in for a handshake and a pat on the back, made awkward by the fact Marlon was sitting. "Happy to see you're getting out and living your life again."

Marlon peered around the room to determine if it was some elaborate trick. Why the hell was Asher talking to him? What was his angle? "Uh, yeah. Laura invited me, so I figured I should give it a shot. What's going on with you?"

Asher sat next to Marlon on the sofa. "I wanted to say I'm sorry for everything you've been through, and for making you uncomfortable a few months ago at the coffee shop."

Marlon flashed a reassuring smile. Maybe he didn't need to worry. "Thanks, but you didn't do anything."

Asher shrugged his statuesque shoulders. "I know, but I was friends with him, and I believed him at first. I was an idiot."

Although Marlon agreed with the sentiment, he didn't

want him to feel guilty. "Lots of people did. Nobody realized what he was capable of."

Asher's dark brown eyes flickered up at Marlon's. "I bet you think since I play on the team, I must still be tight with him, but I swear I'm not. Most of the guys cut him off. Shit got way too weird with him. That's actually one of the reasons why I wanted to talk to you at Noir."

Marlon wasn't expecting him to say that. He assumed everyone took Parker's side. "I'm glad people are starting to see his true colors."

Asher grinned and tapped Marlon's shoulder with the palm of his hand. "Yeah, well, I'll leave you alone now and let you get back to the party. See you around, man."

The conversation didn't go as badly as Marlon had expected. He was socializing with people and not acting weird—an incredible feat for him.

---

Anna and Quinn returned for a quick check-in with Marlon to see how he was handling being there. After insisting he wanted alone time and they should get back to the party, they parted ways again.

The living room became crowded as new partygoers arrived. Marlon walked toward the back door for some fresh air. If he opened it, he would have to confront the scene of the crime. An internal argument between right and wrong raged on inside of him. He wanted—no, *needed*—to do it.

He took a few deep breaths and turned the knob, hurling the door open. The initial steps out to the porch were the toughest, but after a few seconds, it became easier. His palms relaxed on the railing as he peered out at the backyard.

The expansive wooden deck overlooked several mature pine trees. In the yard below stood a cobalt woodshed, behind which the attack took place. His eyes fixated on the spot as he choked for air. There was the spot where his life changed forever.

Pine in the chilly air hit him with force, sending his mind on a rollercoaster. His pulse quickened, prompting him to grip the wooden railing tighter. A million images danced around his head as he squinted at the manicured lawn. Why did he go to the party? Was he retraumatizing himself by going back to that house? Should he walk down there? No, he couldn't handle it. Or could he? Parker wasn't there, and Marlon wanted to face his fears.

Marlon exhaled through his nose as he trudged down the stairs. His legs became so shaky, he could hardly stand. "It's just a shed. Stop freaking out," he whispered to himself several times.

Before he knew it, he was retracing the path he followed on the night his life almost ended. Within a few more steps, he stopped short of the spot where Parker forced him face down on the ground.

His trembling fingers traced along the wood exterior of

the shed. His eyes squeezed shut as the memories of that night flooded back to him: Parker walking him over there. Kissing him on the lips. Marlon rejecting him. The slap to his face. The repeated blows until he could no longer resist. Fingers wrapped around his neck. Desperate hands yanking his pants off. The ripping of flesh. He could still feel it, but it was only a memory.

His eyes darted open to find nobody there. He was all alone. Nobody to hurt him.

Having experienced enough flashbacks for one night, he raced back up to the deck. He stared out into the distance, trying to collect his thoughts. That wasn't as hard as he pictured it being. Marlon from a few months ago could never have imagined doing it.

A hand grasped the rail next to his as a male's voice shattered the silence. "Is that where it happened?"

Marlon jumped backward and almost lost his balance. He thrashed his head around. It was Blake. "You scared the hell out of me."

"Sorry about that, buddy. Are you okay?"

"I'm fine. I just needed a break from the action."

"Understandable. Sorry for barging out here like this, but is that where it happened?" Blake asked, pointing at the shed.

Marlon's eyes closed, and he nodded.

"Is this your first time here since that night?"

"Yes." Why was he asking that? Why did he care about

the case so much? Since Marlon returned to the university, all of their interactions had been awkward like this.

"How does it make you feel?"

Marlon stared straight ahead with a blank expression and inhaled the crisp air. "Uncomfortable." And Blake wasn't helping with his line of questioning.

Blake rocked his head and frowned. "That asshole deserves to fry for what he did to you and other people."

"The justice system doesn't see it that way, unfortunately," Marlon said in a frustrated tone.

Blake's face relaxed. "Do you ever want to kill him? Has the thought ever crossed your mind?"

Chills shot down Marlon's arms and neck. "No, I don't believe in that. If I hurt him, I'd be the one in trouble. It's not worth it."

"All I've gotta say is he better watch his back. Everything he did will come back to bite him in the ass," Blake whispered, his head swaying.

Marlon gave a hesitant nod.

"Sorry about the rant. What are you majoring in at Pine again? I forgot."

"Graphic design, but I'm still not sure if I want to stick with it. What about you?"

"Computer science."

A grin lit up Marlon's face. "Oh, cool. I guess we're both into computer-related stuff, huh?"

"We have a lot more in common than you would imagine," Blake said, gripping the railing so hard that his hands twitched.

Marlon raised an eyebrow. "What do you mean?"

Blake shrugged and stepped backward. "Nothing. Sorry. I should go back inside now. It's cold out here."

There was something off about him, but Marlon couldn't quite put his finger on it.

———

Marlon lingered out on the deck for a little while longer and attempted to gather his thoughts. The agreement with his friends to remain close at the party popped into his head, and he rushed back inside out of fear they would worry for him.

Laura spotted him wandering through the living room and gestured for him to join her.

Since he was last inside, someone turned the music up all the way. Understanding her would be almost impossible. "What's up?"

She tugged his head near her mouth and hollered into his ear. "Dance with me." The stench of alcohol radiated from her pink lips. Her hair was now a tangled, brown mess.

Not wanting to offend the host, he danced with her to a collection of pop and R&B songs from the early 2000s.

Passersby joined in, forming a small dance circle, which engulfed the room within a matter of minutes. That was the most fun he'd had in a while, and his fears and cares subsided. He surrendered himself to the pounding music.

When the sense of responsibility hit him again several songs later, the hairs on his arms raised. "I have to find my friends. Be right back," he shouted at Laura.

She gave him the thumbs up before returning to her sloppy dance routine.

Marlon walked through the home, unable to locate either of his friends. He hiked up the grand wooden staircase, and into the first bedroom he found. Nope, no luck there. The bathroom door sat wide open in the second room he entered, so he checked around the corner. The floor below his feet rattled from the reverberation of the bass-heavy song downstairs.

Quinn smiled at him from the edge of a clawfoot bathtub. "I'm so happy to see you." The slurring of words made it clear he'd had one too many drinks.

"I've been looking for you. Is everything okay? Where's Anna?"

One of Quinn's eyes twitched as he attempted to concentrate on Marlon's face. "Probably hooking up with Ethan or Ian or whatever his name is. Ugh, my head hurts."

"Let's get out of here. Why are you sitting in here?"

Quinn plopped his beer down on the frosted tile floor, shooting a surge of alcohol and foam out of the bottle. "I wanted to talk to you about *us*. What are we?"

A lump formed in Marlon's throat, and his face flushed. "Uh, we're friends."

Quinn rose to his feet and wobbled toward him. "No, but like, there's something more between us, right? I know you feel it too."

"No. We're best friends. Nothing more. I love being around you, but I'm not ready to date anybody," Marlon said, stepping back.

The explanation prompted a pout on Quinn's reddened face. "But we'd make a great couple. You're so—" he hiccupped— "handsome. Give me a chance."

Marlon glared and put his palms up to stop Quinn from advancing. He didn't want him to say another word. It was already awkward enough. "I don't want to hurt your feelings, but you're drunk and need to back off."

Quinn's expression hardened. "Shut up. I'm not drunk."

The words pierced through Marlon's eardrums and made his face burn. "We're leaving now." He clutched Quinn's wrist and dragged him through room after room to locate Anna.

When he attempted to twist a doorknob at the end of the hallway, a woman said, "Occupied."

He knocked and pressed his ear against the thin wood, awaiting a response. "It's Marlon. We should leave now. It's getting kind of late."

Anna groaned. "Is everything okay? Can you give me a few minutes?"

Since the lock only required a flat object to unlock it from the outside, he stuck the corner of his debit card in and twisted. The door shot open, and he barged in. "Let's go."

On the bed lay Anna and Ethan Washington, locked in an embrace. "Sorry, Ethan. Gotta run." She gathered her pumps off the floor, slipped them on, and strutted out the door with her friends.

Marlon raised a brow as he peeked over at her. "What were you doing in there?"

She shoved her bracelets back on her wrist. "Nothing. You showed up before we could do anything."

Quinn's body ricocheted off the walls as they trudged down the hallway. "Yeah, he's in a bad mood."

The sight caught Anna's attention, and she chuckled. "What's his deal? Did he get hammered?"

Marlon's eyes rolled around. "Yes, and he's pissed because I rejected him."

"Oh, awkward." Anna cringed and walked down the stairs.

Saying it aloud put the situation in perspective for Marlon. None of the men he knew could handle rejection.

Marlon stormed out of the front door with his friends and slammed it shut behind him.

# CHAPTER 20

FOUR WEEKS LATER, *THE JUDY FAITH SHOW* RAN TEASERS for an exclusive interview with the unidentified second victim of Parker Sullivan. The episode would air on April 16, a little more than a month before the trial.

Marlon and Anna planned to watch the interview together at her house. They invited Quinn, but he claimed to be busy with a project. Marlon suspected the truth was he didn't want to face him after confessing his feelings at Laura's party.

———

Anna clicked the television remote on, and a coffee commercial played on the screen. "Who do you think she is?"

Marlon shrugged. "I don't know. I just hope this doesn't affect the trial."

Anna flapped her hand at him as she scrolled through

the on-screen TV guide. "It shouldn't since they've already picked the jury. They aren't allowed to read or watch anything about the case."

When she landed on the correct channel, *The Judy Faith Show* banner swooped in, and the usual theme song blared. Judy leaned in toward the camera with a solemn look on her face. "Good evening, ladies and gentlemen. Welcome to a live, special edition of *The Judy Faith Show*. Tonight, I am joined by someone we've all anticipated for months now. The trial of Parker Sullivan in the Pine State University sexual assault case is only a month away. The victim, in that case, will testify in court about his experience. But now, I have one of the other victims of this predator. Cassie, thank you so much for agreeing to do this interview with me."

A tan woman with wavy, black hair grinned. "Thanks for having me, Judy."

Judy peered down at a sheet and back up at Cassie. "Please, tell our viewers at home your name and how you came to know Mr. Sullivan."

"I'm Cassie Roberts, and I went to high school with Parker Sullivan. He played on the football team, and I was a cheerleader, so we spent a lot of time around each other."

Marlon's eyes widened. A cheerleader? He had assumed Parker only targeted nobodies like him.

"Was Parker popular in school?" Judy asked.

"Oh yeah. Parker was the quarterback, so he had lots of friends and people pawing at him. It was kind of pathetic."

"When we spoke on the phone several months ago, you brought up an incident where he tried pursuing you, and you shut him down. Could you elaborate for us?"

Marlon leaned forward in his seat in anticipation.

Cassie exhaled. "He was usually nice to me, but also flirty. He had a girlfriend but would hit on me every chance he got. One time, during junior year, he spanked my butt. I called him out in front of his friends, and he freaked out on me. He called me a slut and told me to leave him alone. Rumors spread around the school about me trying to steal him from his girlfriend, and it was a mess. But we moved past it and were cool with each other throughout most of our senior year."

Marlon's stomach churned. The same situation almost happened to him. Parker didn't handle rejection well.

Judy's maroon-lipped grin dissolved as she stared at Cassie. "This is going to be painful for you to talk about, but could you describe the night he assaulted you? What happened, and where were you guys?"

Marlon's pulse quickened, and his eyes fixated on the television screen. He kept reminding himself it was an interview, and there was no reason to stress over it. He needed to focus.

Cassie shifted in her seat. "He invited me out to see a movie one night and said several of our mutual friends planned on coming. I said yes."

"And what movie did you see?"

With an uncompromising stare, Cassie said, "We didn't. Parker picked me up and said our friends would meet us at the theater. After driving for a few minutes, I realized he was going the wrong way, so I tried to tell him, but he ignored me. Several miles later, he pulled over in a parking lot and said, 'I've waited so long to get you alone.' I thought he was joking, so I laughed at him. That pissed him off. He glared at me and slapped me across the face. He said, 'What's so funny?' and grabbed me by my hair and forced my head in his lap."

Tears filled Cassie's eyes, and she paused. "He told me if I bit him, he would kill me. I believed him. And then ... *it* happened."

Marlon's trembling hand fumbled with the remote as he increased the volume.

Judy slid a box of tissues over toward the woman. "Take your time."

Cassie dabbed a tissue at her eyes and nose a few times. "It went on for what felt like an eternity, but I realized it lasted for about seven minutes. I stared at the clock in his car the whole time, trying to imagine I was someplace else."

When the show cut to a commercial, Marlon and Anna turned to face each other.

The partial interview left Anna with a stunned expression. "Can you believe that?"

Marlon glared at her. "Yes, because I went through a lot of the same things."

Anna sighed. "Of course she's telling the truth. But I mean, he did that shit to other people, and nobody said anything about it."

"It wouldn't surprise me if there are others out there that he did this to—men and women."

Marlon tried to process his thoughts as the commercials played. The interview was bittersweet for him. On the one hand, it was vindicating because somebody else was saying they experienced the same thing with Parker, which confirmed it wasn't just a misunderstanding for him as some people implied. But the details were triggering. Was this how the trial would go? Parker's on-air outburst on Judy's show months prior left him equally frazzled. If he could hardly watch a television interview, could he handle recounting his assault in front of dozens of audience members?

The show's song played, and Judy returned to the screen. "Welcome back, everyone. Once again, I am joined by Cassie Roberts, a victim of alleged rapist Parker Sullivan. Thanks for tuning in with us tonight. Cassie, what happened after the assault you described to us moments ago?"

Cassie's eyes focused on the desk. "He pulled his pants back up and just stared at me. I didn't care. He already ruined me. I was a virgin by choice, and wanted to wait for the right person. He wiped the smeared lipstick off the corners of his mouth and told me I should get dressed. When I asked him why he raped me, he laughed and said if I told

anyone, he would hurt me. He also said nobody would believe me because his parents were so respected and well-
known. I believed him. When he dropped me off at my
house, I sat in the shower until the water ran cold."

Marlon's blood turned to ice. That was exactly how he
felt after his assault.

"I'm so sorry. When did you encounter him next?" Judy
asked, lowering her tone and resting her hand on Cassie's.

Cassie sniffled. "I missed a few days of school but eventually had to go back. Nobody knew what happened except
for Parker and me, or so I thought. The first day back at
school, everybody acted differently around me. I found out
that Parker had recorded a video and shared it with some of
his friends. Somehow the video spread between some of our
classmates. I opened my locker one day to find some screenshots of the video inside. While I was ripping them apart,
Parker walked by and winked at me. I almost vomited."

He gulped and shook his head. This was too similar.

After giving Cassie a moment to breathe, Judy looked
at the camera. "Now, I am sorry if this comes across as insensitive, but a question people keep tweeting to us is why
you didn't report this to the authorities."

Cassie lurched forward in her seat. "I did! I ended up
telling my parents what happened, and they were pissed. We
drove to the police station and reported it. Mrs. Sullivan
contacted me that night. She called to apologize, said they
were seeking therapy for Parker, and wanted to make things

right. She offered to give me fifty thousand dollars if I took it back and agreed not to go public."

Cassie paused and sighed. "At first, I said no. But she told me if I pursued charges, they would find him innocent anyway. He was seventeen, and his father was the former governor, so they had ties to the justice system. I guess I felt like she threatened me, and I just wanted the whole thing to go away. My mom was battling breast cancer, and we needed the money for medical expenses. I agreed to take the settlement and to remain silent."

Marlon's brows snapped together. She reported it, and they talked her out of pressing charges against Parker. That could have been him. He was thankful he left the state when he did.

Judy placed her fist over her chest and dropped her mouth open. "Oh, my stars. And what happened after you accepted the money?"

"I tried to forget about the assault. Then one day, I was watching the news and found out what Parker did at Pine State University. I knew that guy was telling the truth because the same thing happened to me. I couldn't let him face the same ridicule and shame that I did. When I saw how people were talking about him online and in the news and stuff, I felt so bad. I had to go public."

Judy leaned forward and squinted. "What did you do with the money? Did the Sullivan family make you sign a non-disclosure agreement?"

"The money paid off some of my mom's medical bills. She passed away last March, unfortunately. They made me sign an agreement, and by doing this interview, I'm breaking the terms. But I don't care about the consequences. The truth needs to come out. My dad wrote the Sullivans a check back in September for the amount they gave us. I also called the King County Sheriff's office to see if they wanted my help."

Marlon's heart fluttered, thinking about Cassie trying to help with his case.

"I am so sorry about your mother. So, you paid the Sullivan family back the money they gave you? Why did you do that?" Judy asked, her eyes focused on Cassie's.

Cassie straightened her posture. "Because I felt dirty. Like his family paid me for their son raping me. The thought alone is almost as disgusting as what he did to me. What could I use their dirty money for? School? A car? Why, so it could remind me of what happened?"

Judy pressed a pen to her lips and peered at Cassie. "You're right. That was disturbing. Do you regret not pursuing charges against Parker? Do you think you could have prevented him from doing this again?"

Cassie moved her head side to side in contemplation. "Yes and no. I've heard horror stories about trials. I mean, hello, *Law & Order* is enough to change anyone's perspective. I'd like to think I'm a brave person, but definitely not that brave. I guess I worried about people not believing me, kind of like they did with the PSU victim. The Sullivan family made me think I had no chance at justice. And no, I don't think anything would have stopped this from happening. The justice system almost always sides with the rapist, so I'm sure he wouldn't have gone to jail for what he did to me. But if somebody doesn't stop him now, he will continue doing this to others."

Marlon nodded in agreement. Cassie was right. It surprised him that he hadn't given up yet. Justice seemed so far away, but he needed to push forward.

The show's song echoed through the television as Judy refocused her body toward the camera. "Time for a break, but when we come back, I will read a statement from the Sullivan family."

The anticipation became too much for Marlon, and words flew out of his mouth at a hundred miles per hour. "What do you think they said? I can't believe this is happening. That could be me. Can you imagine?"

Anna gripped Marlon's wrist to calm him. "I know, but you have the trial in a few weeks. Everything will be okay."

He shook the thoughts from his head. "Yeah, you're right. Sorry. I wonder what his family said about Cassie."

Anna walked to the kitchen and grabbed a bag of potato chips off the counter. "Don't expect too much. They tried to cover up their son's crimes."

The show resumed, and a devilish grin displayed on Judy's face. "And we're back with Cassie Roberts. Now, when we scheduled this interview, our producers reached out to the Sullivan family for a statement. In most cases, they don't receive a response, but to our surprise, they did. I'll read it to you now."

A white screen with black text covered the two women's faces. When the words appeared, Judy read them aloud.

*The allegations made by Cassie Roberts are disturbing, as our son, Parker, considered her a close acquaintance in high school. The two quit speaking several years ago, and it is distasteful of her to make such heinous accusations over four years after this alleged incident took place. We will consult with our attorneys to discuss any legal action we may need to take against her for defamation of character and outright libel. To clarify why she received a fifty-thousand-dollar payment, our family runs an annual Mary L. Sullivan Scholarship in honor of Walter's sister, who passed away from lupus at a young age in the 1980s. Each year, our board members select one exceptional student with outstanding academic and volunteer achievements. The year Cassie and Parker were seniors in high school, she won the scholarship. Attached is a copy of the scholarship check and the annual newsletter*

*released by the board announcing the win-*
*ner. This woman received a scholarship, did*
*not pursue charges, and can provide no proof*
*an attack took place.*

The revelation made Marlon squeeze Anna's arm. "What the hell?"

She glared at him as she rubbed her arm. "Ouch."

A second display replaced the first with a scanned piece of cream-colored paper. Once again, Judy recited the text:

*MARY L. SULLIVAN SCHOLARSHIP:*
*WINNER ANNOUNCED. We would like*
*to congratulate Cassie S. Roberts on receiv-*
*ing this year's Mary L. Sullivan Scholarship.*
*Our board selected Cassie based on her ex-*
*emplary volunteer history, commitment to*
*after-school activities, such as volleyball and*
*cheerleading, and her 4.0 GPA.*

Below the newsletter was a copy of a check from the Mary L. Sullivan Scholarship Foundation to Cassie.

The two women appeared on the screen again, and a grave expression covered Judy's face. "So, what are your thoughts, Cassie? Did you receive a scholarship from them, or what?"

Cassie glared at Judy with an incredulous stare. "I never applied for that scholarship. They're liars!"

Judy shuffled her papers and cleared her throat. "Is it

possible they made the check out to you from the scholarship fund?"

"Maybe, but I didn't read the check when they gave it to me. If I knew what it said, I wouldn't have accepted it."

Judy pursed her lips and leaned in. "Did you accept any further compensation from them aside from the fifty thousand dollars you received and refunded to them?"

Her head shook back and forth with fury. "No, not at all. Mrs. Sullivan tried to refuse the money when we gave it back to her and said she couldn't believe I was stupid enough to return it. I told her I hope her family rots in hell for what they did."

Judy nodded. "Thanks for agreeing to this interview, Cassie. I appreciate your honesty with us this evening, and I wish you the best of luck."

Cassie stared into the camera. "Thank you for having me. Before I go, I want to say one thing. Parker, we're coming for you. See you in court."

Marlon turned to Anna. "This is crazy."

"Yeah, his family is garbage," Anna said, frowning.

Marlon's eyes rolled up at the ceiling. "I feel bad. She's been through so much. I can't imagine living through all this and never getting justice. And think of how it must feel knowing he did this to someone else after you."

"I wish she would have pushed for charges back then. I mean, I understand why she didn't, but still. I couldn't do it. No amount of money can take away the pain."

He shrugged and exhaled through his nose. "If his family offered me the money, I wouldn't accept it. But I get where she's coming from. A trial is long and stressful on its own, let alone with a dying mom."

"How many other people do you think he's done this to at Pine? You can't be the only one."

"I don't know. Even if I did, I'm sure everyone would be too afraid to speak out against him. Look how powerful his family is. They buried Cassie's case. I hope everyone he hurt will be brave enough to come forward someday."

Anna smiled at him. "I don't know if you realize this, but you're the face of a movement. I'm so proud of you for having the courage to pursue this thing and help the people who aren't there yet."

His cheeks reddened as he grinned back at her. "Thanks. You're my best friend, and I'm lucky to have you in my life. Thanks for standing beside me and helping me through this. It means the world to me."

She winked. "You couldn't get rid of me, even if you tried."

# CHAPTER 21

**A NEARBY STUDENT BLASTING MUSIC IN THEIR EARBUDS**
captured Marlon's attention as he glanced up and back
down at his notepad several times, trying to stay focused on
his assignment. The student lounge was designed to be a
quiet sanctuary of sorts—a distraction-free place one could
go to work on a paper or read a book and unwind without
someone bothering them. Nowadays, the Pine State University lounge was more like a frat house—loud, sometimes
stinky, and annoying.

Marlon huffed, flipped his notebook shut, and yanked
his phone out of his jean pocket. No matter how hard he
tried to focus, he couldn't stop thinking about Quinn. He
spent the entire Introduction to Sociology class that morning staring at him, hoping to catch his eye, but to no avail.
Things had been uncomfortable again for far too long, and
Marlon couldn't bear leaving things that way before the upcoming summer break.

His finger hovered over the Call button for several seconds as his mind played through a quick list of things to say. How was he supposed to recount what happened at Laura's party, tell Quinn he forgave him, and pretend it never happened? Nothing would take back Quinn confessing his affections for him. Those words would always be there, hiding below the surface.

A brunette-haired girl sitting across from Marlon in the lounge spritzed five squirts of a cheap-smelling, sugary perfume on herself, filling the space with the aroma. The overpowering fragrance gave Marlon an instant headache.

He stared her down, and she took the hint by flinching and shoving the pink bottle back into her purse.

Sometime between him glancing between his phone and the reeking woman, he bumped the button on his screen. He raised the ringing phone to his ear.

"Uh, hello?" Quinn said.

"Hey, it's Marlon. Wh-what's going on?"

Something slammed in the background. "I just got in my car. Why'd you call?" Quinn's voice was cold. This was the tone Marlon had grown accustomed to since that night—a hint of ever-present bitterness and rejection.

"Just wanted to see how your classes are going."

"They're all going fine."

Marlon paused. "Nice. Mine are about as good as they can be. I'm kind of looking forward to summer, though."

"You and me both," Quinn said with a sharp sigh.

It was a long shot, but it was worth a try. Marlon cleared his throat to tell Quinn the real reason he called. "There's no way to sugarcoat this, but I know things have been awkward between us. I wanted to see if maybe we could meet for lunch today and talk things over, just you and me."

The line fell silent for several seconds, leading Marlon to wonder if the call had ended.

"I don't know how to … I'm sorry. I didn't mean for things to be weird. I was drunk, and I know it's no excuse. So, let me know a time and place, and I'm there," Quinn said, his tone less harsh and biting than before.

Marlon's heart fluttered. "I have an idea. How 'bout I grab subs for us, and we can meet at Cypress Park in an hour? We could do a little picnic, if that's cool with you."

Quinn chuckled. "Well, if you're buying, I can't say no to that. Sure, sounds good. See you then."

"Okay, bye," Marlon said before pressing the red button. He gripped the phone to his chest and let out a sigh. Never in his life had he been so conflicted. He wanted nothing more than to give Quinn a chance and see where things went with him, but he also didn't want to risk ruining their friendship. Then, there was the even bigger issue of the trial. With only weeks to go, he couldn't afford to lose focus and let a potential romance distract him when his future depended on the outcome of this. Love would have to wait.

———

Marlon walked along the sidewalk at Cypress Park—the same place where his friendship with Quinn ended all those months prior when he suspected him of masterminding the Pine State University website and email hack. Marlon picked that park because of the symbolic value it held regarding their relationship. Things were rocky between them again, and he hoped to fix things.

Birds chirped in the luscious, green trees above. Two women played in a match on the tennis court ahead of him, and to the right, screaming children filled the crowded playground. He wandered along the path to the secluded spot Quinn had promised him in his text message minutes prior.

Marlon turned the corner and spotted Quinn sitting at a picnic table, staring out into the distance at some trees. Marlon broke his focus when he stepped on a small branch, prompting him to turn.

"Well, look who it is," Quinn said, smiling.

Marlon placed the large sandwich on the table and opened his arms for a hug. "God, I've missed you."

"Same, but I think you already knew that."

Marlon's ears reddened. Only a few seconds had passed, and the awkwardness was already coming out. He couldn't tell if Quinn was still bitter about it or if he was making light of the situation. Either way, it was uncomfortable.

DALE ROBBINS

Quinn motioned for him to sit at the table and took the seat across from him. He opened the sub and grabbed a quarter-piece of the massive sandwich.

Butterflies danced around inside Marlon's stomach, ruining his appetite. He longed for the chance to talk to Quinn, and now that he had him here, the words wouldn't come out.

Quinn looked up at him. "You wanted to talk?"

Marlon nodded. That was the moment when he needed to decide what he wanted out of the friendship. If he wanted a relationship, that was his opportunity to tell Quinn and take things to the next level. But if he hoped to keep things on a friendship level, they would also need to discuss that.

"Here, I'll go first," Quinn said. "I'm sorry I said that stuff to you. I don't remember everything, but I know it was wrong. To be honest with you, I *like* you. But I also realize you have a lot going on and maybe that isn't in the cards for us. Right now, or ever. I kind of wanna hear your thoughts on it, and if you think I'm silly for feeling that way."

"No, no. You're not silly at all. I also—" Marlon struggled to think of how to word it nicely. "There are some similar feelings for you. But you're right, there's a lot happening in my life, and I don't know if I'm ready for … that. I'm sorry."

Quinn bit into the sandwich, and his eyes stayed glued on the table. "Don't worry, I understand. No matter what happens between us, I'll still always care about you and be

202

there in any way I can. You mean so much to me. I don't think you realize it."

The statement was like a punch to the gut for Marlon. Quinn laid out all his feelings for him, and all he gave in return was a 'no, thanks.' Did he deny himself the opportunity to feel that way for someone out of fear of being hurt? Or because he didn't think he deserved to be happy? The thought made his head hurt.

After letting Marlon take it all in, Quinn continued, "That was a lot. Sorry. What I'm trying to say is I'm fine with us being whatever you want us to be—best friends, just friends, or something more. It's up to you."

Marlon smiled. "I'm so lucky to have someone like you in my life. You're so good to me. You've been nothing but sweet and understanding. That's more than I could ever ask for in a friend."

"You deserve it. You're gonna do big things. I'm just happy to be along for the ride. Thanks for always giving me a second chance."

Marlon's brow furrowed. "Second chance? You didn't do anything wrong. Honestly, you never have. I'm quick to react sometimes, and it always seems to come back to bite me in the ass. Sorry if I made you feel bad about sharing your feelings. That took courage."

Quinn shrugged. "I've always thought honesty was best. Whatever happens, as a result, is whatever is meant to be."

"I'm gonna miss you this summer. Please don't leave?"

Quinn laughed. "I'm not sure how my family would feel about that, but hey, if you can find me a place to stay, it's a deal."

Unsure of whether Quinn was joking or serious, the thought popped into Marlon's head to offer for him to stay at his apartment over the summer. But staying in his apartment was more of a boyfriend thing and less of a friendship thing. Plus, it would mean another person tagging along for the grueling, embarrassing trial. No, he couldn't do that. While he wanted Quinn around for support, there was no way he could share all the details while looking at him in the audience.

"You okay?" Quinn asked, snapping Marlon out of his thoughts.

"Oh, yeah. Sorry. I'm doing that thing where I'm all spacey and my mind drifts."

Quinn smiled and pointed at him. "Honesty. I love it."

"So, what do you have planned for the rest of the school year and summer? Anything fun or exciting?"

"Super exciting stuff, like several reports, all the finals, and a project. I can't wait," Quinn said, laughing at himself. "No, not really. I'm most likely flying home a day or two after classes end, and I'm not sure what I'm doing back in Colorado yet. My family is gonna drag me to Florida for our yearly summer vacation, but I'm not a beach person."

Marlon chuckled. "Oh, I'm *so* sorry, Mr. I'm Going on

Vacation. I hope you're okay."

"Yeah, yeah, I guess it makes me sound a little spoiled and ungrateful. I swear I'm not one of those silver-spooned Pine kids. It's not so much the beach as it is my family. I've been making that trip for most of my life, and it's exhausting."

"No, I know what you mean. At least your sister seems cool, so you've got one person. And you'll have me blowing up your phone the whole time, so you won't be alone," Marlon said.

Quinn raised a brow. "Is that a threat?"

"More like a promise."

Quinn chewed on his sandwich and peered back up at Marlon. "Are you going to be okay with the trial and all? Have you been preparing for it?"

Marlon swallowed hard. "I'm trying to block out any feelings related to it. I don't want to stress myself out and overhype it if that makes sense. But I'm supposed to be meeting with the prosecutor soon to go over some practice questions and make sure I'm ready."

"I know you're gonna do great. You got this."

A weight lifted off Marlon's back for a moment, hearing those words. He wanted to believe them.

# CHAPTER 22

THE LINE TO ENTER THE CLUB WRAPPED AROUND THE SIDE
of the building. A red velvet rope stood between Marlon and
his first nightclub experience. He smoothed his white T-
shirt out and slid the bottom part into his pants. The music
pounding inside The Velvet Room made the ground shake
beneath Marlon's feet, adding to his anxiety.

"You good?" Quinn asked, gazing into his eyes.

Marlon nodded. "Yeah. This is just new to me."

"It sucks going to a club when you can't drink," Anna
said, cringing. "Sorry, guys."

"I don't drink anyway, and this was Quinn's idea."

Quinn's eyes widened, and he chuckled. "This was one
of the few bars we could get into since it's college night."

Anna shook her head. "I think Marlon's trying to say
he didn't want to go out in the first place. He'd rather be at
home, watching *Twin Peaks* or something."

"That's exactly what I'd be doing," Marlon said.

Anna stepped forward in front of the burly security guard. "IDs out, guys," she whispered to her friends.

The bouncer grabbed Marlon's driver's license, squinted at it, and handed it back before drawing a large X on the top of both of his hands.

Marlon stared at the black ink—a silly and almost embarrassing symbol of his age.

Quinn's hand rested on Marlon's shoulder, breaking him out of his daze. "Are you ready to go in?"

Marlon smiled at him. "Yes."

Anna gripped the handle on the massive wooden door and pulled it open, sending a flood of piercing noise and blinding strobe lights out into the streets. Her friends passed her through the entrance, and they stopped a few feet inside next to a dark-colored leather sofa.

Marlon spun around, taking in the entire décor—the towering, red velvet curtains lining the wall, the flashing red lights above the dancefloor, and the two bars, centered along opposing walls with the dance area between them. Was this what everyone looked forward to throughout their teenage years? A place like this? If so, it didn't live up to the hype.

Anna cupped her hand to the side of her mouth and shouted, "I'm gonna grab a drink. Do you guys want anything? Water? Soda?"

"I'm fine, thanks," Marlon said.

"Water?" Quinn asked.

"Sure thing. Be right back." Anna strolled over to the

right-side bar.

Quinn tucked his hands in his pockets and glanced around, making eye contact with Marlon several times before looking away.

Marlon's cheeks flushed. Things didn't need to be so uncomfortable between them. Even though they had discussed their mutual feelings for each other and stayed friends, the thought of taking their friendship to the next level continued to plague Marlon, and he was sure Quinn sensed this.

"So, uh, what do you think?" Quinn asked.

Marlon swallowed hard. "It's cool. Different from what I imagined, though."

"Is it not up to your standards? I'll have you know this is the fourth highest-rated nightclub in this part of Seattle, mister," Quinn said.

Marlon laughed. "You're really selling me on the place. Have you considered a career in real estate?"

"Okay, let me try again. Overpriced alcohol, shady employees, dusty red velvet curtains on the walls—probably soaked in years of semen, spilled drinks, and mildew."

Marlon continued to laugh. He loved how Quinn always had a way of making him forget about his problems and feel normal again, even if only for a moment. "That's the most honest description of a place I've ever heard. I'd buy it."

"If political science doesn't work out for me, I have a

back-up plan," Quinn said with a smug expression.

Marlon's brow furrowed. "Oh, please. The scores you got on your finals were amazing. I need to have you take my tests from now on."

Quinn chuckled. "So were yours. I'm proud of you. You were all worried about it for nothing."

Anna walked up behind Quinn, holding two clear plastic cups. "Were you guys having fun without me?"

"We always have fun without you," Marlon said in a serious tone before cracking a smile.

Anna rolled her eyes. "Rude. Hey, let's go dance. I love this song."

The three friends wandered over toward the middle of the dancefloor, surrounded by dozens of strangers—some of whom shuffled side to side, but none were actually dancing.

Anna took a sip from her red-to-yellow gradient drink and moved her hips around. Quinn followed, shimmying his shoulders.

Marlon closed his eyes and let the music take over his body. He was safe. He had his friends, and nothing else mattered. That was the last piece of fun he'd have before things became serious again.

"Okay, I see you, Marlon," Quinn shouted.

Marlon grinned back at him. Once he survived the trial, life could be more like this for him. His name would be out of the press, his title of 'Pine State University rape victim' would vanish, and he would have another chance at privacy and a sense of normalcy again. The thought made his shoulders relax, and he allowed himself to sink into the music. None of the other hundred patrons mattered, just him and his best friends.

———

Rows of empty seats lined the courtroom. Marlon eased the chair out and lowered himself on it. A faint creaking noise echoed through the space. That seat was the one he would sit in and recount everything that happened to him—every single disturbing detail. No amount of mental preparation was enough. He needed to rip the band-aid off.

The clack of footsteps approaching the stand recaptured his attention.

"Marlon?" Kenneth Hughes asked. He would be the prosecuting attorney for the trial.

Marlon turned toward him. He shook the nervousness from his face and forced a smile. "Sorry. Go ahead."

"We'll run through several scenarios, and I need you to give me your best answers. Can you do that for me?"

Marlon nodded and studied Kenneth's features to allow himself to be more comfortable with what was to come—his rich-toned dark skin, short, black hair laid in waves, and his kind smile. Kenneth was the good guy. He made a mental note of that.

"First, I will be me—the prosecutor. Remember what I

told you," Kenneth said as he shifted and walked away. When he twisted back around, his face slackened.

Marlon gulped, his throat like damp sandpaper. He couldn't mess it up.

"Mr. Woods, how old are you?"

"Twenty years old."

"And how do you know the defendant?"

"From Pine State University."

Kenneth shook his head. "Be more detailed than that, but not *too* detailed. The keyword in that question is 'how' and not 'where,' make sense?"

"Yes. Let's reset. I shared a psychology class with Parker Sullivan at Pine State University."

"And how often did you speak to him?"

Marlon's eyes closed. "Only a few times throughout the semester. He complimented me once, and we worked on a project together, and then I saw him at parties and—"

"Too much. Narrow it down to a shorter response. Focus on answering the number part of the question and why you spoke with him."

Marlon's stomach burned. Out of the three questions Kenneth had asked him so far, he had butchered two. Was that what the trial would be like? If so, he wasn't as prepared as he had hoped.

"How often did you speak with the defendant?" Kenneth asked.

"Not often. We spoke a few times in class and at parties."

"Great job. That will segue into the inevitable questions about Laura Carpenter's party and what happened. It's going to be uncomfortable for you at first, but I want you to focus on me and on the answers. Okay?"

Marlon closed his eyes again. Kenneth's strong, musky cologne filled his sinuses and left him on edge. It was too similar to Parker's. How could he make it through the actual round of questioning if the person asking the questions reminded him of his rapist?

"Mr. Woods, you mentioned speaking with the defendant at parties. Where did these parties take place?" Kenneth asked.

Marlon's eyes darted open. "Uh, uh, outside. I mean, no, they were off-campus, usually at people's houses."

Kenneth squinted, appearing to consider rejecting the answer. "And how many of these parties did you attend?"

"Three during my freshman year."

"Good. And at how many house parties did you see the defendant?"

"All three."

"Let's change roles now. I'll be the defense attorney. Like I told you, he won't be as nice. I'll dial it down some but prepare yourself," Kenneth said.

Marlon gulped.

"Mr. Woods, why were you at parties where alcohol was

being served if you were only nineteen at the time?" Kenneth asked in an aggressive tone.

Marlon leaned back in his chair. "I don't know. It was college."

"So that justifies you breaking the law?"

"No?" Marlon said in a low voice.

"How much alcohol did you consume on the night of June 6?" Kenneth asked, his voice unwaveringly harsh.

"A few drinks, I think. I don't remember."

"If you don't remember how many drinks you had, Mr. Woods, how can you accurately recall an alleged assault?"

Marlon's eyes burned. The question hurt more than it should have, but he was right. How was he going to handle a defense lawyer asking these questions when he couldn't even answer the prosecutor's practice round?

"Answer the question, Mr. Woods."

"It happened. He did this to me."

"What did he do to you?"

"He raped me," Marlon shouted.

Kenneth stopped in his tracks, and his expression softened. He walked toward the witness stand. "Are you okay?"

Marlon huffed. "I'm not ready. I can't do this."

"That's why we're doing this, Marlon. We need to make sure you're prepared to answer these questions in front of an audience. I know that sounds scary, but we'll keep practicing. Okay?" Kenneth gave a reassuring half-smile.

Marlon adjusted his posture. "Let's try again."

# CHAPTER 23

**THE TRIAL WAS TWO SHORT WEEKS AWAY, AND MARLON** wanted nothing more than to fast-forward and forget about everything. All of the progress he had made since returning to Washington in August risked unraveling at the sight of his rapist in the courtroom. He couldn't allow this to bother him, though. He needed a break from the madness, so he planned to see a movie at the local Pine Place Cinema.

His eyes fixated on his phone for several minutes, and he contemplated inviting Anna and Quinn to join him. But since he hadn't given himself much alone time, going solo would be the best thing for him. Plus, Anna had a date with some guy she met on a dating app, and Quinn mentioned needing to pack for his trip back to Colorado in two days.

Marlon threw on his clothes from the night before and rushed to the car. It was a quarter past nine, and he had fifteen minutes to reach the theater before the movie started.

———————

Cars lined the crowded parking lot. The place should have cleared out soon since the last showings for most films were about to wrap up for the evening. Marlon pulled into the closest available spot he could find, a straight shot to the front doors.

Flickering lamps overhead illuminated the parking lot, dampened from a drizzle earlier in the afternoon. A gentle spring breeze whistled through the air, blowing his hair around. He walked toward the entrance, fumbling his car keys into his pocket.

Approaching the outdoor ticket booth, he locked eyes with the man behind the counter. Adam Poole. Their last encounter, when Adam berated him in the drive-thru of Burger Hut months prior, left Marlon reeling for weeks.

Seeing one of his most aggressive tormenters froze Marlon dead in his tracks, and he contemplated the best course of action. He could run back to his car and leave, or he could try to go to another ticket person. Unfortunately, there weren't any other employees working in the booth. He had made it that far, and he sure as hell would not let some asshole stop him from being there.

Marlon approached the counter with a suspicious stare. "I'd like one ticket for *Eleventh Angel.*" He remained focused on the showtime board behind Adam to avoid locking eyes with him.

Adam's body tensed. "Marlon, I-I'm so sorry, man. I don't know what—"

"It's fine. I said I'll take one ticket for *Eleventh Angel*."

Adam winced. "Don't worry about it, man. I'll pay for the ticket."

Marlon glared. "I don't need your money. Just give me the ticket. I don't want to make this more awkward than it already is."

"Look, I was wrong for what I did. And if it makes you feel any better, I'm not friends with Parker anymore. He's a rapist and an asshole. I didn't mean to hurt you. I guess he brainwashed—"

Marlon raised his palm at him. "Give me the fucking ticket. I don't want to talk to you. You don't deserve any of my energy."

Someone behind Marlon in line gasped, prompting him to turn and look at them. The woman looked away.

Adam sighed. "I understand. The total is fourteen dollars and twenty-five cents."

After receiving the payment, Adam shakily slid the flimsy rectangular ticket to Marlon.

"Thanks." Marlon stomped toward the entrance. He reached the theater in time for the previews to start.

———

Credits rolled on the screen, and Marlon left the building and walked back to his car where only a few other vehicles remained in the parking area. His phone vibrated with a new text from Quinn.

*Packing is sooo boring. Fml. What r u up to?*

Marlon smiled. He wished he had invited Quinn out to see the movie with him, but he was happy he had finally done something he enjoyed on his own. It helped provide some much-needed clarity on all the uncertainty in his life.

*Sorry. Just saw a movie. Wanna do lunch tomorrow?*

He tapped the button to send the message. That palpable awkwardness between them diminished more as the days flew by. This lighthearted in-between stage was what Marlon craved all along. The hope for a happier future appeared to become more of a reality.

Marlon's phone notified of a new message again, and he clicked the screen back to life in hopes of it being Quinn. He paused outside the theater entrance, and a new text from his mother displayed.

*You're too cool to call your mom??? LOL kidding! Love you honey. Call tomorrow. I'm going to bed now.*

Marlon chuckled and slid the phone back into his pocket. When he neared the car, he spotted a guy walking toward him from the restaurant across the lot. Unable to distinguish the stranger's face through the blinding street-lights, he brushed it off. As he was about to reach the driver's side door, the mystery man sprinted in his direction.

Marlon's stomach ached with anticipation, and his mind raced. Who was this person? Why were they running toward him? He fumbled with his keys, but the figure reached him before he could open the car.

The stranger reeked of alcohol and a hefty amount of musky cologne. "Marlon, is that you? I knew it. Damn. I shouldn't be talking to you."

No. No. No. It couldn't be. The voice bore into him like sharp daggers, sending chills throughout his body. "Don't touch me. Get the fuck away. I'm calling the police."

Parker Sullivan put his hands up in the air. "Whoa, don't do that. Please. I want to talk to you."

Marlon backed away with clenched fists. It couldn't be real. "Get away from me. I'm serious … I'll—"

"Stop, it's not that serious. I wanted to tell you I missed you. We had a good time, you and me," Parker said, slurring every other word as he stumbled forward.

"A good time? You *raped* me, and I've been in a living hell ever since. Don't tell me we had a good time when you know that's a lie." Tears filled Marlon's eyes.

Parker's jaw dropped, and he squinted at Marlon. "Get over yourself. *You* wanted *me*. You were practically begging for it. If anything, I did you a favor."

Marlon placed his hands on his chest. "Did me a favor?

How? You raped me and ruined my life."

Parker chuckled as he jabbed his index finger at Marlon. "Ruined *your* life? You were a nobody before me. Nobody gave a damn about you. Now, you're the perfect little victim. I hope you're happy. You ruined *my* life."

"You raped me, just like you raped Cassie. You need help. Leave me alone. You aren't supposed to talk to me." Marlon pulled his phone out and continued backing away as his attacker inched closer to him. "I'll call the cops."

Parker lunged forward and snatched Marlon's phone out of his hand. "No, you won't. We gotta talk about this. You have to drop the charges. I can't have this on my record. Haven't I suffered enough? We both need to move on with our lives. Come on, what will it take to get you to drop it? Do you want money?"

Seeing his cell phone in his rapist's hand sent Marlon into a frenzy. Parker would kill him if he didn't escape. He stumbled as he jumped toward him to retrieve it. "Give me my phone back. I'm not dropping the charges."

Parker shook his head and took several steps toward him. "I'm not giving it back until we sort this out."

Marlon backed up against his car. He considered taking a chance and running but wasn't sure if it would further anger him. Besides, he had nowhere to run, and Parker could run much faster than him. "Go away. Stop doing this."

Thunderous footsteps of a bulky person sprinting toward them echoed from behind Marlon.

Parker's eyes peered up at the approaching person. "No way."

"Get away from him. You better back up, man."

Marlon closed his eyes, convinced someone was coming to Parker's defense. He braced himself for a showdown. All the nightmares about a situation like this were coming true.

A powerful thud rang out in front of him. His eyes darted open to see what happened.

On the damp pavement lay Parker, groaning.

Adam Poole towered over him with clenched fists. "I told you to leave him alone. You shouldn't be here."

"Adam, you … you saved me," Marlon said.

He patted Marlon's shoulder. "I was outside vaping, and I saw you guys. Do you want me to call the police?"

"I don't know." Marlon's voice trembled. "I didn't … I didn't expect this."

Adam kicked Parker in the ribs a few times as he rolled around on the ground in apparent pain. "Get your ass out of here before I knock you out."

Parker struggled to stand as he clenched his side. The punch to his face bloodied his nose and left him various shades of red. He scowled. "Fuck both of you."

Adam raised his fist at Parker again. "See you in court, asshole."

Parker almost lost his balance as he backed away. He hobbled in the direction he came from and faded into the darkness.

Adam scanned Marlon for injuries. "Are you okay? I'm so sorry you had to deal with him."

He picked his phone up off the ground. "I'm fine. I'm not sure what would've happened if you hadn't come to my rescue."

"It was the right thing to do. I'm so sorry about what happened last time you saw me. Stupid me believed in his innocence, and I took it out on you. I was an asshole. But as more evidence came out, I realized how guilty he was. I thought about reaching out to you a while back, but I didn't know if I should. All I want to say is I'm sorry for any pain I caused you. I hope I can make things right."

Marlon nodded at him. He never thought he'd say those words, but Adam meant them. He truly meant them. "I forgive you."

Adam's face tensed then relaxed. "Thanks, man. I hope Parker rots in prison."

"Me too."

"And look, I understand if you have to report this. I'm still on the clock, so I might get in trouble, but I don't care since—"

Without giving it a second thought, Marlon rocked his head. "I'm not reporting it. The police are useless, and I'm sure it'll only complicate things."

"I feel like he's done this before," Adam said, pressing his lips together.

"What do you mean? With that Cassie girl who was on

*The Judy Faith Show*?"

Adam exhaled out of the side of his mouth. "No. I mean, yes, with her, but there were other girls. Since I know the full story now, I remember him hooking up with a few girls at parties and some sketchy things happening. I don't remember all their names, and some of them don't go to our school anymore, but one of them was Charlotte."

Marlon's brow furrowed. "Are you serious? Charlotte Knapp? She hooked up with Parker?"

"Yeah, that Charlotte. I don't know if I'd call it hooking up, though. She was drunk. I tried talking to her about it a few weeks ago, but she pretended not to know what I was talking about. She got pissed at me for bringing it up." Adam paused and stared off into the distance. "I feel like it's my fault. I could have said something, but we were drunk, stupid kids, and I didn't think Parker could do something like that."

That explained so much about Charlotte's behavior and helped put things in perspective for Marlon. "It's not your fault. I'm sure she's dealing with it in her own way. Everyone handles trauma differently. She'll talk about it when she's ready."

Adam's eyebrows rose. "I wish more people would come forward so they can put the son of a bitch behind bars for the rest of his miserable life."

"Me too. The trial is all I can think about these days. It's weird because I went so long without talking about what happened. I don't know how I'll handle having the cameras on me, knowing it's broadcasted everywhere."

Adam rested a hand on Marlon's shoulder and offered a comforting smile. "You'll do fine, man. Tell your story, and that should be enough. Don't worry about what people say. People will talk shit either way. At least they'll be talking about how terrible of a person Parker Sullivan is."

"You're right, I guess. I wish it would all be over already. I hate not knowing."

"If you need anything, I'm here for you. Hey, look, I've gotta go back to the theater and clean up before the boss notices I'm missing. But I hope you have a good night." Adam patted Marlon's back and stepped away.

Marlon struggled to find the right words to express his gratitude. "Thanks again."

———

Marlon stirred in bed, and his eyes fought back as he attempted to open them. He glanced at the clock and saw it was nine-thirty in the morning. He had slept for eight and a half hours. The night's events felt like nothing more than a wild dream.

He grabbed his phone and called Anna.

She answered within two rings. "I was just thinking about you. What's up?"

"I saw Parker last night, and I—"

"You what? Where? What happened? Holy shit."

"I saw him." He took a deep breath. "I saw him at the movie theater. I went to see *Eleventh Angel* and ran into him in the parking lot. Anna, he confronted me."

"What? He's not supposed to have any contact with you. What did he say? Did he hurt you?"

"No, but he told me to drop the charges," Marlon said, the words flying out of his mouth. "He took my phone from me, so I couldn't call the police. He was drunk, but Adam saved me."

She gasped into the phone. "Adam, who? Johnson or Poole? Not Adam Poole, after he—"

"Yes, Poole. He punched Parker in the face and kicked his ass. I don't know what would have happened if he hadn't been there to help."

"The same guy who treated you like shit last year? Wow. I'm glad you're okay. Did you call the cops? Please, tell me you did. He deserves more charges for this."

He sat silent for a few seconds. "No, I didn't call the police. I don't want to make things—"

"You NEED to report it," Anna said in an admonishing tone. "This is serious."

Marlon's eyes rolled. She didn't have to make him feel any worse about it than he already did. "I'm not telling the police. It's complicated. I mean, he didn't hurt me, and I don't know if they would do anything about it anyway."

Anna sighed. "All I'm saying is it might help your case."

"But what if it doesn't? What if he were to spin it as I found him in a parking lot and kicked his ass? They would charge me if he did, and I don't want that kind of drama."

"I didn't think of that. I'm sorry. You're right. Let's forget about it. How are you doing?"

Marlon's eyes bounced up to the ceiling. "I'm so nervous about the trial. What if my testimony sucks? I've worked so hard to get to this point. I can't fail."

"You won't fail," Anna said, her voice soft and mellow. "You're going to do an amazing job. I believe in you."

"Thanks. I guess I need to stop stressing over it until the day comes."

"Good idea." Her phone buzzed. "Hey, sorry to cut this short, but my mom is calling me. I'll call you later to see how you're feeling. Okay?"

"Sounds like a plan. See ya."

Marlon clutched the phone to his chest and sighed. Only a few more weeks, and it would be over. He just needed to hold on a little longer.

# CHAPTER 24

THE MOMENT MARLON WAITED ELEVEN EXCRUCIATING months for had arrived: day one of the trial.

Walking to the courtroom took an eternity. With every step, his heart thumped louder. It was about to happen, and there was no turning back. The air in the hallway was thick with coffee and lemon-scented floor cleaner—a combination like Noir Coffee, but somehow a lot less comforting. The doors to the room swung open, and the glare of dozens of eyes overwhelmed him. As he neared the stand, his legs weakened, and a lump formed in his throat.

Someone held a bible in front of him and asked, "Do you swear to tell the truth, the whole truth, and nothing but the truth, so help you God?"

"I … I do," he said, his jaw trembling.

Kenneth Hughes rose from his chair and thinly smiled at him. He tucked his hands into his pockets. "Can you please state your full name for the record?"

That was the easiest question he would answer all day, so he couldn't mess it up. "Marlon Augustine Woods."

"Thank you, Mr. Woods. You are a student at Pine State University, correct?"

His eyes fixated on Kenneth. "Yes."

"How many years have you attended school there?"

"Two years."

"Thank you. And, if you don't mind, what is your major?" Kenneth asked, moving his hands around.

The sea of eyes in the audience left Marlon confused and uneasy. He cleared his throat and looked at Kenneth again. "Graphic design."

"Would you call your first year at Pine State University normal?"

"Objection, Your Honor. Immaterial," a man shouted from the defense table, prompting Marlon to jump.

Kenneth turned to the judge and placed his palms together. "Your Honor, I need to establish that nothing out of the ordinary occurred between August and May of last year."

"Overruled, and the witness will answer." Judge Palmer stared down at him from his desk.

Marlon swallowed hard. Wait, what was the question? The disruption caused him to lose focus, and his eyes darted from side to side as he attempted to recall the question. "Uh, yes, as normal as it could be."

"Thank you. Did you make any friends during your

freshman year at the university?"

"A few, I guess."

The prosecutor's eyes locked on Marlon's, and he softened his voice. "Could you explain how you know the defendant?"

Marlon's face turned crimson, and he didn't dare glance at his attacker's table. "We shared a psychology course during my second semester last year."

"Were you ever invited to attend any parties?"

"Yes."

"How many parties would you say you attended?" Kenneth asked, twisting back around toward Marlon.

"Three during my freshman year."

Kenneth shot a comforting smile at him. "Did you notice the defendant, Mr. Sullivan, at any of these parties?"

He shifted in his chair. The burning question would come any minute now. "Yes. He was at all three parties."

"Did he talk to you at any of them?"

Marlon squinted as he contemplated. "Yes, at two out of the three."

"Did any of these conversations seem flirtatious to you?"

"Objection, Your Honor. Speculation," the same man from the defense side called out.

The judge lowered his glasses at Kenneth. "Sustained. Rephrase your question."

"Did Parker make any sexual advances toward you?"

Kenneth asked.

This was the moment he had waited almost a year for. Time to speak his truth. "Yes."

Several audience members murmured, and Judge Palmer banged his gavel to quiet the room.

"How would you describe the nature of his advances?" Kenneth asked.

How could he phrase his answer without saying the words he dreaded most? "Um, well, I heard he—"

"Objection, Your Honor. Hearsay," the defense attorney said.

Judge Palmer peered down at him. "Sustained. Stick to the facts, Mr. Woods."

Damn it. He couldn't make that mistake again. He needed to remember how he practiced that part. "When we talked outside, he kissed me on the mouth."

Kenneth nodded at him as to reassure him. "What date did this incident take place?"

He took a moment to suck in air through his nose and close his eyes. A night he would never forget. "June 6."

"Where did the party take place?"

"Laura Carpenter's house," Marlon said.

Kenneth nodded. "Thank you. Now, did you want him to make those sexual advances, or did you give him any sign that they were welcomed?"

Marlon took a deep breath. "No, I did not want it."

"What did you say to him?"

The memory caused his ears to burn as they glowed fiery red. "I thought it was a joke at first. I laughed. When I realized he wasn't kidding, I told him I was flattered, but I wasn't interested in him."

"And he respected your wishes, correct?"

That question differed from the ones they had rehearsed during the practice rounds. "Um, no. He did not."

A somber expression covered Kenneth's face. "What did he say?"

The question left Marlon more embarrassed than he had expected. Tears welled up in his eyes. "He slapped me across the face, grabbed my hair, and said, 'How fucking dare you? Nobody says 'no' to me, faggot.'"

An uncomfortable silence filled the room as Kenneth glanced around. "Did he then respect your wishes and leave you alone?"

A single tear coursed down Marlon's cheek. "No."

"Tell us what happened next."

Marlon peered up at the defense table, eyes locking on Parker's face. The image of his rapist sent shivers down his spine. "He … he raped me."

The room buzzed with gasps and whispers, and the judge silenced the audience once more. "Order in the court."

"I'm sorry. I understand this is painful, but can you describe what he did?" Kenneth asked.

Why was it so difficult for him? They had practiced.

"Well, he, uh … he punched me in the face several times, leaving me with a bloody nose and bruised eyes. Then he shoved me to the ground, climbed on top of me, tried to choke me out, and yanked my pants down. He stuck his tongue down my throat for a minute, flipped me onto my stomach, spread my legs apart, and he … he forced himself inside me. He didn't use any lube, so the pain was terrible. He pulled my hair and ended up ripping some out." Marlon rubbed his head and found it almost impossible to see through his tears.

Kenneth slid a box of tissues toward Marlon. "Did you say anything to him while this happened?"

"I screamed at him to stop," Marlon said, raising his voice.

Kenneth stepped back. "How long did the sexual assault last?"

"I'm not sure. I lost track of time after it started."

"What happened after the attack ended?"

"He laughed. He told me nobody would believe me if I tried to report him. I lay there on the grass for a while before I ended up leaving. I was so tired, and I didn't know what to do."

"When did you report it to the police?"

Marlon attempted to inhale through his congested nose, still reeling from speaking the words into existence. "The next morning."

"After you reported it, did you stay in Washington?"

"No. I left and flew home to Salem, Ohio to be with my family for the summer."

Kenneth glanced down at his notes. "At the time of the attack, were you aware that Parker was recording a video on his phone?"

"No."

"When did you come to find out about this?"

"When someone posted the video and some screenshots online a week after it happened."

Kenneth's hand rested on the witness stand. "How did this impact you?"

"Surviving a rape was bad enough, and then the whole incident was available for the world to see. Not only would I have to live with the memories, but the pictures and videos also haunted me." The memory left him numb.

Kenneth winced at him. "Thank you, Marlon. I'm so sorry this happened to you. No further questions, Your Honor."

Marlon gulped, unsure if he could handle the next part. The prosecutor questioning him was hard enough. He couldn't imagine what this asshole defense lawyer was about to say.

When the floor cleared, David Samberg rose out of his chair and rocked his head. "That is a sad story, Mr. Woods. Is it true you approached my client on several occasions before the night that you engaged in sexual intercourse?"

The implication left Marlon scowling. Sexual intercourse? What the hell was wrong with him? "I asked him to work on a project with me for our psychology class."

David's sweaty forehead wrinkled. "Didn't you initiate contact with Mr. Sullivan on the night in question?"

"No. Well, I mean, when I recognized Parker at the party, I waved, and he came over and talked to me."

"So, to clarify, you admit to initiating contact?" David asked, his mouth stuck open as he panted like a dog in heat.

"Yes, I guess. But I didn't know—"

"Have you ever expressed any romantic interest in Mr. Sullivan?"

"No. Never," Marlon said, moving in his seat.

"If that is correct, explain to me why you talked to a classmate about him via text two weeks before the incident? Defense Exhibit H, Your Honor." The defense lawyer yanked a piece of white paper from a folder. "And I quote, 'Parker complimented me again today. He's so thirsty for me,' followed by a laughing emoji. I mean, it doesn't get any clearer than this, Mr. Woods."

Several members of the audience gasped, prompting the judge to slam down his gavel once again.

Now he was using Marlon's own words against him and trying to twist them to fit his agenda. Marlon's jaw clenched. "I said he hit on me, but I never said I liked him. I was shocked because I knew he flirted with girls in class. Everyone called him a player."

"Objection. Hearsay," David shouted, his face beet-red.

"Sustained. The jury will disregard the witness's last statement," Judge Palmer said.

Marlon's cheeks flushed. He reminded himself there were cameras and judgmental pricks watching.

David smirked. "Have you ever had sexual intercourse with any of your other classmates?"

Marlon's stomach twisted in knots. What kind of question was that? Would he have to answer it?

Kenneth jumped out of his seat. "Objection, Your Honor. Immaterial."

David nodded in the prosecutor's direction and then at the judge. "The number of partners he's been with establishes a pattern."

Judge Palmer stared at the two lawyers. "Overruled."

Marlon glared at the defense attorney. He hoped his answer wouldn't ruin the trial. "Yes."

"How many students have you had sexual relations with?"

"Two. Three if you include Parker, but that wasn't consensual."

David's mouth twitched. "When you attended these parties, did you consume any alcohol?"

"Yes."

David's thick finger clutched his bulbous chin as he squinted. "Mr. Woods, please explain to me how you legally drank when you were only nineteen. Last time I checked, the legal drinking age in the United States is twenty-one."

Recalling how he and Kenneth rehearsed the question, he responded, "Since I am under the legal age, I shouldn't have consumed alcohol."

David glanced at Marlon and raised an eyebrow. "You said you left the state after it happened. Assuming he assaulted you, why wouldn't you want to stay and assist with the investigation?"

"Because I couldn't face the embarrassment. I needed to escape. After what Parker said—" As he peeked up, he saw Parker glaring at him, freezing him in his tracks.

"What I have a hard time understanding is why you returned to Pine State University. If Mr. Sullivan raped you, as you claim, why would you want to go back? I know *I* would search for another school."

Was he not entitled to go home, be with his family, and come back to battle his demons? Should he stay trapped in Ohio because that rapist pig thought he owned Washington? Hell no. The rage inside Marlon boiled over until he burst. "Leave the school forever and let everyone else win? My entire family begged me to stay home, but I couldn't. I needed to be strong and show I wouldn't let some bastard with rich parents keep me from pursuing my dreams."

The defense attorney placed his hand over his heart. "Objection, Your Honor. Argumentative."

Marlon's shoulders tensed, and his mind raced. Oh, wasn't David great at playing the victim? How did he sleep at night knowing he did this to rape victims for a paycheck?

Judge Palmer gazed down at Marlon. "Sustained. Careful, Mr. Woods."

David wrapped his arms behind his back and swiveled toward Marlon. "Is it fair to say this was nothing more than a night of passion, which led to a case of buyer's remorse?"

"Objection, Your Honor. Inflammatory," Kenneth shouted out through clenched teeth.

David sneered at Kenneth and then back at Marlon. "Withdrawn. Nothing further, Your Honor."

Marlon stared at Kenneth. He wanted him to say something or stand up and fix this, but Kenneth shook his head at him and sat back down.

"Next witness," Judge Palmer said.

Marlon stood, and his body became numb. He couldn't process what had just happened. Was it a good thing or a bad thing? Did the defense attorney make himself look like a total asshole, or did he paint Marlon in a bad light?

———

He barged through the doors of the courtroom and rushed to the restroom. The stall door crashed shut, and he let out a deafening cry. How stupid was he for thinking the trial would go smoothly? It should have come as no surprise that they tried to make him out to be the bad guy.

The bathroom door creaked open. "Marlon? Are you in

here?"

"Yes, Anna. Go away."

The door jiggled. "Let me in."

He opened the stall and collapsed into his friend's arms. "I can't believe what happened."

Anna patted his back and gripped him close to her. "It'll be okay. Trust me. That guy made a total ass out of himself. Between the testimony and both victims being here, it's not helping Parker at all."

The comment broke Marlon out of his crying spell, and he leaned backward and rocked Anna by the shoulders. "What do you mean?"

Anna pulled away from him. "Cassie Roberts is in the audience."

# CHAPTER 25

MARLON OPENED THE BATHROOM DOOR AND WATCHED A young woman with long, black hair in a white floral sundress exiting through the front door. As she strolled out of the building, he hurried into the lobby to follow her.

He walked outside into a swarm of photographers and news channels waiting for him out front, catching him off guard. Flashbulbs and cameras blinded him. Several reporters emerged from the flashing lights.

"Are you worried they won't convict him?" a woman shouted, extending a microphone to his face.

Marlon knocked the first microphone away, and another appeared in front of him.

"How did it feel to face your attacker in court today?" a male reporter asked.

"What do you plan on doing after the trial ends?" a third reporter shouted.

Standing in a daze, he covered his eyes with his hands

and pushed through the sea of faces. "Leave me alone."

Marlon ran until the cameras no longer blinked. He looked in all directions before running toward someone down the street who resembled the other victim. "Cassie. Wait."

The person hesitated and turned around, staring at him for a moment before grinning. "Marlon? I'm so glad to see you."

"I wanted to find you before you left."

Cassie's expression softened. "Is everything okay?"

He stuck his hand over his chest, leaned over, and breathed. "Yeah, but I need to talk to you. You're the only person who understands what it's like."

She smiled and pulled him in for an embrace. "Why don't we walk to the park and talk?"

As the two walked away, several reporters mumbled in the background.

"Smile for the camera," a guy in the distance shouted.

Cassie flipped him off, grabbed Marlon by the hand, and ran. They cut through several nearby streets until the voices diminished.

A shaded spot under an old tree caught their eyes, and they both sat on the dry grass.

Marlon bit his lip and gazed at her. "How did I do up there today?"

"You were *amazing*," Cassie said, the corners of her eyes creasing.

"Thanks. I can't believe how much of an asshole his lawyer is."

Cassie shrugged. "Right? But you handled it so well."

"I never imagined I would actually be here, testifying against Parker. Not that long ago, I wasn't sure I even wanted to live after what happened. But this … this is so hard. It's not fair."

Her lips pressed flat. "Yeah, I learned the hard way that nothing is fair. But we've made it this far, and that's something to be damn proud of. At least we stand a chance at justice. Some people aren't as lucky. We survived what he did to us, so we can and will survive this."

"True." He paused and struggled to find the right words to say. Birds chirped in a tree overhead, filling the silence. "Did you really accept the scholarship?" The color drained from his face as the question left his mouth. Why would he ask her a question like that?

Cassie's dark brown eyes flitted up at his. Her expression hardened for a moment before relaxing again. "No. I swear. I thought it was a regular check that I could use to pay for my mom's medical bills. And Mrs. Sullivan forced me to take the money and told me I had no other choice."

Marlon frowned. "Wow. It makes me wonder how many other people Parker has done this to. Thinking about them scares me more than anything."

"I think about the 'what ifs' all the time. Until I found out about you, I thought I was the only one. But if I knew he would do this again, I never would have accepted the money. I can't help thinking I could have stopped this from happening to you." Cassie's voice weakened as her eyes welled up with tears.

A breeze whipped through the park, tickling Marlon's skin. He tapped Cassie's shoulder with the palm of his hand. "Stop it. This wasn't your fault. Parker is the only one responsible for what happened. The only way he can be stopped is with a conviction."

Cassie sniffled. "But what if they don't convict him? I don't know what I'll do."

Marlon battled with the same thoughts leading up to the trial. Maybe Cassie wasn't as invincible as she made herself appear in interviews. Perhaps they had more in common than he thought. They were both emotionally damaged people, terrified of what the future had in store. It relieved him, knowing she, too, experienced hopelessness for the case. She didn't radiate that fake optimism everyone else did. At least he wasn't alone.

Marlon shook the blank stare from his face and forced a halfhearted smile. "No, that won't happen. He's guilty, and I don't think the defense is doing a good job of proving his innocence."

Cassie chuckled, wiping the stream of tears from her cheeks. "Yeah, you're right. That David guy is an idiot, and he isn't making Parker look any better."

Inevitable silence crept into the conversation as Marlon

kept his thoughts to himself. He didn't want to risk asking anything rude like he did moments prior.

"What are you doing after the trial?" Cassie asked.

"Finishing school. Things have been better for me over the last few months, and I'm finally getting my life back on track. What about you?"

"Aw, that's beautiful. I'm thinking about going back to school for nursing. I've always been passionate about helping people. I'm also considering moving home again. Portland is nice, but Seattle is where my heart is. Who knows, maybe I can go to Pine State." Cassie winked at Marlon.

"Oh god, the news sites would explode. Can you imagine the two of us in one school? Judy Faith would die of a heart attack."

"Yeah, you're probably right. She's pretty annoying. But have you thought about doing an interview with her?"

"I don't think I can. We'll see how the trial goes. It was hard enough to talk about it today. How did you do it?"

"It was weird at first, but you get used to it. I did it because it felt like the right thing to do. The way I see it is every time I talk about it, I might save someone from going through what we went through. You know what I mean? Maybe I can make a difference in someone's life."

He grinned. "That's true, and I'm so happy you did the interview. Are you sticking around for the rest of the trial?"

"No, I have to go back home tonight. I came today because I wanted to be here for your testimony. But I'm so happy we finally got to meet."

———

Hours later, Marlon and Anna sat on her overstuffed brown couch and chowed down on lo mein. Marlon grabbed the remote and turned on the television, flipping through several channels before a news banner caught his eye.

Judy Faith's stern face appeared on the screen. "… the Parker Sullivan trial, which just wrapped up day one of testimony. We received word that someone photographed the two victims, Cassie Roberts and Marlon Woods, embracing each other moments after Marlon testified. There's no word yet on how they are coping, but as we heard earlier, he recounted his attack on the stand today. Parker himself may be testifying tomorrow. Stay tuned for the latest."

Anna rocked her head. "Fuckin' vultures."

Marlon's eyes rolled around. "Tell me about it."

"Do you think he'll testify? Surely not, right? It would only hurt him and his case." Anna peered up at him.

"It wouldn't surprise me. I'm sure Parker thinks he'll win after what happened today."

"Hey, don't say that. You did great up there. If he wins, I'll lose all faith in humanity."

Marlon was so lucky to call her his friend. She always

had the ability to cheer him up. "Thanks. And I'm glad I had that talk with Cassie earlier."

"Me too."

Marlon smiled. "She made me feel good about testifying."

"That's great. And I'm always here for you if you want to talk about it." She bounced her shoulders and grinned.

"Thanks, that means a lot." He chewed his lip and hesitated before posing his next question. "What would you think of me doing an interview? Like, with Judy Faith?"

"If you want to, I support it."

He sighed. "I think everyone expects me to, so I don't wanna let anyone down."

"Who cares what everyone expects you to do? Do what makes you happy."

Marlon nodded, giving her a once-over. She was right.

Anna held the remote to his face and changed her tone. "Well, Mr. Woods, what's it like having the coolest friend in the whole world?"

He chuckled. "I wouldn't know."

She gasped and bumped him with a decorative couch pillow. "Hey, take it back."

"You asked," Marlon said, struggling to stop laughing.

Anna altered her voice again to mimic a dramatic news reporter. "The viewers at home are dying to know: What movie would you like to watch?"

"Well, Connie, I'd love to watch something with death

and sadness," Marlon said in a similar voice. "There isn't enough of it in the world. Back to you in the studio, Rebecca."

They both laughed.

"Did you talk to Quinn today?" Anna asked.

Marlon pulled his phone out and checked his messages. "Eh, he texted me last night to wish me luck, but nothing else since."

"How long is he back in Colorado? He kept telling me different dates."

Marlon glanced up at her from the 'good luck, handsome' message from Quinn on his phone. "I'm not sure, but he might try to come up for a quick visit in July."

Anna pouted. "I feel bad that he couldn't be here for the trial. He wanted to support you."

Marlon's heart fluttered, thinking about Quinn. He also wanted him there, but the thought of sharing this terrifying experience with two other people he cared about left him uneasy. "It's okay. It would have been awkward anyway, because of the testimony and stuff."

"How are you gonna handle that whole situation with him? Have you talked any more about it?"

Marlon looked skyward. "Yeah, a few times, but I'm still confused about what I want. I kind of like him, but I also only see him as a great friend. I'm trying not to ruin things between us considering what happened with the last guy I crossed that friendship line with."

"I'm sure you'll figure it out over the summer. There's no rush. Did you talk to your mom yet today?"

Marlon nodded. "She called earlier. I'm so happy she isn't here to see this shitshow."

Anna scrolled through a list of movies on the television as Marlon's mind wandered back to his conversation with his mother. She promised not to watch the trial, but he wasn't sure how true that was. Did he expect too much from her? She said she was proud of him for being strong, but staying strong was becoming exhausting.

"This one?" Anna asked, pointing the remote at the television screen.

Marlon's eyes widened. "Sorry. Sure."

No matter what happened, he could get through it. He made it that far. No turning back.

# CHAPTER 26

THROUGHOUT THE NEXT DAY OF THE TRIAL, SEVERAL experts testified on behalf of the prosecution. They reviewed the findings of the rape kit, the emotional effects of a sexual assault, and Parker's state of mind during the attack. One psychologist discussed her diagnoses for Parker in great detail and explained her suspicions that his family's wealth and notoriety made him feel immune to any consequences for his actions.

Many members of the audience and the jury struggled to stay focused throughout the day, as most of the expert testimony dragged on for an eternity. One expert read aloud several pages from a medical book, but not without David Samberg objecting to every other sentence. After a police officer testified about his interview with Parker at the time of his initial arrest, the prosecution wrapped up their testimony. The defense would proceed with their witnesses the following day.

———————

Sleeping was impossible, but Marlon couldn't wander into the courtroom with no rest. He awakened to a blinding white light. After blinking several times, he recognized Anna standing over him.

Her hands clapped over his face. "Wake up, sleepyhead. Almost time to go."

He wiped the sleep from his eyes and stared at her. "What time is it?"

"Ten past eight. I thought you set an alarm on your phone, but I guess not. Hurry up and get ready."

Marlon lunged off the couch and darted toward the bathroom. He washed his face, tidied up his hair, and changed into a maroon dress shirt and blue pants. Almost finished, he hopped out of the bathroom while simultaneously trying to secure a black boot on his left foot and stumbling to the floor.

Anna laughed. "That was fast."

Marlon struggled to lace up the second boot. "What's the time now?"

She checked her phone and squinted at the screen. "Twenty past eight."

He snatched his keys off the table and walked toward the door. "Let's go."

They arrived at the courthouse in time to find a close

parking spot and secure their seats at the front of the room.

At nine o'clock, Parker, David, and Judge Palmer entered the courtroom. David and Kenneth both approached the judge and spoke for several minutes before the attorneys returned to their tables.

The defense lawyer gazed up at the bench. "Your Honor, I would like to call my client, Parker Lyle Sullivan, to the stand."

Marlon's heart raced beneath his shirt, leaving his pulse thumping in his ear. His worst fear was about to manifest.

The courtroom erupted in conversation, prompting Judge Palmer to slam his gavel several times to quiet the room.

Marlon peered over at Kenneth, who smiled at him. The smile told Marlon this was a good thing. He hoped Kenneth would destroy him.

Parker rose from his seat and approached the stand. He answered the "do you swear to tell the truth" question and sat in the chair.

"Mr. Sullivan, how are you doing today?" David asked.

Parker shrugged, wrinkling his ironed, spotless white button-up. "Okay, I guess. I mean, I'm here, so I could be better."

Marlon's lips pinched together. Parker had no right to act inconvenienced by all of this because he wasn't the victim.

"How long did you attend school at Pine State University?" David asked.

"Three years."

"In your three years at the university, did you ever get into any trouble?"

Parker shook his head. "No, never."

"What did you major in?"

"Business."

"And what did you do outside of class in your free time?"

"I volunteered with my mom. We served meals at the homeless and domestic violence shelters all the time. Other than that, I played football for the Pine State University Bears."

The attorney gave an impressed nod at him. "How admirable of you. Where did you meet Mr. Woods?"

"We went to school together and shared a psychology class. And we were at the same parties sometimes."

"So, would you say you considered him a friend?"

Parker chuckled, exposing his pearly white teeth. "No, we weren't close. Whenever we ran into each other, we mostly only talked about class."

"When was your first non-school-related discussion?"

"The first time I remember talking to him was after class one day. We were gonna work on a project together, and I told him we should hang out at the library. He got all weird and said he wanted to do it at his apartment instead, but I said I couldn't because I didn't like guys." Parker scrunched up his face.

Marlon's ears burned. How dare Parker paint him as a predator? That wasn't how their conversation had gone.

Anna glanced over at Marlon before returning her eyes to the witness stand.

David's mouth opened as he let out a deep sigh. "Ah, so you got the impression he was flirting with you?"

"Yes, I did. Someone told me he got dumped by his boyfriend and—"

Kenneth rose out of his chair and stuck up his index finger. "Objection, Your Honor. Hearsay."

"Sustained." Judge Palmer squinted at David.

The defense lawyer refocused his attention on his client. "When was your next interaction with Mr. Woods outside of class?"

"Laura Carpenter's party."

David turned toward the jury. "My client is referring to the June 6 party at classmate Laura Carpenter's family home."

Marlon tensed. He had skipped over their entire conversation at another party months prior. Was it going to come up later on? What was their plan?

"What happened on that evening?" David asked.

Parker stared up at the light fixture and creased his tanned forehead. "I had a few drinks, and me and Courtney got into an argument over whose family we would spend our summer vacation with. I didn't want to go to Aruba again since I'd been there so many times. I was annoyed, so I started to leave, and that's when I ran into Marlon."

Marlon's stomach rose into his throat, hot and fiery.

Parker's eyes bounced over to his, followed by something else in the distance. "We walked around outside and talked for a few minutes about school and stuff. He brought up how beautiful the stars looked. This sounds crazy, and I swear I'm not gay, but there was this strong spark between us because I was so drunk. We kissed. Kissing turned into making out, which led to clothes coming off, and we ended up having … we had sex."

Marlon's throat tightened. *Sex?* No, Parker raped him.

"Did you force Mr. Woods to have sex with you?" David asked.

A flush crept across Parker's cheeks. "No. I understand what I did was wrong because I had a girlfriend, and I apologized a million times for that, but I did not rape Marlon. If anything, he preyed on me because I was drunk and had a lot on my mind."

Marlon struggled to maintain his composure. He wanted nothing more than to jump over the stand and punch Parker square in his face.

All eyes in the courtroom shifted between Marlon and Parker.

Marlon glared at Parker, who locked eyes with him.

"Did he tell you he enjoyed the experience?" David

asked.

Parker half-smiled. "Yes. He kept saying, 'Don't stop' while we were doing it."

Marlon's teeth gritted together. Where the hell did Parker come up with that? The blatant lies became more than he could handle.

David turned around and tried to redirect his client's attention. "Listen, I need to ask, are you gay?"

"No, I'm not. I was drunk." Parker's jaw clenched as he exhaled through his nostrils.

"Well, I will save Mr. Hughes the trouble of asking this, but why would you engage in sexual intercourse with another man if you are not interested in men?"

Parker tensed and fumbled with his red satin tie. "I was drunk and confused. But I didn't force anyone to sleep with me, that's for sure."

"Did you have any further contact with Mr. Woods after that night? Moreover, did you ever threaten him in any way?"

"No, never," Parker said, his voice filled with frustration. "When I woke up the next day, I felt terrible about what I did to my girlfriend and tried to make things right with her. I deleted Marlon's number and didn't talk to him or think about him."

Marlon's eyes tightened on Parker.

David attempted to block Parker's view of Marlon with his body. "Thank you. What was your initial reaction to the police investigation?"

"I thought he was jealous because I didn't text him."

"Objection, Your Honor. Speculation," Kenneth said in a stern voice.

Judge Palmer glared down at the witness stand. "Sustained. Stay on-topic."

Before David could rephrase the question, Parker continued, "They lied about me—Marlon and Cassie. I never raped them."

*Them.* The revelation made Marlon's ears ring. He learned in his pre-trial conversations with Kenneth Hughes that the only way to introduce Cassie's case would be for Parker or his attorney to bring it up. Now, they had to acknowledge it.

"Since you brought her up, did you sexually assault Cassie?" David asked.

"No. We were friends and hung out all the time. There were feelings building between us during our friendship, and one day, it just happened."

Anna nudged Marlon's knee, prompting them to exchange confused glances.

David crossed his arms. "What happened?"

"We had sex. She gave me a blowjob on the way to the movies. We couldn't wait any longer, so we pulled into a parking lot. She initiated the whole thing. I thought she enjoyed it."

Marlon's forehead wrinkled. That wasn't how Cassie

described it. Parker was such a disgusting liar.

David flashed an uncomfortable smirk and continued, "How did this case and the media frenzy impact your life?"

Parker glared at Marlon. "It ruined everything. If I knew having sex with some guy would get me expelled, arrested, and bashed by the media, I wouldn't have done it. I can't show my face in public without having someone follow or threaten me. It's not fair." He rubbed his left eye to prevent a nonexistent tear from streaming down his face.

"Thank you for your honesty, Mr. Sullivan. No further questions, Your Honor."

The defense attorney retreated to his seat, and Kenneth Hughes stood, smoothing out his tie.

"Mr. Sullivan, several experts testified yesterday. One of them described you as having antisocial personality disorder or—in layman's terms—they called you a psychopath. Do you agree with this conclusion?" Kenneth asked.

Marlon gasped. The gloves were off, and Kenneth was ready for a fight. If Parker couldn't handle keeping it together for a phone interview with Judy Faith, how would he handle a face-to-face confrontation like this?

Parker's cheeks turned a bright shade of red. "No. They're lying. They don't know me."

"Okay. Shifting gears now, would you say you are a popular guy?"

"Yes, I guess."

Kenneth lowered his head and peered up at him. "Do a

lot of girls flirt with you?"

Parker chuckled, and his shoulders relaxed. "Yes, but I'm used to it."

Kenneth raised an eyebrow and glanced around the courtroom. "And why is that?"

A smug expression washed over Parker's face. "I don't know, I'm well-liked, and I would say decently attractive. I get good grades. Ladies love that."

Marlon and Anna looked at each other and rolled their eyes.

"Is that so?" Kenneth pulled a sheet of paper out of his folder. "Could you read this for me?"

Parker leaned forward and folded his arms. "What is it?"

"A copy of your grades from the last semester you attended school before the incident," Kenneth said as he placed the paper in front of him.

"Objection, Your Honor. Immaterial," David shouted from the defense table.

Kenneth faced the judge. "Mr. Sullivan is saying he was a popular, smart guy, which speaks to his state of mind. Official records can substantiate one of those two things."

Judge Palmer lowered his glasses. "Objection overruled."

Parker glanced at the sheet of paper for a few seconds before tossing the page aside. "This is stupid. I don't understand how this is important."

Marlon's stomach twisted, and he leaned forward, resting his hands on his knees.

"What was your final grade for your psychology class?" Kenneth asked.

"I shouldn't have to—"

"Answer the question, Mr. Sullivan," the judge said.

Parker sighed. "One point three. D plus."

"And what about your business management class?"

Parker squinted. "One point six seven. C minus."

"What was your overall grade point average for the semester?"

"One point eight."

"So, that would be a low C?"

The room hushed, aside from the tapping of Parker's foot on the ground. "Yes, something like that."

Marlon fought the urge to smile.

Kenneth flipped through his notepad. "As Mr. Sykes stated yesterday, the average college grade point average is around a three point one. So, that would put you somewhere in the lower percentile, correct?"

Parker's fist clenched. "Are you going to ask me a question or continue talking shit about me?"

Judge Palmer slammed his gavel. "Mr. Sullivan, stick to answering the questions."

Kenneth inserted the paper back into his folder and walked toward his table again. "Mr. Sullivan, how many people have you engaged in sexual relations with?"

"Objection, Your Honor. Immaterial. What is the relevance of this question?" David shouted, pushing the seat back and standing.

Kenneth shook his head. "It relates to the defendant's sexual history, which is the reason we are here in the first place."

Marlon nodded. He had a point. If he had to answer that question, so should Parker.

"Overruled," Judge Palmer said.

"Dozens. Maybe a hundred," Parker said.

A woman gasped in the audience. Marlon turned around and saw the blonde-haired elderly lady he recognized as Parker's grandmother crying. He spun back around in his seat and smirked.

Kenneth continued, "How many of those encounters would you consider consensual?"

Parker growled and slammed his fist down on the table. "I don't need to force anyone to have sex with me."

Several people around Marlon huffed, chuckled, or both.

Judge Palmer hit his gavel once more. "Mr. Sullivan, if you have another outburst, my officers will escort you out of the courtroom in handcuffs. Do you understand me?"

Parker's head hung low as he inhaled loudly several times. "I never forced anyone to have sex."

"How many of your sexual partners were men?" Kenneth asked

"Listen, I'm not a fag … Uh, I mean, I'm not gay. I don't understand why that matters."

Kenneth cocked his head to the side. "Mr. Sullivan, you implied earlier you only engaged in sexual intercourse with Mr. Woods because you were drunk. I need you to clarify if he was the only male with whom you've ever had sexual relations. And as a reminder, you are under oath."

"When you say sexual relations, what do you mean?"

"Any sexual contact."

Parker's shoulders dropped, and he looked away. "I only did stuff with guys three times. But I'm not gay, I promise. I was just curious."

Marlon's stomach burned. Three? That meant he wasn't the first guy he had assaulted.

A member of the audience giggled, and Judge Palmer banged his gavel.

Kenneth smiled. "Out of those three times, how many different men did you 'do stuff' with?"

"Three," Parker said, rubbing the back of his neck.

Kenneth glanced at the jury before asking his next question. "When you have sex with a woman or a man, is it slow, fast, aggressive, gentle?"

"The sex might be rough sometimes, but that's how a lot of people like it."

"Rough? Could you explain?"

"Some girls like when you pull their hair and stuff."

Kenneth raised his eyebrows. "How often does that

happen? And how do they go about requesting this?"

"They don't have to say anything. I can just tell."

"You can tell? So, they don't say they like it rough, but you assume they do?"

"Yes. If they didn't like it, they would tell me to stop."

"Referring back to what you said about your encounter with Mr. Woods, you stated that he said, 'Don't stop' several times while you were having intercourse. Is this correct?" Kenneth asked.

"Yes."

"Could you repeat what he said, how he said it?"

Parker chuckled. "Um, sure. That's weird, but okay. 'Don't stop. Oh, don't … stop.'"

"And when he said this, did he speak in a normal voice, whisper, or shout?"

"I guess he shouted. He said something like, 'Don't … Stop' a few times."

Marlon's blood turned cold, leaving goosebumps in its wake. That was how he remembered saying it.

Kenneth didn't speak for a moment, allowing Parker's words to sink in for the courtroom. "Ah, so there was a pause in there. So, you admit Mr. Woods yelled the words *don't* and *stop* at the time you allegedly raped him?"

Parker's arms folded, and he glared at Kenneth. "I didn't rape him. He flirted with me for several months, so I gave him what he wanted."

"So, what he wanted was for you to rape him? Did I

hear you right, Mr. Sullivan?"

"No, uh, no," Parker said, stammering over his words. "He wanted to have sex with me, so we did."

"Did you take photographs and videos?"

Parker's ears turned red, and he sank in his chair. "Yes, but I didn't think it was a big deal. Nobody else was supposed to see them."

"Did you upload them on any website? They ended up on the internet somehow."

Parker's head lowered as his eyes met Marlon's in the crowd. "No. Someone hacked my iCloud and shared the files. I tried to stop it from happening, I swear to God. I'm not sure who leaked them."

"When did you first discuss that night?"

"Other than with my girlfriend the next day, it was after the pictures and videos got posted online. I told my parents what happened."

"How did they react?"

"Mom was pissed at me. She destroyed my ... Never mind," Parker said, shooting his attorney a pleading stare.

Kenneth walked closer to the stand. "Elaborate."

Parker twiddled his fingers. "Mom took my laptop and phone and broke them so nothing else would leak. She set them on fire and buried the pieces somewhere in the garden."

Marlon gripped Anna's wrist and stared wide-eyed at her. Mrs. Sullivan knew all along and helped Parker cover it up.

Kenneth's brow furrowed. "Why would she do that? Is this something she does often?"

"She was mad at me for being stupid enough to take them again."

"Again? What do you mean by 'again,' Mr. Sullivan?" Kenneth asked.

Parker's shoulder raised and fell. "The same thing happened after I hooked up with Cassie."

"Do you mean she destroyed your devices after your encounter with Cassie?" Kenneth asked, his voice thick with suspicion.

Parker gulped. "Uh, yes, because I took pictures and stuff. But I was only seventeen, so I understand why she did it. I was underage."

"If you were innocent, as you say you are, why did you attempt to throw away the clothes you wore the night of the party and let your mother destroy your devices?"

Parker closed his eyes and bowed his head. "I was scared and didn't know what to do."

"What were you afraid of?"

"It looked bad for me, and I didn't think anyone would believe me."

"So, you would rather destroy any evidence that could prove your innocence because it looked bad?" Kenneth rocked his head as he backed away.

"Yes."

"Nothing further, Your Honor." After a moment, he turned toward Marlon and smiled at him.

The room grew silent for a minute as both parties prepared for the next witness.

The defense attorney stood and cleared his throat. "Your Honor, I'd like to call our next witness to the stand: Susan Sullivan."

# CHAPTER 27

A MIDDLE-AGED LADY WITH A CHAMPAGNE-BLONDE BOB and piercing blue eyes stomped through the aisle in a beige pantsuit and dark brown stiletto heels. Upon entering the witness stand, she was placed under oath.

The defense attorney stood. "Good afternoon, Mrs. Sullivan. I would like to talk to you about your son, Parker. Is that all right?" His voice was soft and sweet like cotton candy, a drastic change from the one he used on Marlon.

Mrs. Sullivan flashed her bleached-white teeth. "Yes, I would love to clear up any misunderstandings."

David nodded. "Thank you. Can you please tell me about your son and his childhood?"

"Parker had what I would consider to be a normal upbringing. He earned perfect grades, attended honors classes, took part in wrestling and football, and had lots of friends. When Parker was six years old, my husband became the governor of Washington. So, Parker spent much of his childhood at the Governor's Mansion in Olympia. That was before we settled in Seattle after Walter left office. You could say Parker was the ideal child."

David smiled at her. "Did he ever get into any trouble, either with the law or at school?"

Mrs. Sullivan huffed. "Heavens, no. Anyone who met Parker adored him, including his teachers and classmates. People often remarked on how kind and giving he was."

"Thank you. I wanted to get an important question out of the way: What happened to Parker's cell phone and laptop after his encounters with Ms. Roberts and Mr. Woods? Earlier, he stated that you destroyed them. Can you explain to the jury why you did this?"

"I hate to admit this, but I'm not tech-savvy." She chuckled and shrugged. "As a mother, finding out my son recorded himself having sexual intercourse embarrassed me. I couldn't fathom the thought of what would happen if the pictures leaked on the internet. If I suspected anything illegal happened, I would have reported it to the authorities. The reason I destroyed the devices was to ensure they didn't leak and ruin his life. I didn't think I could remove the files forever any other way."

"So, you didn't attempt to cover up an alleged crime by destroying his devices?"

Mrs. Sullivan gasped and clutched her hand to her chest. "No. I would never do such a thing."

"The last thing I need to ask you is if your son confessed

to assaulting Marlon Woods?" David asked.

"No, sir, he did not. Someone told me—"

"Objection, Your Honor. Hearsay," Kenneth shouted.

Judge Palmer glanced down at Mrs. Sullivan. "Sustained. Stick with the facts."

"No, Parker never told me he hurt anyone."

David nodded. "Thank you for your candor, Mrs. Sullivan. Those are all my questions for you today."

Kenneth read through his notes, creating an unmistakable sense of anticipation in the room. "May we take a brief recess, Your Honor?"

"Yes. Court is in recess until eleven-thirty," Judge Palmer said.

With that, Marlon grabbed Anna's hand and ran out of the courtroom into the hall.

"Can you believe this? Oh my god, I'm struggling so hard to keep my cool," he said, almost out of breath.

"It's almost over," Anna said. "Kenneth did a great job making Parker look bad, and I'm sure he's about to destroy his mom."

Marlon shook his head. "She's untouchable. Did you see how she was trying to set it up like her family is perfect, and her son didn't do anything wrong? Makes me sick."

"We'll get through this together, I promise. But first, we need to eat. Come on, lunch is on me."

Throughout lunch, the two friends ate in silence while

Marlon contemplated the outcome of the trial. The testimonies were ending, and he was more confused than ever. His mind drifted back to his confrontation with Parker two weeks prior. He couldn't give up now. He needed to snap out of his fog.

His eyes locked with Anna's before he stared down at his food again. "Do you think Kenneth has anything on Mrs. Sullivan? I never talked to her, so I don't know why he's waiting."

"Honestly, I wouldn't be surprised," Anna said.

———————

The two friends reached their seats in time to catch Mrs. Sullivan taking the stand once again.

Kenneth wasted no time cutting to the chase. "Mrs. Sullivan, you admitted to destroying evidence that could corroborate the alleged sexual assault of Cassie Roberts. You also destroyed computer and cell phone evidence in this case before investigators could seize the devices. Is that correct?"

Marlon's eyes widened. Was he going to ruin her like he did Parker? He sure hoped so.

Mrs. Sullivan leaned back in her chair and composed herself. "I destroyed Parker's laptop and cell phone to protect him from the images leaking on the internet. As far as I knew, and still believe, the encounters were consensual."

Kenneth peered down at the piece of paper in his hand

and back at Mrs. Sullivan. "Did you watch the video or look at the pictures on the devices before destroying them?"

Mrs. Sullivan shook her head and peered at him with mock innocence. "Of course not. Why would I want to see my child having sex with someone? That is disturbing, Mr. Hughes."

"Wouldn't the photos and videos clear up any doubts about his innocence? By destroying them, you took away anyone's chance of having evidence to prove either innocence or guilt," Kenneth said, his voice chastising in tone.

"Mr. Hughes, I did not and do not have any doubt about my son's innocence. I don't need to watch such smut. Again, had I suspected anything, I would have called the police right away. I am a good, law-abiding Christian woman."

The comments prompted an eye roll from Marlon. Oh, sure she was. And the sky was green.

"So, it is your sworn testimony you had no knowledge of your son breaking any laws? You also didn't take part in helping cover up any alleged crimes, and you didn't doubt your son's innocence?" Kenneth asked.

Mrs. Sullivan nodded in acknowledgment. "Correct."

Kenneth raised his eyebrows and index finger. "One moment."

He strolled over to the prosecution's table, picked up two pieces of paper, and sauntered to the judge's bench. "If I may, Your Honor, I would like to enter State Exhibit X into evidence."

Marlon adjusted his posture, his heart racing.

"Objection," David shouted from the defense table. "What is this evidence, and why didn't I have a chance to see it?"

Judge Palmer lowered his glasses at Kenneth before scanning over the paperwork. "Both of you, approach the bench. Mr. Hughes, explain how and when you came into possession of this?"

Both attorneys argued for several minutes, provoking the audience to whisper to each other.

"What do you think it is?" Anna asked, her voice shaky.

"I'm not sure, but I don't want to get my hopes up," Marlon said, never breaking eye contact with the scene unfolding in front of him. He had hoped it was the smoking gun the case needed.

Kenneth and David stepped away from the bench and back to their respective sides. The defense attorney's face said it all: the new piece of evidence pissed him off. He leaned over and confided in the lawyer sitting next to him.

Judge Palmer slammed his gavel down several times to quiet the crowd. "I will allow State Exhibit X into evidence, as its existence was only discovered today."

Kenneth approached the witness stand. "Mrs. Sullivan, take a close look at State Exhibit X and tell me if you recognize it."

"Sure." She read over the papers, and her eyes widened.

"How did you get this? Where did you find it?"

"Do you recognize that item?" Kenneth asked.

Her mouth hung open. "I … Yes, I do. This is a text conversation between Parker and me. But I don't understand how you got this when—"

"Thank you, Mrs. Sullivan. Since you recognize this text conversation, would you mind reading the messages to the jury?"

Marlon and Anna gasped at each other.

Mrs. Sullivan ran her hands through her hair, causing it to be disheveled. "I don't understand why that would be necessary."

David hopped to his feet, almost knocking over several drinks on the table. "Objection, Your Honor. Why does she need to recite these messages? The texts are—"

Kenneth turned to face the bench. "Your Honor, if I may. These messages are in her own words, and it is imperative for the jury to hear her words in her own voice."

"Overruled. The witness will read the messages," Judge Palmer said.

Mrs. Sullivan's shoulders sank. "I … Okay … On June 7, I said, 'Parker, what the—um, excuse my language—what the fuck is going on? Answer your damn phone. Sergeant Miller called and told me someone is accusing you of raping them at a party last night. We can't go through this shit again. And it was a *man* this time. Wait until your father finds out. Have your laptop and phone ready for me when

I get home.'" She glared at the prosecutor and her son.

Marlon squeezed his friend's hand, and the two exchanged shocked and confused glances. That meant she knew about it, and the police had told her.

Kenneth neared Mrs. Sullivan. "You testified that you had no prior knowledge of an assault. So, what prompted you to say 'again' and 'this time' when referencing the attack?"

"Listen, I … I'm not sure why I said that. Maybe it was an autocorrect issue. Like I said, I'm not tech-savvy and—"

Kenneth bowed his head and stopped her. "Please, proceed with reading."

Mrs. Sullivan's eyes darted up at him. "Parker replied with 'Mom, I don't know what you're talking about. I didn't rape anybody.' And I said, 'You better hope this doesn't go public. I'll see what I can do.' Listen, I didn't mean it like that. I was confused, and I wanted to protect him."

"Let me help clear up any confusion." Kenneth pressed a button on a projector, prompting the text messages to appear on a screen. After turning to face her, he glanced back at the monitor and read aloud.

> SUSAN (7:54 p.m.): *You fucked up this time. After what happened with Cassie and Olivia, I thought for sure the therapy would have helped you. Grow up!*
> PARKER (7:56 p.m.): *Why r u bringing this up??? It's in the past. So what if I had sex??*

*SUSAN (7:59 p.m.): With a MAN, Parker? That is disgusting. We raised you better than that. We are CHRISTIANS. Your father is running for office again soon. This better not ruin things for him or so help me GOD.*

*PARKER (8:08 p.m.): I'm done talking about this. Leave me alone.*

*SUSAN (8:10 p.m.): No, you're NOT done talking about this. You're in big trouble if this goes to trial. I don't want the world knowing my son is a FAG and a RAPIST.*

After he recited the last message, Kenneth paused and gestured toward Mrs. Sullivan. "Could you explain what you meant by the last sentence?"

Mrs. Sullivan squirmed in her seat. "I … I didn't write this. Someone hacked my phone or something."

Marlon reminded himself he needed to stay calm. He couldn't get his hopes up. The messages guaranteed nothing for the case.

"These text messages contradict your earlier testimony," Kenneth said. "So, what is the truth? Did Parker assault someone else to your knowledge? Or had you never heard any allegations of a sexual assault?"

Mrs. Sullivan stared at her son for a moment, and her face relaxed. "I'm exercising my Fifth Amendment right to remain silent."

Several jury members turned and peered at each other.

The statement didn't appear to faze Kenneth, and he turned away. "Thank you, Mrs. Sullivan. No further questions."

David rose out of his seat. "Your Honor, may I redirect with my witness?"

"Yes," Judge Palmer said.

"Did you observe your son committing any crime?" David asked.

Mrs. Sullivan sighed. "No, Mr. Samberg, I did not. He is innocent, as far as I know."

"Did he ever confess to committing a crime?"

"No, he never confessed to doing anything illegal."

"Thank you, Mrs. Sullivan. Nothing further." The defense attorney returned to his seat.

———————

Throughout the afternoon, several more defense witnesses testified, including Parker's friend, Justin Sanchez, who attended the party and saw them walking around outside, the taxi driver who drove Parker home that evening, and a psychologist who examined him. At last, the trial day ended.

Parker whispered into his lawyer's ear.

"Your Honor, we will begin tomorrow with another defense witness, Courtney DuPont," David said.

Marlon sighed. Courtney testifying wasn't the least bit shocking, as he wondered when they would call her.

"Thank you. Court is adjourned until tomorrow at nine," Judge Palmer said.

# CHAPTER 28

MARLON COULDN'T STOP THINKING ABOUT WHAT HAD transpired in court and how it might impact the outcome of the trial. On the one hand, the prosecution pulled out a last-minute smoking gun of sorts. But the fact that Mrs. Sullivan knew about the rape all along left him disappointed.

After getting dressed and heading to the courthouse the next morning, he awaited Courtney's arrival. Several scenarios ran through his head about how her testimony would go. Would the defense paint her in a positive light and make the jury believe her? Would the prosecution pick apart her story like they did with Mrs. Sullivan? More frightening than anything was the fact that she attended the party and had exhibited a lot of hostility toward him ever since. This provided her ample opportunity to lie about what happened.

The prosecutor glanced at his wristwatch before locking eyes with the judge. "Your Honor, she is twenty-three minutes late. We can't wait all day for the defense's witness.

We need to proceed."

Judge Palmer nodded. "I agree, Mr. Hughes. If the witness isn't here within the next five minutes, the defense will have to move on."

David and Parker exchanged glances.

Almost as if planned, Courtney came barging through the courtroom doors. She sashayed up to the stand like she was on a catwalk at Fashion Week in Paris and beamed at the crowd. Her outfit consisted of a thigh-length dress and knee-high boots. "*So* sorry I'm late. It took me a while to get ready this morning."

Marlon's brow furrowed.

The judge's forehead creased. "Ms. DuPont, taking longer than usual to find clothing is no excuse for tardiness. Show some respect for the justice system."

Her cheeks flushed. "Sorry."

After Courtney took the oath, David slid his chair back and stood. "Ms. DuPont, please explain to the court your relationship to Mr. Sullivan."

She grinned at him. "You can call me Courtney. Parker is my boyfriend."

"Thanks, Courtney. How long have you two been in a relationship?"

"Two years, three months, six days," Courtney said with a self-impressed shrug. "I'm great with dates."

David chuckled. "In your two years, three months, and six days together, did Parker ever harm you in any way?"

Like an out-of-work actress, she gasped and put her palm to her chest. "No. He would never hurt a fly. He's a cuddle-muffin."

Marlon's nose wrinkled with disgust.

"Have you ever witnessed him hurting anybody else?"

She shook her head. "No, he wouldn't do that."

"Thank you. Now, I hope you don't mind, but I'm going to ask you a few personal questions about your relationship. Is that okay?"

Courtney giggled. "Sure, I'm an open book."

"Has Parker ever cheated on you?"

Courtney's soft expression melted, revealing how hard she struggled to suppress tears. "Yes."

"Can you tell me how many times?"

"Once," she said, her voice flat.

Marlon's eyes rolled. Parker raped more than one person while they were together, but Courtney insisted on continuing to live in denial.

David wobbled around the floor. "Who did he cheat on you with?"

"Marlon Woods." She glared at him in the audience, and he returned the favor.

"How did you come to find out about this?"

Courtney sighed. "Parker told me the next day."

David crossed his arms and raised a bushy eyebrow. "How did you react to this news?"

"I was upset. Like, how could he cheat on me? And to

do it with a *man*? I mean, imagine the thoughts racing through my head. I did not want to date a homosexual. But he reassured me it was a drunken one-night stand, that it wouldn't happen again, and that he didn't like men."

"When speaking with you about that night, did he refer to the encounter as a sexual assault, rape, or anything of that nature?" David asked.

"No, and I know him too well. I mean, we've been together for over two years now. He would never do that to anyone. In all the times he's explained it, he referred to it as a hookup."

"Thank you, Courtney. Those are all my questions for you. Thanks for your honesty and bravery today." David smiled and returned to his seat.

Kenneth approached the stand. "Ms. DuPont, did you know about your boyfriend engaging in sexual activities with any other men?"

Courtney gawked at him. "Ew, no."

"So, you aren't aware of his confessed encounters with at least three men?"

"Well, no, but I don't care. I love him."

"Can you describe your first sexual encounter with your boyfriend for the court?"

David hopped out of his seat. "Objection. Immaterial. What is the relevance of this probing question?"

Kenneth turned to the judge. "Your Honor, the defendant allegedly had forceful sexual encounters on many occasions and, by his own admission, 'likes it rough.' So, Ms. DuPont's perspective is essential here."

"Overruled. The witness will describe as instructed," Judge Palmer said.

Courtney swallowed hard. "We were at a party and walked around outside and talked. After we got back inside, he pulled me into the bathroom, and we did it."

"What did you do? Please, be clearer. Who initiated the sexual contact?"

"He started it," Courtney said, shifting in the chair. "Um, we made out, took our clothes off, and had sex."

Kenneth's brow furrowed, and he glanced around the courtroom. "Did you *want* to have sex with him?"

Courtney's face scrunched. "Are you asking if he raped me? I am not a goddamn victim if that is what you're suggesting. Of course, I—"

Kenneth peered up at the judge. "Objection, Your Honor. Argumentative."

"Answer his question, Ms. DuPont," Judge Palmer said in a stern voice.

Courtney folded her arms like a scolded child who didn't get their way. "Yes, I wanted to have sex with him. I mean, I didn't tell him I wanted to, but I did want to."

"What indication did you give that you wanted it?"

She squinted. "I think I wanted to. Like, I was drunk, but I didn't mind it. And I was flirting with him, so I think he figured out I liked him."

Marlon's eyes widened at the realization Courtney didn't understand what she was implying.

"And the sex—what was it like?"

She glanced at Parker and down at her hands. "It was rough. I mean, that's how he likes it, so I don't care. But that was the first time I had rough sex, so I needed to get used to it."

"Now, what you've told me about your first sexual encounter is that he initiated it, the sex was rough, and flirting was your way of consenting. Is this correct?"

Courtney's eyes welled up with tears. "He didn't rape me. I'm not a victim. I'm his girlfriend, and he loves me. He wouldn't hurt me. Parker, you love me, don't you?" She sprawled her hands out on the stand and rose out of her seat.

The judge slammed his gavel. "Order."

The stunt left Kenneth shaking his head. "Did you look at any of the photos or videos of the incident involving Mr. Woods and your boyfriend?"

Courtney rubbed her eyes. "No. I didn't want to see my boyfriend cheating on me."

"How did you feel when you found out he stood accused of sexually assaulting another man?"

"Disgusted. I knew he wouldn't ever rape anyone, and he definitely wouldn't do it with a guy. Parker isn't gay, okay? I know that for a fact."

Kenneth stared at Parker and back at Courtney. "How do you know this for a fact?"

Courtney's lips parted as she huffed and rolled her eyes. "Duh, he's dating me."

"Ms. DuPont, the partner somebody dates does not imply their sexuality. Is it possible—"

"Objection," both David and Parker shouted in unison.

"I'm not gay, and this line of questioning—" Parker shouted.

David stared at his client and then looked at Judge Palmer. "Your Honor, is this necessary?"

Kenneth smirked at the pair. "Withdrawn. Last question for you, Ms. DuPont. Do you know who released the pictures and videos of Parker and Mr. Woods?"

Courtney pressed her hair behind her ears. "Yes."

The courtroom erupted in a temporary pandemonium as journalists and audience members whispered to each other.

The confession made Marlon shake Anna's wrist. "What? How?"

Anna's mouth slipped open as she rocked her head. "I don't know, but I thought they would have asked her."

Before Judge Palmer could quiet the room, Courtney continued, "It was me. I released them."

Marlon gasped louder than appropriate, unable to contain his shock.

Silence filled the courtroom, and Kenneth and David exchanged bewildered glances.

"How is that possible if you stated you didn't see the

pictures or videos?" Kenneth asked, a hint of amusement and confusion present in his tone.

"I didn't open them. When I saw the thumbnails and the date he took them, I knew right away what they were. I was going to break up with Parker and never talk to him again, so I uploaded them without a second thought. I wanted to embarrass him, that's all. Parker, I'm so sorry."

Parker leaned over and whispered in his lawyer's ear.

Kenneth nodded. "Thank you for your time, Ms. DuPont. No further questions."

David raised his hand. "Uh, Your Honor, may I re-exmine the witness given the new information?"

"You may proceed," Judge Palmer said.

"Did you really post the pictures and videos to the internet?"

"Objection, Your Honor. Asked and answered," Kenneth shouted.

The judge lowered his glasses at David. "Sustained. Ask another question."

David cocked his head to the side. "As Parker's girlfriend—or, I'm sorry—*former* girlfriend, why would you do such a thing?"

"I wanted to get back at him and—I'm sorry, what do you mean by *former* girlfriend?" Her forehead creased.

"No further questions for this witness, Your Honor."

The judge dismissed Courtney, and she sobbed as she stormed out of the room.

Anna turned toward Marlon. "What … was … that?"

"There's no way," Marlon said, his eyes still focused on the witness stand.

David flipped through some paperwork for a minute before standing. "Your Honor, the defense does not wish to call any additional witnesses and rests its case."

"We will adjourn for today and begin with closing arguments tomorrow morning. Thank you." Judge Palmer banged his gavel.

———

After rushing home to avoid the onslaught of reporters, Marlon and Anna watched television to kill time. Almost every news channel they scrolled past was discussing the trial and today's proceedings. They flipped through the channels before settling on *The Judy Faith Show*.

The image loaded in time to show Judy shaking her head. "In other news, can you believe the bombshell in court today? My goodness. Joining me is special correspondent Melanie Nguyen, who attended the trial of Parker Sullivan today. What can you tell me about the feeling in the courthouse this morning?"

A young Asian woman appeared on the screen. "Thank you, Judy. Yes, I've been at the trial since day one, and let me tell you, the vibe in the courtroom today was totally different from yesterday. Ms. DuPont's statements regarding her own sexual encounters with Parker were difficult to listen to, and she seemed oblivious as to what she implied."

"And don't get me started on her confessing to releasing the photos and videos. I mean, who does that? I understand wanting revenge against your cheating boyfriend, but why would you feed the prosecution their entire case? Had she not released them, we may not be here today discussing this. What a stupid thing for her to do," Judy said.

Melanie nodded. "You're right, Judy. We have yet to hear from Ms. DuPont regarding her testimony, but I'm interested to see how this plays out in court tomorrow. As it stands, it's not looking too good for Mr. Sullivan between testifying to his version of events yesterday and inadvertently confessing. Also, those now-infamous text messages between Parker and his mother, Susan Sullivan, the former first lady of Washington. The jury will have a hard time deliberating on this one."

Judy's eyes rolled. "They shouldn't, though. All signs point to guilty, guilty, GUILTY, and the deeper we get into this case, the more obvious his guilt becomes. I wonder how his defense will try to spin it in their closing arguments tomorrow. They saved Ms. DuPont for the end in hopes of her being a strong character witness, but that failed."

Marlon turned the television off. "Hey, is it okay if we skip closing arguments tomorrow?"

"Are you sure? Don't you want to be there?"

Marlon's expression hardened. "This is all really over-whelming. Besides, all they're gonna do is summarize everything they already said."

"Aren't you required to go, though? I don't want you getting into trouble for—"

"No. I talked to Kenneth earlier, and he said it's up to me whether I want to be there for the closing arguments. But I can't handle this anymore. Am I stupid for not going tomorrow? Be honest."

Anna offered a warm smile. "No. Let's do something fun instead. I'm sure we won't miss anything. And even if we do, Judy Faith will tell us all about it."

# CHAPTER 29

**THE NEXT MORNING, MARLON AND ANNA GRABBED** breakfast at the Double R Diner. Worried about the possibility of someone recognizing him, Marlon donned a hoodie and Ray-Bans.

Anna slid her empty plate to the side and locked eyes with Marlon. "Hey, since we're already here, we might as well check out the filming locations for *Twin Peaks*. I remember how much you loved that show."

Marlon gasped. "Really? Do you want to? Oh my god, that would be amazing."

Anna grinned. "Let's do it."

———

At their last stop of the day, Anna clicked her phone and checked the time. "Do you think we should head home and see what's going on? I wonder if there are any updates."

The excitement of their outing made Marlon forget about the impending verdict. The smile melted from his face. "Yeah, we probably should."

While Anna drove them back to her place, Marlon couldn't help checking the news for an update on the case. A popular news agency pinned an article about the trial and pending verdict to the top of their website, which Marlon read in silence.

> *Jurors are still deliberating on the verdict in the Parker Sullivan Pine State University rape case. Deliberations may last into the morning.*

Anna glanced over several times. "What are you reading?"

Entranced by what he saw on the screen, Marlon hardly heard Anna speaking to him. "Oh, sorry. I was reading about the case. The jury is deliberating now, and they might not have a decision until tomorrow."

Anna chewed her plum-tinted bottom lip. "Does it mention anything about what happened today?"

He stared down at the phone once again and read from it, paraphrasing what it said. "The prosecution focused on the testimony of Parker, Mrs. Sullivan, and me. They said the evidence proves his guilt, between the text messages with his mother, the rape kit, and the pictures and videos. Kenneth told the jury to send a strong message to other rapists out there by convicting Parker."

He scrolled down until he got to the part that scared him the most. "And the defense tore my story apart. They said Courtney tried to ruin her boyfriend out of jealousy. David also said Parker shouldn't serve time in prison because he experimented with another man and—"

"Excuse me? Experimented? What kind of *experiment* is a rapist doing?"

The implication of what the defense attorney said made Marlon frown. "I know. I can't wait until this is over."

Anna placed her palm on his arm. "Everything's gonna be okay. This will all be over soon, and then you can focus on healing. They'll find him guilty. Don't worry."

"Will they, Anna? The odds are always stacked against the victim. In a perfect world, everyone would believe and accept a victim's story, and they wouldn't have to deal with a trial. But look at what the last year of my life was like. Nothing would shock me at this point."

"Stop. He's guilty, and there's so much evidence proving his guilt."

"I hope you're right, but we'll see."

———

The next day, they woke up early and hung out in Anna's apartment to monitor the news. A decision could arrive at any moment, and neither of them wanted to miss the opportunity to be there when the time came.

Marlon's phone vibrated, and he yanked it out of his pocket. "Hello?"

"Hi, this is Kenneth Hughes, and I received word moments ago that the verdict is in. Come to the courthouse as soon as possible."

———————

The twelve jury members entered the courtroom, and the foreman, Mr. Alford, made eye contact with the judge. "Good morning, Your Honor."

Judge Palmer smiled. "Good morning. Could you please hand me the envelope with the sealed verdict forms?"

The foreman bowed his head. "Yes, Your Honor."

The judge peered over the papers before handing them back. "Would you please pass those to Deputy Horne?"

After they passed the forms off, the judge shifted in his seat. "Ladies and gentlemen of the jury, I urge you to listen carefully to the verdicts as Mr. Alford reads them. After he concludes, I will ask you if these are your verdicts. I'm also warning the audience to remain quiet. Any outbursts will be grounds for removal from the courtroom. Mr. Sullivan, please stand and face the jury as they deliver the verdicts."

All three men at the defense table rose out of their chairs. It was the moment everyone anticipated. Twelve months of madness came down to less than two minutes of reading.

Marlon drew a deep breath and reminded himself to stay calm and focused. His pulse thumped fast and hard.

Mr. Alford cleared his throat and squinted at the piece of paper in his hands and back at the crowd in front of him. "Superior Court of Washington, King County. In the matter of People of the State of Washington versus Parker Lyle Sullivan, case number 94-4-77377-0-SEA. We, the jury, in the above-entitled action, find the Defendant, Parker Lyle Sullivan, *not guilty* of the crime of rape in violation of penal code section 9A.44.050(A), a felony, upon Marlon Augustine Woods, as charged in count one."

Not guilty. The words reverberated through Marlon's ears as numbness crept over his body. Quiet cheers and gasps muffled in the background. It was as if someone had snatched away his hearing. Still, he refused to break eye contact with the panel.

"We, the jury, find the Defendant, Parker Lyle Sullivan, *not guilty* of the crime of sexual battery in violation of penal code section 9A.44.100(A), a felony, upon Marlon Augustine Woods, as charged in count two."

Not guilty. Any shred of hope Marlon clung to died. He lived through that for nothing. There was no justice in the world.

"We, the jury, find the Defendant, Parker Lyle Sullivan, *guilty* of the crime of voyeurism in violation of penal code section 9A.44.115(3)(A), a misdemeanor, upon Marlon Augustine Woods, as charged in count three."

Guilty of one charge. The least severe of them all, according to the justice system. What a joke.

Judge Palmer bowed his head at the group. "Ladies and gentlemen of the jury, is this your verdict, so say you one, so say you all?"

"Yes," all twelve members said in unison.

The judge flashed a smile at them. "Thank you. I want to take this opportunity to thank each of you for the service you've given to us. I know how difficult these cases are to deliberate. You are all dismissed."

Parker and his lawyer clapped and patted each other on the back. David gripped Parker's hand and whispered, "We did it," loud enough for Marlon to hear.

The news left Marlon in a daze, and he sat in silence until Anna shook him.

Black mascara tears stained her pale face. "Marlon? Are you okay? I'm so sorry."

Marlon stared at the wall. "I knew this would happen."

Anna clutched his arm and ushered him out of the court. "I can't believe it. There was so much evidence. How could anyone look at this and believe Parker was innocent? The fact that they only found him guilty of voyeurism is a joke. The prosecutors fucked up the case." She took a minute to catch her breath as her face turned crimson.

Marlon exhaled, and his eyes met hers. "It isn't their fault. They did the best they could. I should have known better than to expect more. This happens all the time in the news. Why would my case be any different?"

Anna rattled her head and scrubbed the black stream of tears from her cheek. "Did you see the bastard celebrating afterward? I wanted to punch him in his stupid face."

The first of many tears flowed down from Marlon's eyes. "Me too."

"Marlon?" Kenneth said, walking toward him with a defeated look on his face.

———

In the days following the trial, the court invited Marlon back to the courthouse to give a victim-impact statement during the sentencing phase of the trial.

A tidal wave of emotions washed over Marlon as he approached the microphone to deliver his written statement he had worked on for several days with Anna and Kenneth to the court. It would be his second time ever speaking about the case publicly, with the first time resulting in his rapist being found innocent on the serious charges.

"Good afternoon, Judge Palmer. My name is Marlon Woods. Five days from today marks one year since Parker Lyle Sullivan raped me. No matter how much time passes, I relive the assault every single day of my life. I see his face in my nightmares. I smell and taste the liquor on his breath as he kissed me. I still feel him tugging at my clothes, and the ripping of my flesh as he forced himself inside of me." He paused. "Whoever said that time heals all wounds was a liar or had never experienced anything like this. No matter how much time passes, the pain is still there."

He caught his breath and attempted to settle his nerves. "I want to describe my first year as a rape victim or survivor, as some people call it. After the assault, I did what they instruct all victims to do: I reported it to the police. I went through an invasive exam, which included a rape kit and having photographs taken of my injuries."

His lip quivered, and he glanced up at the judge. "I cut off all contact with friends and family for a few days until I realized I had nowhere to go but home, which, for me, is Ohio. My mom flew me home, and I dealt with uncomfortable questions from everyone once they found out about my assault from a reporter calling my house. Why did I go to a party? Why did I drink when I was underage? I should have known better. Not that they blamed me for the rape, but the implications were there. If that wasn't bad enough, pictures and videos of my sexual assault leaked on the internet."

Marlon trembled and took a moment to compose himself. Tears cascaded down his flushed face. "Someone posted my personal information, including my phone number and social media accounts. Within hours, the pictures and videos appeared on my timeline for the world to see. I had to delete all of my social media accounts, which, for the longest time, were my only link to many of my friends and relatives. Imagine you survived the worst night of your life, and then you're forced to relive it in news articles and on television."

The gaze of his attacker burned a hole through him. Parker didn't scare him anymore, though. Marlon turned and locked eyes with him. "After *courageously*, as described by the reporters who hounded me for months, returning to Pine State University, I was subjected to a different kind of torment. Friends of Mr. Sullivan's harassed me—under his orders, I'm sure. These attacks took on many different forms. In one instance, one of his friends dumped a drink and some food on me in a drive-thru after saying homophobic, awful things. In another, which I'm sure everyone is familiar with, someone hacked the school servers and shared images of my rape with everyone. I also endured many months of bullying both on and off campus—people confronting me about what happened, accusing me of lying, and sometimes threatening me."

Marlon's fingertips grazed the scar on his wrist as he fumbled with his sleeve. "There were times I wished he would have killed me during the rape. I often thought about how much easier this case would be if I were dead. The burden of proof would no longer lie on me, as my dead body would serve as evidence of what happened to me. Over the last year, I've also spent every waking moment trying to figure out why he chose me. What did I do or say to make him decide to rape me? It's a thought that will never go away, no matter how much time passes."

Speaking for so long caused Marlon to cough into his

arm as he inhaled through his congested nose. "Your Honor, although the court only convicted Mr. Sullivan of the lesser charge of voyeurism, it is about time the criminal justice system does its job. Keep the criminals locked up and the community safe. I can't fathom the thought of this happening to someone else. Can you? I understand you have the final say on sentencing, but think of the example you are setting for other students, both at Pine State University and at other campuses across the nation. Show them it is not okay to rape someone, and it is also unacceptable to record and share the attack. Considering the violent nature of the incident, I ask you to sentence him to the maximum sentence allowable by law. Thank you."

As he gathered his papers and trudged away, the judge nodded. "Thank you, Mr. Woods."

———

Parker Sullivan received a sentence of ninety days in jail and five thousand dollars in fines. In the eyes of the law, the cost of raping someone and ruining their life was worth less than a used car.

# CHAPTER 30

A PRODUCER FOR *THE JUDY FAITH SHOW* CONTACTED
Marlon the day after the sentencing, and he agreed to do an
interview on the show to discuss the verdict. He needed the
world to hear his side of the story. The truth.

A few days later, he flew to Los Angeles to tape his interview. Unlike Cassie's live interview on the program, his
would be pre-recorded and played later in the evening. That
way, if it became too much for him, he could take a break
and restart the questions.

———

The director gave the thumbs-up, and a devilish grin covered Judy Faith's heavily made-up face. "Ladies and
gentlemen, welcome to a special edition of *The Judy Faith
Show*. Tonight, I am joined by a guest you should all be
familiar with by now. Over the last few weeks, we were all

glued to our television sets as we watched the drama unfold in the Pine State University rape trial against Parker Sullivan. Jurors returned a verdict of not guilty on all but one count last week. Joining me is Marlon Woods, the victim in that case. Marlon, thanks for doing this interview with me."

The camera panned to him. It was his moment, and he was more freaked out than ever before. But he couldn't mess up because the entire country would judge him.

"Thanks for having me," he said, his voice shaky.

Judy flashed her best sympathetic smile. "I can only imagine how difficult the past week has been for you. How are you holding up?"

Marlon sighed and peered into her eyes, relieved she had started with an easy question. "I'm okay. Overwhelmed, I guess, and a little pissed off, if I can say that."

"Of course you can, Marlon. You can say whatever is on your mind. Now, I'm sure most of our viewers are familiar with your case, but would you mind describing your relationship with Parker before the sexual assault?"

"Parker and I were in a psychology class together. Outside of school, we only talked a few times before that night, mostly at parties." Marlon chewed on his bottom lip after answering, anticipating her next question.

"You described the assault in great detail on the stand, but could you briefly walk us through what transpired?" Judy asked with a frown.

"We were at a party. I had two drinks and was about to

leave for the night, but I couldn't find my friend Anna any-where. Outside, I ran into Parker Sullivan, and he asked if I wanted to go for a walk with him. Since I had nowhere else to be, I said yes. We walked up and down the road and talked about our hobbies and interests. Based on our brief conversation, he seemed like a nice guy. When we got back to the house, he told me there was something he wanted to show me in the backyard."

His mind drifted. "Sorry, this is painful for me to talk about." He took a shaky breath. "We got to this blue shed in the backyard, and he tried to kiss me. I laughed and thought for sure that it was a joke. I mean, he had a girl-friend and seemed straight, right? I assumed he was messing around or trying to be funny. But when I realized he was serious, I told him I was flattered, but I wasn't interested. That set him off."

Judy sat forward in her chair and winced. "I'm sorry, Marlon. I wonder what went through his mind. I bet this confused you."

"Yes. His face turned red, and he said, 'How effing dare you? Nobody says no to ME.' He slapped me across the face, beat me, and tried to strangle me. When that didn't work, he tugged at my clothes, and after shouting and trying to resist, I gave up. He pulled my pants down around my an-kles and yanked my shirt off." The memory tormented him, and the impulse to cry grew stronger.

Judy shook her head and glanced up at him. "Oh, my

goodness, I am so sorry. What kind of man does that?"

Marlon took a deep breath. "After he violated me, he laughed. He made fun of how pathetic I sounded and said I should feel honored he would, um, have sex with me. I cried, and he said there was no point in reporting him because nobody would believe me. I lay there on the ground for like thirty minutes until I found the strength to leave. Then, I caught an Uber home, fell asleep, and drove to the police station the next day."

Judy pressed her mauve lips together in a hard line. "Thank you. How brave of you to share your story once again. What happened after you reported it to the police?"

"I did an exam and a video statement with a detective. They suggested I fly back home to Ohio. The semester had ended anyway, so I flew home and didn't talk about what happened for several days." He took a moment to compose his thoughts. "My family didn't know at first."

Judy placed her fist over her chest and let out a dramatic gasp. "Oh, darling. Is that so? When did they find out?"

"A few days after I came back home, a journalist called the house and asked my mother for a statement. They somehow found out my identity and the details of the case. They described the information they received, and she almost fainted when she found out."

Judy gave an incredulous glare. "So, you're saying your family found out through the media? Those vultures almost destroyed your life, didn't they?"

He looked away. Her show was the most unrelenting of them all. "Yeah, they did."

Judy's forehead creased. "Please tell me about the pictures and videos. When did you find out about those?"

Marlon broke eye contact, staring at the fake potted plant next to him. "I didn't know he took any until the leak happened. Within hours, my phone was ringing nonstop with unknown numbers calling me, and somebody posted the pictures on my timeline." Tears welled up in his eyes. "But I didn't actually see them until someone hacked the university's server and shared the screenshots through the website and email system. Seeing it made a terrible nightmare become more of a reality for me."

Judy stared at him with a somber expression and passed him a box of tissues. "I'm so sorry. After you spent the summer with your family in Ohio, you returned to school. This was something I've discussed at length on the show. May I ask what prompted your decision?"

He dabbed a tissue at his eye. "I needed to go back. Everybody warned me to stay away, knowing people would bully me. But I had to face my demons. If I stayed home in Ohio for the rest of my life, I would have let him and his friends win."

"What was it like for you after you returned to Pine? You mentioned experiencing bullying and an incident where somebody threw stuff at you during your victim impact statement. Could you elaborate on that for us, please?"

"The first few months were hell. I returned to Pine with one friend. Making friends is hard when you're known to the world as 'the PSU rape victim.' You never know who you can trust." He thought about her secondary question. "And the bullying got bad. People harassed me all the time. The worst part is I don't think many of them thought of it as harassment. I guess they thought they were funny. But people calling you terrible names, sharing your assault pictures online, and pouring drinks and food on you in a drive-thru is not my idea of funny."

Judy frowned and shook her head. "What possessed those people to act so foolishly? It's like Parker Sullivan was some god, and they worshipped the ground he walked on. We heard some of this throughout the trial. For instance, his mother, Susan, the former first lady of Washington. What did you think of her testimony, and the bombshell evidence that came out during it?"

He let out a quiet chuckle. "I could tell she was trying to convince everyone her family was perfect. She rehearsed everything so well, but I don't think she expected anyone to recover those texts. Hearing people read them was so painful. How could she know about this and try to cover it up? Especially when she talked about Cassie in her messages."

Judy gasped and flopped her hand out on her leg. "I couldn't believe she perjured herself for her son. This is still a developing story, and I'm not sure if you are aware, but the state charged her with perjury following her testimony.

What are your thoughts on this?"

A grin covered his face. "Yeah, I read about that. She deserves charges for breaking the law. That whole family—oops, I'm not sure how much I'm allowed to say without getting into trouble."

Judy turned toward the camera and flashed a malicious smirk. "I say put Parker in a jail cell with Mommy and throw away the key. Come on, she had some nerve saying the things she did. A 'good Christian woman,' my ass."

Marlon nodded. She said what he had wanted to say.

She cleared her throat and corrected her posture. "Sorry. Speaking of Cassie Roberts, have you spoken with her since the verdict? How has she handled the disappointing news?"

"No, I haven't talked to her since the first day of the trial, after I testified. I hope she's doing okay."

Judy pulled out an index card and read from it. "Cassie released a statement earlier this afternoon. She said, 'After taking time to process the news of this verdict, I realized our justice system needs some major reform. Victims should not suffer through sharing their stories to have a group of ignorant, self-righteous pricks tells them their case wasn't tragic enough to convict someone. My thoughts are with Marlon and the other victims. I'm sure we are not the only people who suffered at the hands of the slimy Sullivan family.' What is your opinion on her statement?"

Marlon's eyes widened. "Wow. Yeah, I understand

where she is coming from. It's messed up because you're forced to relive your trauma and pain, just to have no real closure. Now that I've had time to think about everything, I don't blame the jurors or prosecutors in this case. They did the best they could with what they had, which sounds crazy because my rapist will walk the streets again in a few months. She's right, though—our system sucks."

Judy inhaled and let out an emphatic sigh as she grabbed his wrist. "I agree with you, Marlon. There was an abundance of evidence in this case. There were the witnesses, the videos, the rape kit, and the experts who testified against him. And yet it still wasn't enough. I cannot tell you how shocked I was, and I have been doing this for twenty-six years now. To call his sentence a slap on the wrist is the understatement of the century. People spend more time in jail for petty theft and drug possession."

Marlon nodded.

"Were you as surprised as the rest of us by the verdict?" Judy asked.

"It didn't shock me. Was I upset? Yes. But was I surprised? No. I think my friends and family took the news harder than I did because I was expecting this all along. When you're the victim of a crime, you're used to feeling let down."

"I interviewed one juror in the case earlier today, and this was what she had to say about the verdict." Judy swung around in her seat and pointed at a screen behind her.

A video clip played, and a red-haired, middle-aged woman appeared on the screen. Based on the differences in backgrounds and lighting, it was clear she and Judy were in different locations in the pre-recorded video. "Yes, Judy, the evidence was key here."

"If that is the case, Melinda, please explain why you returned a verdict of not guilty. I mean, hello, what more did you need in terms of evidence?" Judy asked in the video.

"It's complicated. We deliberated for nine hours on the charges. Many of us initially voted guilty on all charges, but a few of the other jurors held out on not guilty. After many hours of this, they convinced us to change our votes to not guilty on several charges."

"What was the reasoning behind that? The whole thing makes no sense, Melinda. Did the Sullivan family plant a mole in the jury panel, or what?" Judy rolled her eyes.

Melinda chuckled. "No, that didn't happen. The thing we kept going back to was the fact that Parker is straight. The way they explained things to us was a straight man wouldn't rape another man. He would rape a woman. Their logic made sense when I thought about it."

Marlon's stomach twisted in knots. Why would Parker's sexuality matter? Parker raped him.

Judy flailed her arms around in the video. "Are you kidding? Melinda, are you telling me one of the deciding factors was the defendant's sexuality? Well, how the hell do you explain him having sex with another man? I mean, it is the only other logical explanation, isn't it? Nobody held a gun to Parker's head and said, 'Hey, go have sex with this guy.'"

"Yes, but there was more to it, of course. That was just one of the main points they made. The best way to describe what Parker did would be curiosity. Sometimes, college students experiment with each other. I'm not saying I condone that behavior, but it made sense," Melinda said with a shrug.

Judy laughed sarcastically. "Experimenting would involve him hooking up with a man one time, but Parker admitted to having sexual encounters with three different guys. And who knows how many of those encounters were consensual? Let me ask you something, why did you return a guilty verdict on the voyeurism charge if you didn't think there was sufficient evidence to convict him on the rape charges?"

"Um, while we didn't have enough evidence of a sexual assault, we realized Parker recorded his encounter with that young man without his consent. When they played the videos and showed us the photographs, it was clear he didn't know Parker was recording. And in all our minds, that is a real problem with kids these days. They're so attached to their devices that they don't consider the real-world consequences of their actions, including filming sexual acts without permission."

The clip ended after Melinda finished speaking.

Judy turned her attention back to Marlon. "What are your thoughts on that?"

His pulse quickened. "I can't believe that was how they decided on the verdict. It blows my mind. Why would his sexuality matter when he's a rapist?"

"Many rapists and child molesters don't care about the gender of their victims. They get off on the sense of power they feel from it. It's normal for a sexual predator to go after both male and female victims. I can't believe this wasn't common sense amongst those jurors. But, you know, they clearly brought in Seattle's finest," Judy said in an unimpressed tone, accompanied by a signature eye roll.

Unsure of how to react to her statement, he nodded.

Judy glanced down at a card and back at him. "What do you think of the other victims? What do you want to say to them? So far, in the last four days, five women and one man have come forward with allegations of rape and sexual misconduct against Mr. Sullivan. Several of them are also alleging the sicko recorded their assaults."

Marlon looked at the camera and softened his expression. "They're all so brave. Take it from me, I understand how hard it is to speak out and share your story. But the more you talk about it, the easier it gets. You have each other for support, and I'm here to help in any way I can."

"I understand you are familiar with one of the young ladies speaking out against him, am I right? Charlotte Knapp is a classmate and an acquaintance of yours?"

The question reminded him of how shocked he was when he read Charlotte's statement a few days prior. "Yeah,

Charlotte and I know each other from school. I'm so proud of her."

"Where do you go from here? What are your plans?"

He winked at Judy. "You'll have to wait and see."

Judy peered over to him and beamed. "Thank you so much for joining us today, Marlon. God bless you, and best wishes on your journey."

"Thanks again for having me."

Judy shifted to face the camera. "Ladies and gentlemen, that's all the time we have for tonight. Remember to take care of each other and hug your children extra tight. They need all the love we can give them. Goodnight."

As the show's theme song filled the room, Marlon leaned in and whispered in Judy's ear.

"And cut!" the director shouted.

Marlon's phone vibrated several times, tickling his thigh. He had forgotten to power it off before walking out onto the set. He slid it out of his pocket and clicked the screen. A new message from Quinn displayed.

> *Florida is sooo boring without u. Can't wait*
> *to see u guys in a few weeks.*

Judy sighed and twisted toward Marlon. "Oh, thank god. Now we can talk. Are you going to do it?"

Marlon's chest tightened. "I guess I don't have a choice now, huh?"

# AFTERWORD

Did the verdict piss you off? It should.

This book doesn't have a fairy-tale ending because this is the outcome most victims experience. In the United States, only 0.7% of rapists receive felony convictions. Yes, there is a zero and a decimal point before that seven. This is the reality of the American criminal justice system, a system that mostly favors the accused. An oft-reported factoid people cling to is the number of false accusations; however, this only accounts for roughly two to eight percent of all allegations. Although it's not covered in the news regularly, male rape cases are more common than most would expect. According to RAINN, one in thirty-three men report an attempted or completed rape. And that's just the number of people who were brave enough to acknowledge their trauma. To add on to this statistic, male college students aged eighteen to twenty-four are five times more likely to experience sexual assault than non-students.

While not every case has an attacker like Parker Sullivan, we see examples of this in the news every day. Wealthy perpetrators have the added protection of money, legal aid, and public opinion on their side. The victim not only has to live with what happened to them, but they are also commonly subjected to brutal bullying and ridicule.

Writing this book forced me to revisit my own trauma, bringing back feelings I forgot existed. But I was one of the lucky few to receive justice, which is something everybody deserves.

We need to change our laws for the safety of sexual assault survivors. We need to change our laws to protect our future.

# ACKNOWLEDGMENTS

Many of the statistics in this book were provided by RAINN (Rape, Abuse & Incest National Network).

Thank you to the survivors, including those brave enough to come forward and those living with their painful secret every day of their life. You inspired me to write this book.

My husband, Christopher Holifield. I'm forever grateful for your love, support, and willingness to deal with many days of me ghosting you to work on this story.

My wonderful beta readers. You contributed to this book in ways you'll never understand. I appreciate your honesty and insight.

My editor, Stephanie Cohen. Thanks to your keen eye and delicate touch, this book is more than I ever dreamed of. Thank you, thank you, thank you.

My author buddy, Sean Morales. I appreciate you lending your ear and wisdom whenever needed.

My other author buddy, Iona Wayland. Thanks for suffering through countless hours of text and voice messages to help me make this book the best it could be.

Last but not least, thanks to Teenage Dale for having the strength to carry on and live long enough to write this damn book. Look at you, kid. You did it.

# ABOUT THE AUTHOR

Dale Robbins resides in Nashville, Tennessee with his husband, Chris. When he isn't writing, he can be found in the nosebleed seats of a concert, streaming a true crime docuseries, or rewatching *Halloween* or *The Wizard of Oz*. IN OTHER NEWS is his debut novel.

Visit his website at dalerobbinsbooks.com